Harvest of Ashes

J. G. PERKINS

Books by J. Greg Perkins

DARKNESS BEFORE MOURNING SERIES
The Announcers (Book I)

Harvest of Ashes

J. G. PERKINS

CHATWIN
BOOKS

SEATTLE

2017

Darkness Before Mourning,
Volume II: *Harvest of Ashes*

Edited by Phil Bevis and Amanda Knox, with the assistance of Molly Hunt.

Series cover design by Stephanie Podmore. Cover photo by Candace Doyal, modified by Rex Wilder.

Photograph of the author © Annie Brulé, 2014.

This is a work of fiction. No resemblance is intended to any living person.

paperback ISBN 978-1-63398-005-1
hardcover ISBN 978-1-63398-060-0

Chatwin Books
www.chatwinbooks.com

Dedicated to my mother

Prologue

Most of us have some magical Christmas memories. And most of us have also dreaded Christmas. I'm no different.

The compulsion to recreate the good Christmases of our childhood comes from that part of the brain which stays as fixed and constant as the North Star. This is a need that doesn't fade, but instead shines brighter and stronger as the years pass. It is not unique to me, but shared by many.

My magical Midwest Christmas past was something that could be experienced only in the naiveté of youth. Santa's house on the town square. The singing of favorite Christmas carols. The glitter of tinsel on the tree. Lights blinking on and off. Ornaments commemorating each fleeting year. The scent of pine needles. A family pet confused about all the excitement. A carved turkey sitting in the center of the table. Unspoiled white blankets of fallen snow. Sleigh rides. Parties at school. Classmates. The breath-seizing cold. Laughter. So much laughter and love. Love. Love. Love. From mothers and fathers, grandmothers and grandfathers, brothers and sisters, aunts and uncles, great-aunts and great-uncles.

And presents. Presents neatly stacked beneath the tree. Presents talked about at school. Presents wanted. Presents begged for. Unaffordable presents somehow acquired. Or not.

Standing around the table and saying the Lord's Prayer before Christmas dinner. Having everyone *there*—alive and basking in the common joy of being there together. And being safe. Very safe. So safe you couldn't even imagine things being any other way.

Every culture has a time of year particularly important for families, where tradition, faith, history, and sometimes commerce intersect. Where families come together to celebrate their common heritage. And it is a universal desire of parents that their children have positive experiences during these times, as well as warm memories to take away from them.

In America, that time of year is the Christmas season, which started out as a religious holiday in December, and grew over time to become *the* big show in the richest country the world has ever known. Christmas transformed an affirmation of faith and family values into a secular, commercial extravaganza that has come to dominate much of the American economy.

Christmas has now become the real focus of the year for most families, an amalgam of religious beliefs, secular family traditions, and outright commercialism that no one can avoid, even those who are not Christian. Even atheists are caught in the trap.

The pressure on parents is intense, to nurture, to buy, to make the experience *perfect*. And that desire, that pressure, that expectation, is somehow transmitted to their children, who swim in a sea of marketing from which there is no escape.

Everything has to be perfect. Everything has to be special. You can't just give your family memories, you have to give them memories they can *treasure*. Parents strive hard to deliver on these expectations, and many of them manage, especially when their children are young.

Everyone who has tried to provide a *real* Christmas for their family will have had their own experiences, their own stress and turmoil, and feelings and memories of these times. All of us get feelings in the pit of our stomachs when the thought of family Christmas comes up. Some of us may experience joy and warmth, others dread and anxiety. Most, I think, will have a mixture.

I marked myself as an outsider at age fourteen, when I proclaimed myself an atheist in that shrine to Christian faith that was the Midwest of the 1950s. Beyond my public denial of faith, what set me apart in the Kokomo, Indiana, of my youth was a powerful intellect and my lack of a father, whose loss occasioned my atheism. The year 1980 found me—at age thirty-five—with my young family in North Carolina.

I've spent my life largely out of step, being just different enough that the people around me knew I didn't entirely fit in. I thought I was used to it. Then I moved to the South. It wasn't just that I didn't hunt, fish, or like either NASCAR or grits. It was *way* beyond that. I was three-strikes unthinkable—an atheist in the Bible Belt, a damn Yankee in the South, and a PhD in Jesse Helms' country.

Although I worked in the Research Triangle, I lived outside that bubble in Durham. Even in the Triangle, surrounded by plenty of well-educated people from all over, my outspoken atheism set me apart. There might have been others who shared my perspective, but the culture of faith and conformity was so dominant they were silent, even at work, where I was surrounded by fellow scientists. My non-conformity and atheism were so ingrained, there was no other way for me to be. My wife, on the other hand, wanted most of all to fit in, to be accepted.

The first thing a Southerner would ask in those years was, "Have you found a church home?" My answer and my public denial of faith set me apart—people were often shocked beyond words. The waves of faith that crashed daily on my rocky shores left me marked but never eroded. I had questioned god, defied god, and denied god and his hosts of evangelists.

But Christmas was different. To me, religion was a fairy tale, but Christmas was *real*. Christmas had *power*. The strength of Christmas didn't come from thousands of hours of advertising or a culture of deafening materialism. The power of Christmas was rooted in the magical Midwest Christmases of my childhood, followed by a string of losses of people close to me that, over the years, created a void in my heart which needed filling.

The power of Christmas was rooted in family, the love and security I had known and lost.

Christmas was more powerful than god.

For most of us, some Christmases are more stressful than others. For me, 1980 was that Christmas, the *one* most pressure-filled Christmas of all.

It was the first year that my child was old enough to be aware—to remember. The year my family would establish our *own* Christmas traditions. When my wife and I, each with our own unique histories and perspectives, tried to deliver something memorable and magical to our child.

For those of us who either as children never had a perfect Christmas, or who had some and then lost them, the pressures are even more intense. The desire to heal our own childhoods through delivering perfection to our children can be like a racing pulse.

Bringing added stress to me in this period was a pattern of past family losses during the Christmas season, which brought me to a state of gut-gnawing tension and actual physical illness. On a philosophical level, my atheism and certainty in the existence of no higher power contrasted starkly with my strong sense that somehow, awful things were bound to happen, simply because all too often they had.

I was struggling to get past this recurring pattern of loss, back to something closer to the happier childhoods of my youth. This was the reality, and the memories, that I wanted to give my son.

There is the Christmas we want, the Christmas we need, and the Christmas we struggle to provide. But it isn't always the Christmas we get, or can give to those we care about.

CHAPTER I

December 1st

Maybe it was the wind through the North Carolina pines that woke me in the predawn darkness, I really don't remember. I felt my wife Paige sleeping beside me, and knew I didn't want to wake her. I also knew for certain it was December 1st.

The contrast between her warmth next to me, and my sudden sensation of chilling dread that December had begun, felt like the story of the struggle at the heart of my life.

The sound of Paige's breath—knowing she was *there*—brought strength. We'd known one another since first grade, been sweethearts since high school, and been married twelve years. She knew me better than anyone, even Mom.

Her quiet, steadfast presence at my side was what I needed in that moment. Her understanding of what I needed in the now, and her unquestioning willingness to give it, was to me the foundation and strength of our marriage. Awake or asleep, she was there in the way I needed.

The friction that arose between us almost always stemmed from Paige's attempts to have me fully present in our current life, to stop me dwelling on the past, and to try to get me to stop my endless obsession over losses from long ago. She made it clear she believed this would be good for me, good for her, good for our marriage, and most of all good for our young son's happiness.

When it comes to life in the now, she's very supportive—always there. The knowledge she will be there is the single most important thing to me. Trust is almost impossible for me. I don't trust anyone, but I trust Paige to be there. For me—that's love.

What is it to Paige?

The life we had was the one Paige made clear she wanted as far back as high school. A smart, adorable child, a successful husband who loves her, a beautiful home, and an interesting career of her own.

We purchased a vacant lot, so Paige could do what she always wanted to do—design her own home. I was dying to know what the house of her dreams looked like. And over several months her sketches and floor plans took shape into architect's drawings which turned into a light gray two-story Cape Cod with charcoal trim. A picture-perfect house—"one we can live in, that I can manage." I'm so proud I was able to give her what she wanted.

What we have, what we work for every day, is what I've always wanted and needed. So if I have the life I've always wanted—why do I keep obsessing about the worst parts of my past? Paige is right about this.

Paige has always known this time of year is difficult for me. Her tolerance for what she once called "picking at the scabs of past wounds" wore thin some time back, and expired entirely earlier this year. She told me this holiday season, she wanted to focus on having a perfect Christmas with our three-year-old son Brett, and asked me to join her with my whole heart.

I promised her, and vowed to myself this Christmas, and all the years to come, would be different. It's not an easy promise to keep, but I'm going to try.

To vanquish my inner chill, I bring to mind the image of Brett, asleep down the hall.

How did I come to hate December? I didn't always feel that way. The question is enough to make my chest tighten, a warning sign of the asthma that has plagued me for years.

To fight this, I breathed deep, like my wife asked, and thought back to better years… Good Christmases started with Mom…

Mom baking. Santa riding the last float in the Macy's Thanksgiving parade—seen on a small television screen. Decorating the Christmas tree. Wondering at the mysteries inside carefully wrapped presents. Lights on houses. Bundling up against the snow and the Midwestern cold. Drapes left open so you could see the trees in everyone's houses. Nativity scenes in front yards. Kokomo, Indiana dressed up inside and out, with more smiles than at any other time of the year. Mom, Dad, together.

But Mom has always been more than Santa's helper. She raised my sister Ann and I on her own after Dad died, with some help from her brothers.

After we left for college in the Sixties, neither of us ever moved back. Mom not only didn't remarry after Dad died, she never even dated. She stayed in Kokomo and seemed to do well until her job with the city disappeared in layoffs. After that, her life in our hometown paralleled Kokomo's slow decline. By the end, after the deaths of her two brothers and a mother crushed her, there wasn't really a choice about moving her out to join us in North Carolina.

When she arrived just over a year ago, she was like a flat tire, hopeless and seemingly with no goals of her own. But Durham seemed to fit her—this was one place her quiet nature and willingness to listen were a real social advantage. So many Southerners love to talk and are bountiful sources of stories—in Mom they found a willing pair of ears. An occasional nod was all it took to give her the reputation of a brilliant conversationalist.

Between her work, meeting people despite her shyness, and her plans next month to start taking continuing education classes at Duke, she seemed for the first time in my life to be doing things for herself, rather than as wife, mother, daughter.

I slowly and carefully slid out of bed, trying my best not to disturb Paige. The clock sitting next to the bed flashed 5:40 a.m. I spent time every morning and evening taking care of my son, but Brett wouldn't wake for roughly twenty minutes, so I had time to write...

"Where are you going?" Paige mumbled.

I was startled and disappointed by the sound of her voice. My effort to slip out of bed unnoticed hadn't worked—"To the study, dear," I responded softly in my most soothing voice. Hopefully this was all that would be needed.

"Not to work on that stupid play again?" Paige sighed. "Can't you give it a break?"

"I wish I could, it's something I have to do—" I began.

"It'll put you in a bad mood." The urge to respond to this was tempered by the sense I was winning this one—Paige was drifting back to sleep. If she had woken up, we would have launched right into our first argument of the Christmas season. I stood there, trying not to breathe until I was sure she was asleep and it was safe to leave.

Once sure, I tiptoed out of the room. I could go write—the argument was postponed, but not for long. It sometimes seemed there was neither rhyme nor reason to what would upset Paige, and I tried my best to avoid things that might do just that.

Paige wasn't the only one in the family who disliked me writing. Mom refused to read anything after the second poem I'd shown her years ago, and even Brett had said, "Mommy, don't let him write—it makes him too sad." Not exactly a fan club.

Twenty minutes to write isn't much, but it is precious to me, especially in the early morning hours, when I'm the freshest and the flow of words is easiest. Being halfway through the first draft, things were going really well and I was eager to sit down and write. The play was my attempt to deal with some close family losses, and I had the sense that showing it to my mother would allow us to finally talk about some important things we'd never been able to discuss.

Surrounded by silence, I walked into the study and sat at my desk. *This* is the best part of my day. I opened the desk drawer, reaching for the play—and instead saw Mom's letters from the Mayo Clinic, a neat stack held together by a rubber band.

Curious, I picked up the letter dated December 1st—exactly twenty-five years ago, it began, "My dearest children—"

"I'm up!" Brett shouted from his room at the other end of the hall. I rushed to his room before he woke Paige.

The words came fast as I walked through the door—"Is Santa getting ready? When are you putting up the Christmas tree?"

He was sitting up in his bed—a blonde-headed bundle of energy. At three, this was the first Christmas Brett was old enough to understand, and like most American kids—he was all in. He knew December was a special time of year and meant very good things would happen for him.

"Santa's in his workshop at the North Pole at *this* very moment," I said. "And very soon on putting up the tree." I was gratified that, judging by the smile spreading across his face, this was what Brett wanted to hear.

"I'm working on my list," Brett said.

For an instant I struggled with what he meant. Then I remembered: Brett's list was the presents he expected Santa Claus to bring him. It was growing daily.

"What's the last thing you put on it?" I said.

"A John Deere tractor," Brett said. "I really want a John Deere tractor."

"Santa has elves that do nothing but put together John Deere tractors. If you're good, they might make one for you," I said.

"*Really?*"

"Only if you're good."

Brett's face lit up. He wrapped his arms around my neck. Noticing a day's growth of whiskers, he said, "Are you going to shave?" It was time to move on.

Shaving was our morning ritual. Brett sat on the countertop and we both lathered up our faces and went through the usual motions. I used a real razor, he a razor without a blade. Brett never took his eyes off me as he mimicked all of my actions.

The final step to get me ready and out the door for another day at Cornwallis Pharmaceuticals was dressing for work in the study. The study closet was neatly hung with my five outfits for the week. Three dark suits—one navy blue, two gray—alternating with two sportcoats and matching slacks. All conservative. Each hung with the appropriate shirt and tie.

Paige said my color sense was "pitiful" and didn't trust me to dress myself. Perhaps with reason.

Putting on a starched shirt always made me feel like I was putting on armor. Given the sometimes vicious politics at work, maybe I needed it.

During all of this, Brett was relegated to the role of spectator. He closely watched me, especially as I tied the knot in my tie.

"One day I'll have to wear one," Brett said.

I looked in the mirror. Not bad—Paige *was* better at this than I was. Glancing at my watch, I repeated the same words every morning: "It's time to turn you over to Mom."

"Yes, Mom!" Brett cried. This was Brett's little world: quality time with me sandwiching quality time with his mother. There could be no exception.

Brett charged into our bedroom and up to the bed to hug his mom. Paige was wide awake—as if she'd been eagerly waiting for us. After twelve years of marriage, her beauty still stunned me—long blonde hair, clear blue eyes, and one of those Irish-girl faces that seemed untouched by time. She wasn't looking at me—she only had eyes for Brett, and her eyes brightened and cheeks glowed. I know that look—it is the same one my mom had for me.

And then my mouth, all on its own, screwed everything up. "Here's another December…" I said, before I could catch myself.

The sunshine in her face turned into storm clouds in an instant and she darkened with displeasure—"Why must you always *dwell* on such morbid things?"

I don't need this, I thought, *but I did it to myself.*

Brett looked puzzled.

"I'm sorry, Paige," I mumbled, "but this isn't an easy time for me."

Paige got up from the bed and faced me. She sighed. "Don't you think you make it harder on yourself than you need to?"

"How so?" I said, though I knew her reply.

"By wallowing in misery, harping on dates, and writing that *damned* play!" She positioned herself behind Brett and placed both hands on his shoulders. I couldn't help but think she was seeking an ally against unwanted rebuttal.

None was forthcoming. Despite such a promising start, somehow I'd lost the morning. Even so, I attempted a smile. "You're right. I won't mention it again."

Paige relaxed her hold on Brett. "And you'll come home in a good mood?"

"I'll come home in a good mood," I said. I slowly backed toward the door of the bedroom, eager to flee the scene for the comparative safety of big-league pharmaceutical research.

Paige smiled. "We'll be eagerly awaiting your arrival! Come give us a hug."

I reversed direction and complied. Everything was perfect again. Not wanting to risk another blunder, I kept my mouth shut as I rushed out the door and down the stairs.

I left work in the dark, as usual this time of year, after a long, hard day. I felt drained, but I was far from being through for the day. It was time to rally, to be in a good mood when I arrive home, if I knew what was good for me. I'd promised and would be expected to deliver.

As I drove home, I thought about my play. Which was a mistake. Although I was happy with the progress I was making, the subject was so dark that I found myself wiping a tear from my cheek.

I could hear Paige's voice—"Don't write—come back happy."

This isn't helping. I have to think about good Christmases. Good memories.

The best—like when I sang carols and believed in their message.

Small town Christmas when it still felt real—a party held at the post office where my Dad worked—ground outside covered in snow—boots and coats hung by the door—the presence of thirty families keeping us warm—a hundred voices singing "O Holy Night"—our song bringing lightness to dark

I turned into the driveway. By the time I opened the door, a smile was set on my face. My skin felt as though it would crack, but I was ready to perform the good mood I had promised.

CHAPTER 2

December 2nd

The darkness of morning and darkness of evening felt indistinguishable. I was so tired it felt like the end of a long day, rather than just after 6 a.m. at the start of one. Even though it was only Tuesday, I was as wrung out as if it were Friday night at the end of a brutal week.

With all the things going on at work, I have to get there in shape to get something done, and get out the door without saying something that will screw everything up at home. *Twenty-nine more damned December days to go*, I thought, *but only twenty-four matter—I just have to get through Christmas.* I have to get through it without anything happening that will upset Paige or Brett—I promised. I can't mouth off. I can't make even the slightest reference to bad things in the past—particularly their anniversary dates.

Paige says I have an obsession, like a numerologist. If something bad ever happened on a given day, I'd never forget it, and fixate on that date year after year. And not just think of it, but bring it up over and over with Paige, so that the calendar of our life looked like a minefield.

After a few years of marriage—she snapped. Told me to stop obsessing, stop dwelling, to "stop beating yourself up—and me along with you. I've got enough to deal with from my own past."

She's right. Paige knows me better than anyone else, and through her twelve years of telling me that dwelling on my past traumas only hurt me, I both knew she was right—and that I'd never be able to get past them.

I managed to hand Brett off to Paige and make it into the car without getting into trouble, thinking, *This is hard—how can I hold it together?* Think about something good. Mom. No, not Mom *now*. Mom *then*.

Helping Mom pull the Christmas tree decorations from storage. Tinsel, lights, and ornaments were laid out on our living room floor— trying to keep them safe from Boots, our family cat. With Boots as a distraction, it was always a major accomplishment to get the tree in its stand without a tilt to the left or right, backwards or forwards. Once it actually tipped over and hit the floor—ornaments and tinsel flying everywhere. Mom, with a smile on her face and a twinkle in her eye, actually seeming to enjoy the cat's antics rather than tolerate them. Mom.

Driving through the morning darkness—back to work and the same stack of headaches I left behind last night. I'd simply turned off my light, shut the door, and walked away. The work might wait, but the deadlines wouldn't—the FDA had made it clear they would pull one of our leading products off the market if we didn't deliver proof it was effective. I'd generated the data showing this to be true, but as head of my company's Respiratory Section in Clinical Research, it was my job to convince the FDA the drug worked with a giant submission. With countless millions and people's jobs at stake, a lot was riding on my work.

And as the light on Cornwallis Road turned red, it hit me as sad that this particular Santa's workshop didn't have elves to help with my big project. Cornwallis was one green and red light after another. I was on the home stretch to Research Triangle Park but seemed to be taking forever. Red and green. Green and red. I took the red personally. *Christmas.*

I pulled into Cornwallis Pharmaceuticals almost with a sense of relief. I was a success at work. Home was the challenge. My problems at work at least had real solutions that hard work could solve. At home, Paige wanted me to be happy, but she'd settle for me *acting* happy. I'd muddled through last night and this morning without blowing it. I knew she was right that my "dwelling on the past" by talking and—in my play—writing about it would cause me short-term pain, but I believed it would somehow help in the long term. And not just help me, but Mom as well. My gut told me being able to show Mom my finished play would enable us to—*finally*—talk about some long-festering wounds in a way that might help them heal.

It also hurt that the person closest to me made me feel it was wrong to even open my mouth about how I felt. I needed support, but Paige had her own rough childhood, and didn't have the strength to be there in the way I needed her. Her refusal to let me talk about past trauma was what drove me to write in the first place—a way to vent my feelings without hurting the woman I loved. Now Paige was putting pressure on me to stop even that. I didn't know if there was a right answer.

Paige was working on her second Master's degree. I have my PhD. We still couldn't figure things out.

Work was easier. All I had to do at work was deliver.

As usual I was early, so the parking lot was empty and I had my choice of spots.

Passing through the double glass doors, I was greeted by the weathered face of the guard, Betty, sitting behind her desk.

"Howya all doin'," I said to her in my imitation Southern vernacular.

"Doin' jist faine," she responded in kind.

It had taken me almost two years of living in the South to be able to decipher some of the heavier accents with confidence. And it wasn't just the syrupy accents that made folks hard to follow—it was the often elliptical nature of what they had to say.

That was all—no need to flash my ID badge as Betty smiled and waved me on. I made sure to smile back. My face was feeling a little more comfortable than it had been so far this day. More natural. My imagination had Betty pegged as a widowed Southern grandmother, but I'd never asked—and after four years, I knew I never would.

I was officially admitted into the building. With the same brief, unpretentious ritual that would be replicated exactly at the same time tomorrow morning, and the ones after that. I was now ready for the second step of my morning ritual. Equally important as the first: coffee.

Going to get my coffee took me through the same corridors leading to the same stairwell and up to the same fourth floor and the same cafeteria. Every day. Sameness was really important to me. Always was since Dad died. This morning was no exception. So far everything at work was going as I wanted and needed it to go. The same.

The cafeteria was the same as well. Seeing the same identical, smiling women with names I never bothered to read off their badges. Hearing myself ask for the same large black coffee. Saying "thank you" once I received the coffee steaming inside a large paper cup. Seeing more smiles. Smiling back. My face had thawed completely. This part of the day is starting smoothly. Good. As always, feeling the coffee almost burn my hand through the cup. Going to the cash register and reaching for the dollar bill I always put there in anticipation of this exact moment. Having it be there. Smiling again. The skin of my face feeling almost normal. Being smiled at again. Saying "have a good day" as I left. "Thank you, you too" in return.

Two final smiles in the cafeteria. These were the same, too. The same as every morning. As was the mechanical "have a good day" said in departure.

These minor workplace interactions don't seem to matter to most people—but they matter to me. Having lost so many of the people I've counted on in my life, the presence of even small things, predictable and constant, becomes all the more important. Especially in December.

Retracing my steps down the stairwell. Two flights to the second floor. Along the bizarre futurist corridor with its obliquely angular walls. Even the strange can become the familiar. Finally, that familiar right turn and I was back to my home away from home in the medical wing.

My job involved a lot of work, and my office had a lot of room to do it in. A large desk, huge work table big enough to seat six, a white board filling the end wall, and one long wall of windows. Paige hated the decor, which she called "Corporate Modern." Personal touches were my framed etching of Mark Twain on the wall and family photos on my desk.

After sitting down at my desk, I changed my desk calendar to read "December 2, 1980." As I did every morning without exception. Except on this day, the simple gesture caused me to dwell again on past losses—exactly what Paige asked me to avoid. I was almost completely immersed in thinking about this when a voice interrupted my train of thought.

"Howya doin, you crazy bastard." I didn't even have to turn around to know this was the voice of "Pee-Wee" Stewart—with the same insult that greeted me every day.

"Not bad. You receive your new pair of elevator shoes yet," I responded, which as usual elicited a gruff, "You son of a bitch."

Pee-Wee, given name Frank, had played college football despite his short stature and mere one hundred fifty pounds, and was an accomplished boxer who packed the wallop of a two-hundred-pound man. Something I knew quite well because I had been the recipient of a number of them on the basketball court. We prided ourselves on making basketball—and our friendship—a contact sport.

It was Pee-Wee's recommendation four years back that led our boss Herb Spivey to hire me, bringing Paige and I to North Carolina.

Frank was gone from my office as quickly as he arrived. Normally a signal for me to start the daily grind, but not today. Another visitor prevented that.

Alistair Cumberland. A bona fide descendant of the landed gentry in the U.K.—if not before Stonehenge, close to it. His lineage was three or four galaxies removed from my Midwestern background. His ties were either school or regimental—I made a point of never asking which one. He was Herb's boss which meant anything but a casual visit, although he gave it his best shot to appear as though it was.

On this day, the mannered Dr. Cumberland led off with his typical small talk about literature, this time Faulkner, a recent interest of mine. Then he smoothly transitioned the discussion to Russian authors—Chekhov in particular—another of my favorites. How many plays did he write? Short stories? We had just placed a bet on whether the author had been a physician (my assertion, which Cumberland discounted as nonsense) when the conversation was artfully and instantly shifted.

We were talking writers because he knew my interest in literature and book collecting—both serious passions. If I had a boat, we'd talk sailing. I would never be this effortless in managing people—public schools in England clearly had their advantages over those in Kokomo.

He smoothly interrogated as to the date upon which I projected the FDA submission to be mailed. And *if* it was still on schedule. He was preparing himself for this Thursday's meeting, and clearly didn't want to be surprised by any problems. Better to know beforehand than to be caught blindsided in public. I had to admire his skill, while confidently promising, "February first—no delays anticipated."

"That's what I needed to hear," Cumberland replied. He was *absolute* head of Clinical, with my boss Herb and his counterpart and rival across the hall, Darren Drake, as direct reports.

He walked out of my office without saying another word. Or looking back at me. He used his manners when he thought he needed them. When he had what he wanted from you, he was done. He had gotten what he came for and would forget I existed until Thursday.

Work beckoned, but I glanced at my watch and saw Mom would shortly be leaving her apartment for work. She recently shared details of some strange dreams with me, dreams that featured her own death. I might have brushed this off but for the fact Mom had, over the years, had similar dreams about her brothers right before their deaths.

I felt both compelled, and entitled, to call and check in on her.

One ring. Two. Three. Four. I was beginning to think I missed her, but suddenly, "Hello?" Mom's voice sounded frazzled, strained, like she was expecting bad news.

"It's me, Mom. Checking in to see if you're ready for Santa Claus," I said, trying to be funny.

Without wanting to, I remembered her leaving my house after Thanksgiving dinner, even though I had wanted and asked that she stay over. "No. I need to get back before it gets too dark," she had said matter-of-factly, so that I couldn't press the point, and she vanished into the gathering gloom. It had been a lost opportunity, but next time I would be more insistent.

"Not quite ready for Santa Claus, but I soon will be," Mom said. The now cheerful timbre of her voice reminded me of when I was a child, when we got out all the Christmas decorations.

"Don't forget the fudge for Saturday's big game," I said, referring to the upcoming Indiana and Kentucky basketball game, bragging rights for another year unless Indiana met Kentucky again in the NCAAs. "I can't wait until the next installment."

"I've got the ingredients in the kitchen at the ready," Mom said. "Isiah Thomas will have to be at the top of his game if we're going to win."

"I'm afraid you're right on target, Thomas is a great point guard, but it takes more than that to beat Kentucky," I said. Although the

Hoosiers were immensely talented and had great potential, they had yet to really gel.

"How's my grandson?" Mom said.

"He's excited about Christmas, and bugging me to put up the tree."

"The one you bought last year at South Square Mall?"

Suddenly her voice seemed strained again, like her good mood had deflated, helium leaked from a balloon. I wondered if Mom was remembering the debacle of last year's Christmas, when Paige's parents came to visit. Alcoholism is an ugly disease.

Why was I thinking of that? "This is the first year Brett is really into Santa Claus," I mumbled distractedly.

"The very same age as you," Mom observed wistfully.

"The very same age? Tell me about that later, Mom. I've got get back to work."

"I'd like that," Mom said. "I've got to get to the store too. Vince already has the coffee brewing, and will have a cup waiting for me when I get there."

Her work. My work.

"Goodbye."

"Goodbye, Mom."

At 4:30, I called home to talk with Paige and was greeted by a busy signal. Mom beat me to the punch. She always called Paige around this time to recap the day. I dialed Mom's number and received another busy signal, confirming my deduction. They were probably talking about what to buy Brett for Christmas.

Remembering how important the holiday was for me when I was his age, I promised myself again to get with the program. I put that smile Paige asked for back on my face and went home.

CHAPTER 3

December 3rd

Driving home from work, Wednesday, December 3rd. Red and green lights punctuated my thoughts. *Like the road, this month is crawling, when I wish it would be over.* The stress of a heavy workload and getting ready for tomorrow's big meeting had chipped away at me. Making my drive and mood worse, a piece of my car's window trim had pulled loose and vibrated loudly in the wind. Damn car, damn month. Pulling into the driveway, I put on my smile and walked through the door.

Paige and Brett caught me as soon as I entered the family room. Brett beamed. "Everyone's coming, Dad! Everyone's coming! Ma, Papa, Aunt Lynn, Aunt Ann, and Grandma!"

My smile grew brittle. Paige and I planned for Mom to be at Christmas all along, but now there would also be my sister Ann, and Paige's parents and sister. A more incompatible group couldn't be assembled. Images from last year's Christmas fiasco crowded in—*Paige's father's raging alcoholism—raiding the cabinets for Jack Daniels to spike the punch. A week of never knowing when he'd find something to drink—or what would happen when he did. Paige and her sister Lynn never even talk... And my sister... Ann's relationship with Mom is strained even under the best circumstances.*

Paige was watching me intently, gauging my reaction. *It's beyond me, what went through her head to make her do this.*

"It's going to be wonderful," Paige informed me cheerfully.

Brett could barely restrain his excitement. He looked up at me, expecting me to be equally enthusiastic.

"That's great," I said. I wished I could stop thinking—*it's going to blow up in our faces.*

I could see Paige relax. She now knew I really had given in to her vision of Christmas.

I'd read some Marquez, enough to recognize magical thinking when I encountered it. Paige's childhood hadn't been easy, and this—a belief the impossible would magically work out—was a youthful coping mechanisms which occasionally resurfaced. But then again, she married me, and that worked out...

For the first time I heard Sergio Franchi's Christmas album in the background. Paige played it every year, regular as clockwork. It didn't seem that long since I had heard it last. Another year of marriage. Brett a year older. Damn calendars.

Paige smiled, saying, "Welcome home, dear, the two of us have been getting ready for Christmas..." Her voice trailed off before she followed with, "It's going to be the best Christmas of all—it's going to be perfect for Brett."

The best Christmas of all... perfect for Brett. The edge in Paige's voice was gone.

It wasn't entirely clear to me who Paige was addressing. Me. Brett. Herself. Or a combination of all three.

"It's going to be a *great* Christmas!" Brett parroted. With everyone coming to see him and nearly a month of holiday excitement ahead, how could it be otherwise?

I coughed. A recurring reminder of an asthma-filled December a quarter century past. For some reason, that suddenly seemed much closer to me—like only yesterday.

"Yes, it will be!" I sputtered. I noticed the decorations from Thanksgiving had been put away. Instead there was a pile of boxes right next to us in the family room, each filled with Christmas decorations, including what seemed liked hundreds of ornaments for the tree. This should have been obvious to me as soon as I stepped through the door, but my mind had been on a double scotch on the rocks—not Christmas.

The decorations needed to be put into place. *After* I put up the tree, that is. This was something I'd intended to do before now, but I'd kept putting off the task. The mound of boxes made clear that Paige and Brett wanted me to get on right away. The scotch would have to wait—but not for long.

The box containing our new artificial Christmas tree was sitting on the floor in the family room as well. I had missed that too upon entering, although I could have easily tripped over it. The salesman claimed it was easy to put together, but the truth of that remained to be seen.

The official launch for Brett's first great Christmas season was to be me wrestling with assembling our store-bought tree. All I had to do was take it out of the box and follow instructions. I hoped in future years Brett would remember this Christmas as warmly as those I recalled from the 1950s.

"I've prepared snacks so we can get started and not worry about dinner," Paige volunteered. She was being less than subtle. Decorating most definitely was on the docket. Her voice left no doubt she expected not just buy-in but immediate action.

"Can you set up the tree? Can you set up the tree!" Brett chimed in, as excited as only Santa could make a three-year-old. To underscore the importance of the question, he began hugging my leg. In other words, I'd do it.

Paige may not have gone to a fancy English school, but in her way she'd maneuvered me as neatly as Alastair Cumberland at work the day before. *Just a different kind of boss.*

"I'll get right on it. I should have it set up in no time," I said with a smile. I hoped my voice didn't betray how I felt.

It didn't, as evidenced by Brett's enthusiastic response.

And Paige's: "We'll go upstairs to get out of your hair for a while."

One of those strange feelings that sometimes came over me chose that moment to visit—and suddenly I didn't want to be alone, didn't want my family to leave. But they did and I was, which left me standing over the box with the tree, thoughts headed in the wrong direction—to the past and not the present. *Dwelling—I promised not to.*

When you've promised your wife to be happy, there's no way to tell her it's not a good idea for you to be alone.

My thoughts went to the play I was trying to finish. Another thing Paige wasn't happy about. And I wasn't supposed to obsess about dates, either. The anniversary of one of those dates was the 4th—tomorrow—something I'd been trying hard not to think about.

Looking at the half-opened box, it seemed an apt metaphor for the play I couldn't get out of my mind. I was pressing hard to finish it, to show it to my Mom as I'd promised at Thanksgiving. I couldn't remember whether she actually said she wanted to see it. Clearly it must be as much or more about the writing as it was in the seeing.

I shouldn't have been surprised Mom was as enthusiastic about my play as Paige. Which meant not at all.

It's not exactly holiday material, with three coffins each having central roles in the play. The only work of mine Mom had ever read were two poems I'd written about death—the second of which she couldn't even finish.

Trying to get this tree out of its box was working as well as trying to stick my memories and feelings back in theirs. Another Christmas, arrived so quickly—*another season of death*—these were *not* the memories I wanted to have or pass along to Brett. What were?

Driving around Kokomo, looking at decorations. Dad driving carefully on icy streets. We decided the west side won our informal yearly contest for best lights and decorations. Forest Park especially. Second place went to the houses on West Main. Eggnog or hot apple cider with cinnamon.

The play was all coffins and corpses. It was crazy for me to be making these associations. Absolutely nuts. For an instant, it was truly touch and go. I went to the kitchen where I took the Dewar's White Label from the cabinet. I debated whether to prepare my drink neat, but decided against it. Scotch on the rocks it would be. Two quick gulps didn't faze me. I was wired. Remembering death did that to me. No amount of alcohol could make me forget.

Clearly, I needed to do something besides think, so further procrastination was out of the question.

My steps were resolute as I headed into the family room. There was no turning back. This wasn't exactly D-Day, but it was Brett's first Christmas tree. My son's very first tree. I could do this. He'd remember it when he grew up. A dazzling sight all lit up and decorated especially for him—just like Mom did for Ann and me.

That thought didn't last long.

Only until I had the box open. "How am I going to survive another Christmas?" not only became a thought but somehow escaped from my mouth. I could only hope I hadn't been heard. Saying this around Paige was unthinkable—even her suspicion I might be thinking it would be just as bad.

I held still and listened with the focus only the guilty can have.

To my relief, all I could hear was soft laughter coming from Brett's room at the top of the stairs.

Laughter—all I could make out, and exactly what I needed to hear. My wife and son sounding happy.

But were they happy enough? They had to be to compensate for how I was feeling. Barely getting by while trying not to get more depressed. As I proceeded to take the branches of the tree from their individual wrappings, my mood soured.

Guilt joined my depression in a whirling tango. This wasn't helping.

My mood was headed in the opposite direction from where it needed to go. Two healthy gulps of Dewar's followed without noticeable effect. My hands began to shake. This was something new and unsettling for me. Regardless of how hard I tried to stop the trembling, I couldn't. At least the ice in my glass wasn't clanking. Not yet. And shaky hands or not, piece followed piece and the bottom of the tree was taking shape.

Sergio Franchi's singing had become the faint strains of Christmas music emanating from Brett's room. I thought Paige was probably rummaging through boxes for wrapping paper and ribbon. She had a lot of work to do in order to get the house ready for Christmas.

Neither she nor Brett had stopped laughing. If only they wouldn't stop. They couldn't—I needed it.

Mother laughed all the time for those special Christmases on East Mulberry—laughed while trying to keep Boots at bay—laughed during each and every one of them without exception—that's the way it had been—

Tomorrow's the 4th. One of December's worst days. The day I lost my first surrogate father—Uncle Norman, and way too many other things to think about.

From upstairs—laughter. Laughter. *Helping me forget—*

Almost but not quite because its sound was shortly uprooted by another unwanted Christmas memory. The first of my bad Christmases, when my perfect childhood train went off the rails.

Twenty five years ago—the Christmas Mom and Dad were gone—gone to the Mayo Clinic because Dad was sick—sick in a way they didn't explain and we couldn't understand—Ann and I pouring over Mom's letters, trying to figure out what was going on. Promises of a return home for Christmas being followed by uncertainty, and then by them not being home for Christmas—Uncle Norman taking care of Ann and me, doing his best to make things normal and give us a real Christmas

Trying not to remember but remembering anyway—

I couldn't remember any laughter from that bad Christmas, although there had to have been some. And not just Christmas Day—I couldn't remember any laughter from the entire damn month.

Two more desperate gulps and I walked into the kitchen to refill my glass with scotch.

Upon my return to the living room, the tree was halfway up, looking so good I imagined smelling pine needles.

Pine needles. Mom's voice was returning to me although she wasn't there in the family room. Her voice returning from when she was young. So much younger than her current age of fifty-nine.

The trunk of the tree had taken shape. Brett's first tree. I had to make it so even Paige considered it perfect.

Another sudden burst of laughter from upstairs. Brett's. He sounded happy. He had to be happy! Paige, too. It would take both them being happy to help me get out of this depression. To make my plastic smile a real one.

I was almost done with my scotch, and the tree was finally done. I set it far enough from the wall so there would be room for mountains of presents to surround the base of the tree. Just like the way things were when I was young.

All the neatly wrapped boxes with their ribbons and name tags—

I looked up and saw three stockings hanging from the mantle. Paige's, Brett's, mine. I was noticing them for the first time. None for Boots. By no means unexpected, yet I suddenly found myself missing her anyway. And wondering what had happened to her stocking. I didn't have it. Perhaps Mom did. If not, there was an outside chance it was with Ann. I decided to ask her the next time we talked.

My stomach growled. Dewar's was a poor substitute for food. Two more sips and it was finished, and my stomach began burning.

Two double Dewar's and no dinner somehow got me thinking about the apple pie Mom brought for Thanksgiving. With vanilla ice cream. One of my favorite recipes. I wasn't really hungry, I was missing Mom, and decided to call and see how she was. It wasn't too late. I just wanted to hear her voice.

I dialed her number. Paige's and Brett's voices came from upstairs. I couldn't make out what they were saying.

No sooner had mother answered the phone than Brett charged into the room.

"I want to talk! I want to talk!" the toddler demanded. There wasn't the slightest doubt in his mind that he would be granted his wish.

Paige walked in as I was handing over the phone. She walked to the couch and sat.

Brett's voice bubbled over with excitement as he answered and announced, "Hi. Mar-Mar. I'm working on my Christmas list for Santa." After a short pause he followed up with, "A John Deere tractor." Mother must have inquired as to the last item he put on his list. Their conversation lasted a few minutes longer, and then he handed me the phone and went off to bed with Paige.

It's odd I remember Brett's conversation so clearly, but I have no memory of what I talked about with Mom. Maybe it was the Dewar's, or maybe what was most important for me was just hearing her voice.

CHAPTER 4

December 4th

My morning time with Brett mattered to both of us. I was trying to be here, with him—not someplace else. But the more I tried to not think about painful memories, the harder it seemed to become. I was *not* thinking about my big report today. I was trying to keep my promise to Paige and *not* dwell on the past, or the fact it was December 4th, and everything that means—the things Paige didn't want to hear about.

"How many days until Santa comes?" asked Brett. He looked up at me expectedly, unaware he wasn't the sole object of my attention, or that he was taking me in the wrong direction by asking me to think about what day it is. The 4th.

"Let me see," I begin before my voice trailed off...stilled by a memory from when I was ten years old.

Uncle Norman beside me on the train platform in Logansport—I'm waving goodbye as Mom and Dad shrink from sight—for Dad's operation at the Mayo Clinic—at least that's what they said—

"Don't you know?" Brett demanded, trying to capture my attention.

Uncle Norman was always vocal about Paige and I having children.

"How many days until Christmas Eve?" I managed to ask Brett.

And another four years ago on this date, when I was thirty one—

December 4th—the phone ringing—mother's voice—"Norman choked on a pork chop and turned blue—I held him in my arms—he's on a respirator at St. Joseph's—where Dad died."

Brett was struggling with my question, said, "I don't know. How many days until Christmas Eve?"

Norman chasing me and Ann around the house singing, "This Old Man—" playing games all the time—trying to beat Ann but only winning sometimes—how long was he without oxygen—TEN MINUTES—he's brain dead.

"Twenty more days," I told Brett—more gruffly than I intended.

Twenty more days for me to get through—twenty days to make a perfect Christmas for Paige and Brett—and—Mother.

Brett hugged me around my knees as if he was trying to lasso me in with his arms. "That's a lot, Jack!" he declared. He wasn't about to let go of me, and finally had my undivided attention.

He kept it until we were lathered up for our morning ritual of shaving. At first I saw two images in the mirror—mine and Brett's. One instant it was that way, and the next it was alarmingly different.

Instead of my reflection, Norman's face stared back at me from the mirror—not the addict's face from later in life but the younger one from when he was my role model after Dad died.

I didn't let the blade touch my face until his haunting image was gone.

What was Norman like before the war? I was born in 1945, so my only memories of him are from afterward. That horrible scar through his shoulder—from a German sniper's bullet that shot him off a tank—did more than disfigure him physically. It also led to a lifetime of pain, and addiction to painkillers. He once said, "I never really came back from the war." I sometimes had the sense during his lifetime that he was haunting himself, so it shouldn't have been a surprise to see his face in my mirror.

The war hadn't been easy on my uncles—aside from Mike, who was still in school. Steve, who died a few months before Norman, spent a year in a German POW camp, an experience that so tormented him he was never able to speak of it.

I had to get out the door and to the office—petty politics and an intense workload may not rank with fighting the Nazis, but it still wasn't a cakewalk.

After shaving, I walked Brett to our bedroom to hand him over to Paige—one look and she knew my mind was someplace else. "I'm afraid to hazard a guess as to where your mind is now," she said immediately. Paige was staring a hole through me. She had me—I was still thinking about Norman.

"Today is my presentation before senior management," I said.

Paige's eyes remained unrelenting. But instead of pursuing the point, she turned to Brett and said, "How's my absolutely most favorite person in the whole wide world?"

Apparently I was off the hook—for the time being. Not wishing to press my luck, I said, "Gotta get the show on the road."

Paige avoided looking at me. "Please come home in a good mood," she said, quickly shifting her attention to Brett.

I was free to go. Past the tree that had somehow become totally decorated while I was sleeping. With those first few steps, my mind turned to my presentation in the Cornwallis Pharmaceuticals boardroom. I had essentially memorized it. As I turned the ignition my thoughts reverted to Paige, Norman, and Mother.

Paige literally hated Norman for something else. Hated him to such an extent she said he should've been shot.

These are old landscapes never revisited without pain. Disturbing me so much I wondered—*how can I stay grounded in the present?*

I gathered my sources of strength—my young son. My wife. My mother. How can all my sources of strength also be my responsibilities? How screwed up is that? Where does this come from? That's one question I damn well knew the answer to, and I never had to go to a shrink to discover it.

The defining moment of my life was being told two hours after my Dad's death that I was now responsible for my Mom. At thirteen. By Uncle Norman—bastard.

But that responsibility became my strength, and I've carried it through my whole life, through many losses and great pain.

"You were much too young to be told you were responsible for your mother. He had to be an idiot to put that burden on you," Paige said many times through the years. So often she had long sounded like a broken record. One that made me very ill at ease whenever I had to listen to it.

Norman had to be an absolute idiot? Without a doubt. Yet at the time my mind immediately latched onto his words—and took them as Gospel. Snapped them right up and took them to heart.

This obligation preyed on my mind daily, as did those I felt for my wife and son.

I must have driven. Must have parked. Must have. My body did this, but I was someplace else.

Before I knew it—I was at work, standing in the lobby. For an instant I didn't have a clue as to how I got there—or *why* I was standing there. Then I notice the Christmas tree sitting on the far side of the lobby. It's identical to the one that greeted me four years ago today. December 4th.

Identical—down to the smallest detail.

Hearing the news from Mom—calling the hospital—Norman's physician angry at my wave of questions—not wanting to tell me what he knows but giving in to my persistence—"flat EEG indicative of no brain activity"—he's brain dead—like a bomb went off in his head—

riding in the backseat of Norman's convertible through the Indiana countryside, throwing cherry bombs into fields, "Night Train" playing on the radio

This had to stop. I had a huge presentation and had to be here *now*—this was today, not four years ago. I wasn't going to let the pressures of today drive me into the past—I spent too much time there already.

Focus. My eyes were definitely playing tricks on me—had to be. Nothing going on in my head had anything to do with today. I used the thought of the work I had to do in a few hours to push away these haunting images and memories from the past.

I turned away from the tree and walked to the medical wing.

Walking helped me concentrate on the oral presentation in the boardroom. Show time—a few hours away. I'd feel better when it was over.

Switching on the light to my office, I saw the script for my presentation sitting on my work table. I knew the material cold, but immediately started rehearsing it anyway. No kidding around with these guys today.

In the four years since my arrival, I'd qualified as an expert in the field. I literally knew everything of importance about cough and cold products. It sounds boring—but it meant hundreds of millions of dollars. And I was able to show what no one else ever had before: it worked. All I had to do was submit my data to the FDA on time and convince them of this. The simple fact that our most important product *worked*.

Regardless of the importance of this to the company, not everyone was cheering for me. If I failed, Darren Drake would be happy since the department of his chief rival—my boss—would have failed in a spectacular fashion. Bad for the company, good for him. Politics. Pretend they don't matter and you're dead.

By the time I was summoned to the boardroom I was ready. I had honed my presentation beyond further refinement—it was tight. My half an hour or forty five minutes on stage was imminent. "Focus, focus, focus," I chanted to myself. My undivided attention to the task at hand was essential. No screw ups. It had to go without a hitch.

Three flights of stairs separated me from the fifth floor where most of the VPs and the CEO lived. The door to the boardroom opened without a sound. I sat off to the side while the presentation preceding mine finished. No one in the room acknowledged my presence except my boss. Herb nodded his head slightly.

I barely heard my name being called by the VP. It was time for me to speak, and I was moving to stand at the opposite end of the table from where he was. Alistair Cumberland was

sitting in the chair to his immediate right. Darren Drake was sitting to my right. Herb to my left. Both ready to pounce on each other.

All the eyes around the table were glued on me. My voice droned on and on and on, monotonous to such a degree it seemed to become detached from me. Detached to a point where it could be someone else speaking altogether.

Two major studies showed the contribution of each drug in the combination—supportive studies confirming them—complete review of the literature—another study showing the product's absorption into the bloodstream—complete review of safety, no delays in submission to FDA—droning on like a recording continuously until I stopped speaking and there was silence in the room.

"Nicely done, Jack. Nicely done." Cumberland was talking. Darren Drake—wanting to stick a knife in, tried to speak first, but Alistair beat him to the first punch and kept swinging. He was speaking and looking at the VP to make sure he noticed who was running the discussion. Herb was glaring at Darren. If looks could kill, that son of a bitch would have been dead.

"Thank you." Me again. Had to say it while waiting for the inevitable question from the head of Clinical. Couldn't help but wish he'd speed things up.

"With that vast amount of work, you have an extremely aggressive timeline for submission. Are you sure you can make it?" Drake was sarcastic and intentionally ignoring Herb, making him angrier by the second.

"Yes. I'll make it."

"A vast amount of work and a vast amount of data for old drugs. All this work, and you've reinvented the wheel." Drake's voice. Dripping with pride that he'd gotten in the zinger. The son of a bitch was setting a trap.

Herb was predictably livid. On the verge of coming out of his chair.

"He's done what the FDA requires!" my boss's voice sputtered. "Everything that's in the submission is needed."

Sitting at the opposite end of the table next to Cumberland, the VP was enjoying the spectacle. Like a noble Roman at the Coliseum.

Keenly aware he had stolen the show, Darren Drake sat back demurely in his seat. "No doubt that's true, but don't you think he could state the obvious in one-tenth the space? Less wear and tear that way." A constrained burst of laughter erupted around the table.

Alistair Cumberland's "Gentlemen, that's enough." straight-jacketed Herb. The exchange was over, Drake the obvious victor.

Somehow getting lost in the shuffle was my presentation. I was delivering on what I had promised. The next words I heard were, "Thank you, Dr. Lewis," from the VP. I was dismissed, and I walked from the conference room without looking back. This ordeal was over.

Being finished was like a weight off my shoulders. December 4th was about the worst day they could have scheduled this, and I'd been dreading today ever since I'd gotten the memo. But it was done—all I had to do now was go home, have a scotch, and put on my Christmas smile.

Brett greeted me enthusiastically at the door as always. The den sparkled with the lighted Christmas tree and decorations. After Brett had gone over his day and ever lengthening list of presents, Paige remarked almost as an afterthought, "Your mother told me she was under the weather a bit, but wasn't sick enough to stay home from work."

Today of all days—

"Today of all days!" Somehow I was able to stop anything from escaping from my mouth. Instead, I asked, "Did she say what was wrong?"

"Probably the flu," Paige replied, giving me the look. *The* look.

"What's the flu?" Brett asked.

"It's when you don't feel very good and don't want to do anything except go to bed and rest," I said, pretending to be calm.

She had the flu at the Mayo Clinic! It was the most unfortunate of associations. Another.

"She doesn't think it will interfere with the game on Saturday," Paige said. She was reading my mind, and didn't like where it was headed.

Brett smiled at me—crowing, "Indiana is still going to lose."

I have to keep my mind—here—here and nowhere else!

I turned to him and managed to reply, "No, they won't. And they'll beat your precious UNC in two weeks."

Brett laughed. For him this was family fun time—teasing me about basketball.

"Did Mom say she would call the doctor?" I asked Paige.

"She said she'd call him tomorrow," Paige responded.

"I think I'll call her," I heard myself saying. *Yes, call her—call her now and make sure everything is all right.*

"Let's give your father some peace and quiet so he can call your grandmother," Paige said to Brett, who reluctantly followed her up to his room.

Two rings were all that was required for Mom to answer her telephone with a terse "Hello."

"This is your son," I said cheerfully.

Her voice lightened as she responded in kind, "To what do I owe this honor?"

"Why in the hell did you come down with the flu," followed from me.

"Because it appeared to be the best thing to do. This way I can be rid of whatever ails me in

plenty of time for Christmas," she calmly answered.

"Great timing, Mom, great timing," I countered. Then, "If you're not back to full speed by tomorrow, you'll have to call the doctor. Have to keep on top of this, whatever it is. Nip it in the bud."

Some seriousness had tempered the levity in the conversation. Mom chuckled despite the shift in tone. "I'd hate to bother the doctor."

"Why? Besides, I wrote the package inserts for many of the medicines he'd prescribe for you. Also, don't forget I can get them for you for free," I said as reassurance.

"Yes, Dr. Perkins," she said with obvious pride in her voice.

I felt emotionally drained despite what I had just learned. "I had a huge day and think I need to get some rest," I muttered. I could hardly wait until I got into bed.

"Okay. I wouldn't want to keep you from your beauty rest," Mom replied. Her voice was the embodiment of health. "Please give Brett a kiss for me."

"I will." And I did.

After climbing into bed, a few deep breaths had me at the edge of sleep. Waiting there for me was the memory of my mom's nightly ritual, tucking me into bed, kissing me good night. This smile was a real one, as I nodded off.

CHAPTER 5

December 5th

I laid in bed wide awake, staring through the darkness at the ceiling.

As long as I don't move and wake Paige, this time—and my thoughts— can be free and my own.

I heard her slow breathing, felt the covers move that little bit each time. I decided to stay in bed for a bit and let my thoughts wander before going to the study to work on my play, or getting Brett out of bed.

December—made it through the first four days. Big presentation— took a few knives in the back—but still delivered. Made it past the 4th—one of the bad days—without getting caught dwelling by Paige. Trying to keep my promise about Christmas. It's working—Brett's happy and there's peace with Paige—like the Christmas truce in World War I.

Paige shifted slightly, and I held my breath till she settled.

Today's the 5th—another bad date. Damn it—can't think like that. Like one of my Southern friends said, "Don't focus on the ugly—there's something positive in every day." But by the time I was in high school, Mom was already telling me not to not be so morbid, to lighten up, and stop obsessing about numbers...dates...anniversaries...the cal- endar.

The calendar is *not* my enemy. All it's doing is marking time. I live in the real world—I'm not some nutty numerologist. There are plenty of good days, and good things can happen, even on bad dates. Visualize the positive.

Good days—first date with Paige—getting married—buying our first house—Brett's birth—can't top that.

The calendar is not a scary thing. It's not some caricature of a Mayan stone carving with dates dripping blood. Find an image that isn't frightening.

A rectangular calendar floating in midair—day five with a big circle—Dad's surgery, December 5th, 1955. Damn. As if I needed reminding. Something else, better image. Happier. Those goofy paper calendars with the windows everyone had when I was young. What were they called—Advent calendars—you open the windows and find pretty pictures. That's it—a calendar with twenty-five days—with a happy surprise you discover each day

Twenty-five days. Twenty-five years. To the day. Dad's surgery. Damn. Or as Mom said—"Your father's serious operation." She left out *so* much. Why? Despite the careful markings on my mental map, my mind had taken that wrong turn.

Paige would blow a gasket if she knew what I was thinking. She had as many ghosts from the past haunting her. I had to stop taking her places she wasn't strong enough to go. She's carrying enough baggage of her own without me burdening her with mine.

"Blow a gasket—" one of Mom's favorite expressions—wish I had a quarter for every time I heard her pull this out of the hat over the years. Wish I had a quarter—Mom has always liked that one, too.

Clichés. Mom doesn't live for them—but she seems to need them to live.

I'm made fun of her use of repetitive cliches as a chorus, but it sure was something I picked up from her—I'm Captain Cliché myself.

My clichés—how many did I inherit from Mom, and how many did I find on my own. Three, four…all of them? Paige and the guys at work mocked me all the time. What were the ones that started eyes rolling…

Head in sand, writing on the wall, can't teach a dog new tricks, play it as it lies, let her rip, rolling stone, can't bury your head in the sand, the handwriting is on the wall, what goes up must come down, pound foolish and penny wise.

Paige was still deep in sleep, her breath slow and steady. Good. Getting through yesterday without getting caught "dwelling" was tough enough. Having Mom complain of the flu on the same date—the 4th—that Norman basically died in her arms. It's just a date that unrelated things happened on. Coincidences. These things have no connection other than in my mind.

But they come to mind over and over and over again. Like the clichés that Mom and I used so often in speech. It must be something in our brains.

Even though I knew this, even though I knew I shouldn't talk about it with her, if Paige were awake, I was always on the edge of providing a new justification of why this or that particular date bothered me because of something from years ago. Regardless of any of the good things that happened more recently. Can't teach an old dog new tricks. Thanks for the cliché, Mom.

Now was the time to sneak out of bed, work on my play, hand Brett off to Paige with a quick smile, and be off to work. If

I had my druthers, nothing would be said about unmentionable subjects. No opportunity for more friction. Zero.

"If I had my druthers—" Mom's still knocking around in my head—hope her bug decided to go away.

I sat down and my desk—so far so good—picked up the manuscript and recalled the last lines I had written in my play.

"The memories of a boy don't have benefit of the man he will become, and yet those of a man are shaped by the youth he was."

Where was I going with this?

Brett's chirpy voice proclaiming "I'm up!" ahead of schedule ended any thoughts of writing. His voice was more excited than normal. It was one day closer to Santa Claus arriving, and our entire family coming to visit—with presents.

I put the pages back down. No play today. I'd let my thinking run through my writing time. This one time, it was worth it.

Brett shouted "Dad!" almost as soon as I flipped on the light, and then he bounced up and jumped toward me with open arms. My mood brightened considerably. It couldn't help but lighten up, given Brett's enthusiasm and his talk of Santa Claus, an expanding wish list of presents, and the guest list for the upcoming "Big Day."

"I love you, slugger," I said. I always tried to be vocal about my feelings and love for Brett. In part, an attempt to compensate for something I didn't get from my Dad.

I always wanted my Dad's love and approval, but almost never succeeded in feeling like I had either. The one exception was little league baseball. Dad was the announcer, sitting up above the field in the scorekeeper's booth. Sometimes I climbed up the ten-foot ladder and joined him.

I didn't want Brett having to climb a ladder to feel he had my love and approval.

The hole was so big, I looked to Mom to fill it. I used to pester her with questions about whether Dad loved my sister and I. Mom would calmly reply, "Certainly, my dear, but he doesn't know how to show those emotions."

That wasn't going to be me. That isn't me.

Fortunately for me, Brett's excitement had staying power. I managed to hand him over to Paige without getting anything more than a quick, sharp glance in return.

"Have a good day at work," Paige said to me while cuddling a squirming, giggling Brett.

"And don't forget to come home smiling." Thrown in for good measure.

"I'll do my best," I said.

I'll do my best.

My renewed testament to the very best of intentions kept my mind on track through getting to work, flipping on the lights in my office, the morning ritual of getting coffee in the cafeteria, the daily exchange of insults with Frank Stewart.

It wasn't long after my day started going south.

My secretary Crystal led it all off. She had long, raven-black hair that reminded me of mother's when she was young. I could tell something was amiss when she entered my office and didn't greet me with her usual smile. She was clearly nervous and upset, and I had never seen her like this before. I had a tough time even getting her to talk about what was troubling her. It turned out *my* boss was the problem. Before I could get her to tell me what he had done, she practically ran from the room.

I would have to deal with this—later. Later—but what had her so upset? And how was I going to deal with whatever it was?

He was my *boss*. I was startled by the phone ringing, which meant Crystal wasn't answering, as she normally would. I would be getting whoever it was without a filter. Not good. Not good at all since it turned out to be a pissed-off medical researcher from some university yelling at me for not receiving the grant check I'd promised him.

"It's in the mail," I said, without having a clue as to whether it really was. Anything to get him out of my hair *now*. Something else for me to worry about later. Much later, I hoped.

The morning's mail came in and provided my next shot in the ribs. A rejection letter from a prestigious medical journal. On a paper for which I was lead author. I scribbled action notes in the margins of the rejection letter—"Morons!! IT WAS A GREAT PIECE OF WORK!" Back to the drawing board. Re-submit somewhere else. Get on it mid-afternoon today. Maybe tomorrow morning.

Taking a sip of coffee, I took stock of what was quickly becoming a mess of a day. It dawned on me I was already falling behind schedule on completing the filing with the FDA. Management wouldn't be happy, particularly since I told them just yesterday it would go in on time, and on top of that Drake was riding me whenever he had the chance. I'd walked past him in the hallway earlier, and his cheery "How's the submission coming along?" still burned.

A bad day became worse when the phone rang a second time.

Paige, filling me in on Mom, who was staying home from work with what had developed into a clear-cut case of the flu.

Paige proceeded to tell me Mom called our family doctor, Barry Winthrop, to see if an appointment was necessary.

Barry Winthrop was short and in his late thirties, with a full-length beard as if to divert attention from the top of his bald head. Mother said he looked like a flower child from the late '60's. A funny-looking guy, but he was a fellow Midwesterner and we had developed a great relationship with him since we moved to the area.

Barry informed Mom that her condition didn't warrant an office visit, and phoned in a prescription for medicine to lessen her symptoms. Barry advised bed rest for Mom for several days to allow the infection to run its normal course.

Run its normal course.

I shared my quick assessment that, aside from being an inconvenience, this was nothing to be concerned about. "Nothing—to—be—concerned—about." The words flowed effortlessly from my mouth.

Paige readily concurred.

"Too bad she'll miss the basketball game" was all I managed to remark to Paige.

I decided to stop worrying about Mom to Barry. I'd get her whatever she needs when she needs it. That way I could get back to worrying about work—my FDA project and Drake's constant sniping, making Brett's first memorable Christmas a happy one, and staying out of the doghouse with Paige.

No worrying.

Great plan—lasted almost a whole minute.

Why is this happening now?

It was just the flu. Why was I so quick to dwell—to loop?

It's coincidental—a coincidence. I can tell myself this ten thousand times and still not be able to stop trying to find pattern and causation in randomness. My rational mind knows there is no *why*, and that the calendar is not out to get me, but my emotional self needs something and can't stop looking.

No reason to obsess about it, but I was still uneasy. It certainly would be easier to put this out of my mind if her flu would have picked another date.

It was just the flu. This was my field, I was the expert. And I knew more about the medications she was receiving than Barry Winthrop himself. I liked him, and trusted him as much as I could trust anybody, but true trust was impossible for me. But I could trust him for now, because I knew I was in a position to call the shots if I thought I needed to.

From my perspective, there is absolutely nothing to trust in this godless universe—besides myself.

I trust myself, and the things I can reach out and touch.

Right that moment, I wanted to trust Mom was okay, and I dialed her number to make sure. Her voice sounded reassuringly normal to me.

"I understand you haven't shaken your bug," I joked.

"Not quite yet, but I'm well on the way to getting it done," Mom responded in kind.

Well on the way of getting it done. Another Mom-ism.

"What did Barry prescribe for you?" I asked nonchalantly.

"The usual stuff and some Valium."

"The usual stuff" meant the standard medicines for which I truly was the world's foremost expert. The Valium had been thrown in to calm Mom's nerves.

"Call Eckerd's and tell them your grandson and son will be by tomorrow morning and pick it up," I said..

"Oh, good. I'll tell them you're a *doctor*," Mom replied with unmistakable pride in her voice. Pride of what I had been able to accomplish. Moreover that she was my mother.

"Also, before I forget, if you start to feel worse, call me up right away and I'll go sooner," I told her.

"You can count on it, but I don't think it will be necessary."

Mom sounded content. Her flu had been dutifully recognized by her brilliant son, and its resolution was completely in my hands. There was no one else she trusted more, and this included Barry Winthrop. It couldn't have been any other way. Ever since I had been thirteen.

"Don't over-do it, Mom" I cautioned. "You know you're supposed to be in bed."

"I know. I'll behave. I don't want to be sick any longer than I have to be," she replied.

I adopted a no-nonsense tone. "Now you're talking. Remember what you used to tell me all the time: Be good and we won't have anything to worry about." My emphasis on "we" was clear, and she took notice.

"Okay. You've convinced me," she said. "You're aware, of course, you won't have fudge for Saturday's game. That might bring the Hoosiers bad luck against Kentucky." Thrown in as a clear attempt to change the subject.

Bad luck—bad luck?

An allusion to bad luck did not sit well with me, but I concealed my true feelings. "We'll win without your fudge." I added, "Besides, you can make a double batch for the Carolina game."

"It's a deal. I'll be in good shape by then."

I dove into work and used Friday busyness to successfully avoid thinking about anything, now or in the past, that would stop me from getting home with that promised smile on my face at the end of a long work week.

Getting home, I passed all the tests my watchful, wary wife and my happy, bouncing child had for me—my smile intact.

Despite everything the day had thrown at me, I kept my promise, and Brett went off to bed happy while Paige went to work on her thesis.

I had made it through the whole day.

And then. Like a moth to the flame, I went to the one place, one time, one thing, that I never should have gone to.

I returned to my study and closed the door. I opened the top right-hand drawer to my desk. There they were, barely more than an inch of old letters confined by a frayed rubber band. Mom's letters from the Mayo Clinic.

Dangerous territory. Don't open them. Put them back.

Only one—I would look at one. One couldn't hurt. The one from the 5th. Twenty-five years ago.

There wasn't one. The day of Dad's surgery. Mom had her hands full and was too busy to write. Like my perpetual chase for Dad's affection, it wasn't there.

The last time I saw him alive, Dad's hand exerted a pressure on mine. There was something about his grip. Something telling me he was as afraid as me. If not more. I stood at his bedside like that for several seconds, Dad didn't want to let go. Even after he died, I never did let go. Part of me has been frozen, standing in that same spot for twenty-five years, holding the hand of a man who wasn't here *now*, and in many ways, never was *then*.

I began to cry, remembering these things from a quarter century past. As hard as I tried, I couldn't stop. My door was closed and I hoped no one could hear.

It took a while before I could pull it together. After I did, I went into Brett's room and stood quietly, watching him sleep. At peace, without a care in the world, off in some dreamland.

It'll be different for him.

CHAPTER 6

December 6th

It was Saturday, time for the Indiana-Kentucky basketball game. I grew up in Indiana—a state so crazy about college basketball almost no one outside the state can possibly understand, except for the people around me in North Carolina. They are as passionate about their great local teams—Duke, UNC, NC State—as my family is about Kokomo High School and the great Indiana University Hoosiers.

A love for basketball was often one of the few things I shared with colleagues, friends, and neighbors who were North Carolina natives—although my rooting for Indiana, rather than one of the great local schools, is considered as bad in some circles as my atheism is in others. Much to the disappointment of Paige, my Mom and I, Brett drank too much of the local Kool-Aid, and roots for the UNC Tar Heels.

Before tipoff, Brett and I were off on what Paige fondly referred to as a "boys' day out." Going to Eckerd's Drug Store to pick up Mom's medicine and something to fix the annoying rattle on my car. A stop by Mom's for a hygienic hello. Then out to Northgate Mall to so Brett could ride the Christmas train that ran inside the mall.

"I'd better call Mom and tell her we're heading out," I said.

Brett chimed, "I get to see Grandma this morning!"

Paige and I exchanged glances. We sure didn't want Brett catching Mom's bug. I said, "No, Brett. You have to wave at Grandma from the hallway so you don't get sick." Brett's face clouded over.

Paige took her cue. Her teacher voice flicked on like a light switch. "You don't want to get sick over Christmas. If you're good, Dad might just take you to lunch at the Mall."

I said, "It'll be a great morning. We'll get a special treat at the drugstore, and after we get done at Grandma's, we'll go to Northgate Mall for a ride on the Christmas train and have lunch at McDonald's."

The sales pitch worked—Brett beamed and Paige took him to his room to get ready.

Time to call Mom. I made a mental note to take her the pint of cough medicine sitting in the cabinet, regardless of what Barry prescribed. It was my brand, the one for which I happened to be the world's expert. It might seem less complicated than rocket science, but I did pioneering work in this field—and this medicine is represented that. My job was something I'd worked hard for, and I was proud that today my mom would be one of the many people helped by my work.

Walking over to the phone, I noticed my hands were shaking slightly. Three cups of coffee, rather than the usual two, made me jittery. I misdialed Mom's number the first time.

She answered after only the second ring. Her voice came across as calm and collected.

Reassured, I said, "You sound good. Are you sure you can't join us this afternoon? Indiana's going to need all the help we can get." I thought to myself that one or two additional days of rest would be all Mom required before returning to work.

"I'd like to, but aren't you usually the first one to tell me to behave myself, even if it is the Hoosiers?"

"You've got me there. We'll have to pull through without you. Or the fudge." More serious, I continued, "How do you feel?" I already imagined a positive response.

The same strong, upbeat voice replied, "Not bad. About the same. I'm coughing a bit and feel like I have a bug."

"I'm bringing you my own personal cough medicine."

"Does it taste good?"

"Not really, but it works."

"How do you know?"

"I wrote the label and the insert."

"So Mr. Expert—if I can stand the taste, it might do me some good?"

"Quite possibly."

"Wonderful. I'll try it."

"If you'll listen to me about this, why wouldn't you get a flu shot when I asked you to a dozen times?

"I never had one in the past, and don't need one now. Are you going to convince Brett to root for the right team this afternoon?"

"Nice change of subject, Mom. And not likely. I tried to explain the glories of Indiana last year and got nowhere. He's crazy about UNC."

"True. But he's older and wiser now."

I laughed. "I doubt that age will be of any help in this case." I glanced at my watch. Time to get going. "I can hear Brett upstairs bouncing off the walls. Be over in a bit."

Brett babbled enthusiastically as I helped him put on his winter coat. He described in detail the decorations his class had made for his room at nursery school. He wondered who drew his name in the gift exchange. He speculated on what Santa Claus would be bringing for him. He was on a roll—Christmas caffeine. I grabbed the cough medicine from the kitchen cabinet, and we were off.

Brett announced that he would like nothing more than to build a snowman.

"There's no snow today, but maybe there will be before Christmas," I said. "Just like in Kokomo."

The Datsun's wayward aluminum trim caught my eye as I strapped Brett in his seat belt. I hoped the super glue I was about to purchase would solve the problem. Somewhere over the next few days, I'd find time to fix it.

As always, I stopped for gas at Daniel Brothers on Old Chapel Hill Road. This was a family service station, run by folks that hadn't forgotten the "service" part. It was the only place I had my cars worked on. I'd grown tired of paying the "Yankee price" for car repairs—sometimes needed, sometimes not—early on after moving to North Carolina, and had been lucky to find this place. They were fair, and didn't make me feel like I was making personal reparations for the War of Northern Aggression. Brett got out of the car and climbed on the bumper so he could watch me check the oil.

Eckerd Drugs, on the other hand, wasn't family owned. It had all the local charm of the national chain it was. But the toy and candy sections still attracted Brett like a magnet. I headed to the pharmacy, despite his repeated tugs on my arm.

Mom's advance call to the pharmacist meant we found a white sack, a smile and a "Merry Christmas!" waiting for us. The "Merry Christmas," at least, was local.

After I let Brett scout the toy section, I stopped briefly to make a selection of super glue. Each choice promised the same "super" effect, but none specifically mentioned aluminum. Then we combed the store for the treat promised to him. He had selected three or four that he couldn't do without. I simply nodded my head in each instance. Treats and toys versus glue and medicine—I sure was getting the short end of the stick.

The checkout line, as is so often the case in these parts, took a while. With some encouragement from Paige, I'd long since given up getting in a snit about it. The clerks carried on conversations about family, health, basketball, and holiday plans with almost everyone. The downside was that things down here move at the speed of molasses on a cold winter day. The upside was living in a place where folks actually take the time to both notice and care about those around them. Which, if I recall, was Paige's point. Still, it took forever, and I envied Brett not knowing any other way of life.

Mom's Vega station wagon was parked at an odd angle along the curb in front of her apartment. A missing hubcap needed replacing. Odd, not like Mom. She must have been in a hurry to get inside. Another thing to add to my list.

Brett balked when I told him again he had to wait in the hallway—and complained about the heat. I promised he could have a long visit when Grandma was feeling better. I felt the faint pressure of his small hand grasping for my fingers as we walked to the front door and up the stairs to Mom's second-floor apartment. I smiled at the the small wooden Santa Claus on her door.

A cough and a faint rustling accompanied Mom's footsteps to the door. I looked down at Brett. "Please wait here in the hallway while I talk to Grandma." The scowly-pouty face he made was a classic.

Mom opened the door just a crack to avoid contaminating the hallway. She waved to Brett, who actually minded and stayed a step back. I entered her apartment, leaving the door slightly ajar. Mom had on a pink shower cap and was still in her nightgown—not her usual look. She made a point of not getting too close to me.

As we said hello, I placed the sack from Eckerd's on the television set inside of the door, next to a picture of Brett.

"What are your symptoms like?" I asked.

"Moderate cough. Typical flu."

Nothing to be overly concerned about... I looked at Mom and realized she had become an old woman overnight. It was more than the nightgown and shower cap, more than her lack of dentures and makeup. An illusion I had created in my own mind, of Mom as a young woman, had suddenly fallen away.

Mom said, "When I told the pharmacist you were coming, I said you were a doctor who does research on cough and cold medicines."

Her soft brown eyes, eyes I had known all my life and sometimes took for granted, confirmed what I had known all along: Mom was proud of me, and loved me more than anything or anyone else in the world. Although Brett was a very close second—and catching up fast.

"What has Dr. Winthrop given me?" she asked.

"Valium to calm your nerves and medicine to relieve your flu symptoms," I said. "And I brought a little something over for you myself." I launched into a long-winded discourse on the relative virtues of antitussives, antihistamines, and decongestants in relieving her symptoms. Mom half-listened, at first with appreciation, then with slightly crossed eyes. I elaborated on the possible interactions and why f to avoid Valium. I advised her to drink plenty of juice and take Tylenol for her slight fever.

Mom smiled and nodded. "Thank you, Doctor, I feel better already."

Lost in my own erudition, I was too preoccupied to appreciate Mom's sarcasm.

"Go to bed and watch the game. You should be good as new in two to three days," I said.

"I will, but I won't be able to root as hard as I would like. I'll be sure to make an especially good batch of fudge for the North Carolina game in two weeks. I hope Isiah is in top form so I can rub Brett's nose in it when Indiana kills them." Her voice had risen to carry it out to him in the hallway.

Mom waved out the door to Brett as we left.

Northgate Mall was a December zoo. The parking lots were packed, and I drove around playing musical cars until a spot freed up. Brett spotted the empty space first—"There! There!" he exclaimed, winning the game. I pulled into the space.

Brett lobbied for a prize all the way into the mall.

Northgate's main attraction during the Christmas season was the miniature train. "It's directly inside the main entrance. You can't miss it," Mom had said—she was the family mall expert.

Brett's little hand clasped mine, we progressed slowly through the milling crowds.

The train was hardly visible because of all the people gathered around it. Mothers corralled an assortments of four- to six-year-olds. Brett was no different—he could barely restrain himself as the line crept along inch by inch by inch. Brett watched those already onboard with unblinking eyes.

When the line got to to the point I could purchase a ticket, Brett snatched it from my hand, joining the controlled stampede to replace the kids whose ride had come to an end. He managed to outmaneuver everyone to sit at the very front of the train.

His first ride was such a success—we had to go back in line for two more rides. This was not negotiable.

My reward for this was that each time Brett would look straight ahead and refuse to look at his me as the train ran in circles. I went through considerable antics to get his attention before I realized I was witnessing the first stirrings of Brett's independence. He wanted to do this one his own. I wiped a tear from my eye.

An entire shopping center of potential presents finally lured Brett away from the train. I was gratified to feel the slight tug from his hand as we combed the mall. Brett asked my opinion on each prospective gift and requested I include them on the list he zealously guarded at home. There was absolutely no doubt in his mind that Santa would bring him everything he wanted.

He ran from store to store. I thought his supply of energy would be depleted after a half an hour or so, but he was inexhaustible. I had to convince him to stop for lunch at McDonald's by promising him fifteen minutes in the playground.

On the way home to the highly anticipated basketball game, Brett said, "Indiana's going to lose!" After spending much of the day catering to his every whim, I didn't feel affirmed by this.

Paige greeted us. "Did you have fun?"

Brett nodded eagerly.

She looked to me. "How's your mother?"

"Okay."

Brett, wearing his UNC sweatshirt, turned on the television. Paige and I were in our glorious Hoosier cream-and-crimson. A commercial ended and the screen showed Assembly Hall in Bloomington. Game time!

I remembered taking Mom to Assembly Hall years earlier. Now she was under the weather and couldn't join us. The next big televised game was two weeks away, against North Carolina. If I was lucky, I might be able to get tickets.

Our shared passion for Indiana basketball didn't follow a typical mother-son model. Basketball had always been special for Mom and I. It started as a family thing before my Dad died—in fact, one of my earliest memories was from age three or so—Brett's age now—being up on Dad's shoulder watching huge machines build Kokomo's enormous Memorial Gymnasium. It seated 7,200—and was built for high school games. That's Indiana basketball.

After Dad died, Mom and I kept going with basketball. This year was the best yet for us—Jimmy Rayl's year. They called him the "Splendid Splinter," and I still get goosebumps remembering how he could shoot the ball. "Nothing but net," as the old saying goes. Literally, from anywhere on the court.

When I went off to college, Mom watched every Hoosier game, hoping to see me on the screen. Before, during, and after seasons, basketball was a constant topic of conversation.

"Indiana's going to lose!" crowed Brett.

Apostate.

"No, they're not!"

Brett sat beside me in the middle of the family room floor. Books flanked the television set on either side. The starting lineups were being introduced. I missed Mom, and repeatedly glanced over at the front door in the hope that she had changed her mind about driving over.

Indiana played the first half as if they were sleepwalking. They trailed by three points despite my exhortations, expletives, and floor poundings. Brett beamed and Paige glared at my unruly behavior.

I waited until halftime to call Mom.

"Hi, Mom," I said, getting only a cough in reply. A single cough, and no more.

Undismayed, I continued with, "We're playing poorly. If the bounces don't start going our way, we're not only going to lose *this* game, but had probably better concede to North Carolina." Hearing that, Brett made a face and laughed.

Mom replied, "I know. Bobby hasn't got the boys playing the way they should. We'll get them in the second half."

"I certainly hope so," I said. "By the way, how do you feel?"

"A little better, I think," Mom said. "The medicine you gave me is beginning to work."

A little better. Just the words I wanted to hear. I ignored the Mom's ragged breathing. "That's good," I said.

"No, everything's fine. I wish I was better—I don't have time to be sick."

She was fine. She had to be fine. "That's right. I suspect Indiana's lousy play in the first half is due to not having fudge for the game."

"Hah."

Brett took the phone from me and tattled on my behavior during the first half. Not only was I guilty of saying bad words, but also—he claimed—of cheering for the wrong team.

I told Mom I would check in tomorrow.

As the announcer signaled the beginning of the second half, Paige gave me a look that reminded me to be more mannerly during the rest of the game. With Paige and I cheering for Indiana, Brett beside me, cheering—*for Kentucky!*—we were having a good time, passing the Lewis family passion for basketball to the next generation. I wished Mom was here, but she'd be here for the next game in two weeks—unless we got tickets to the game.

Indiana eventually lost. But I still felt like I won.

CHAPTER 7

December 7th

Sunday morning, sitting alone at the kitchen table with only a cup of coffee for company, staring at the empty chair across from me. The one where Mom sat every Sunday morning. *I miss her.* Her company every Sunday morning really mattered to me. Sometimes we didn't even talk.

Not talking about things—we're good at that.

Sunday morning breakfasts with Mom were a highlight of our family week. Mom and I drank coffee and browsed the paper, Paige cooked breakfast, and Brett chattered away about nursery school, his friends, bugs, toys, and other epochal events in a three-year-old's life. Sometimes Mom and Brett sang silly songs she wrote for him—"Great big trucks, going along the highway…"

After breakfast was over, Mom and I would get some quiet time at the table together. This time every week was the glue that held us together. The one day she was fully a part of our household—at home here. If she had her way, every day would be Sunday—she would live with us.

It's really hard—but that just can't be—for now. When I'm making more money, when we get a bigger house, when Mom can't live on her own, when Paige comes around. Paige is pretty firm. But she'll come around. I know she will. Someday.

For now, this was the time we were really together. Except today—Mom still had the flu, and I'm staring at an empty chair.

If we were all living outside the South, we'd likely not have this Sunday ritual. But down here, it seemed everything was closed Sunday morning except churches—so there wasn't much else to do. Things seemed to be slowly changing, and some of the blue laws were even repealed a couple of years back, so you could finally get an actual drink without brown-bagging it in. But not on Sunday, at least around here.

Paige generally wanted to fit in and conform, but in other ways she was part rebel. On the one hand, she always said not being able to get a drink made her want a Bloody Mary on Sunday mornings. And on the other, against my objections, she insisted Brett be baptized—which caused quite an odyssey through churches throughout the Triangle area. I knew it frustrated and hurt her that so many priests and pastors refused to baptize Brett because his father was an atheist—but in truth I found it ironically amusing and less than Christian. After many rejections, the Methodists at Duke University Chapel agreed—with no strings attached. I don't have faith, but I respect people like that who live theirs—not just talk it.

Mom moved down from Kokomo just over a year ago. I flew up and we drove back down to North Carolina in her Vega station wagon. Her meager possessions from a lifetime in Kokomo were neatly packed in a small U-Haul trailer attached to the rear bumper. It was an uncomfortable journey in more ways than one.

Mom ran out of options in Kokomo. She brought Ann and I up by herself, with help from her extended family. After we moved away, she ended up living in her Mom's big old house with her brother Norman and her mother. First her brothers Steve and Norman died, in a span of six months. Then two years spent nursing my grandma through a sorrowful decline left Mom alone and unemployed. Once my grandmother died, Mom fell apart.

Mom was a mess when she arrived, but—flu notwithstanding—was in better shape now. But we had a rough start.

Paige found Mom an apartment less than two miles from our house, across from Duke's East campus. We were working hard to fix it up for her, but it took a couple of weeks after her arrival for us to finish.

So Mom stayed with us at first. And that's where she wanted to be—not on her own in an apartment across town.

Mom wanted to move in with us right away and stay, plain and simple. This wasn't a new thing, and it started shortly after Paige and I were married. What started as quiet conversations became a drumroll after Paige and I bought our first house five years ago, before Brett was born. His arrival ratcheted things up even further. But this was out of the question for the time being.

Telling Mom her apartment was finally ready, that she needed to move out, was one of the hardest conversations I ever had. But it had to be done. Paige and I discussed the matter until we were at the point of exhaustion, and she made clear to me she wasn't going to be happy with my mom living with us.

I took my responsibilities to my mom as seriously as I did those to Paige and Brett, not just as a breadwinner but as a husband and father who was actually present. When these responsibilities conflicted, I found myself torn beyond my ability to cope. I kept thinking one or both of the two immovable objects would move.

But this issue wasn't going to resolve itself or go away. To my mind, there was little question Mom would live with us someday. When we had more room. When. When. I told Mom this on the way to her apartment that first time. Told her as convincingly as I could. Tried to persuade Mom, even though she knew Paige didn't want her to live with us. My efforts to persuade Mom didn't seem to make her feel any better.

She frustrated me then, but I was proud of her now. In just over a year she'd made friends, and was really building a life in Durham. She hadn't worked for years in Kokomo, but she was now working half-time at a feed store, which she seemed to enjoy. And she signed up for continuing education classes at Duke.

She could be sitting at home, making herself miserable, trying to make me feel guilty, and spending all her energy trying to get a chokehold on my homelife. Instead, she's making a pretty decent life of her own. What a pleasant surprise.

Four cups of coffee was enough—as was all this thinking I was doing. Time to get moving.

The car. Super glue. "Guess I'll bite the bullet and fix the car," I said to Mom's empty seat. I thought I was alone, and didn't expect to be overheard.

"I'll help you!" Brett shouted from over my shoulder.

"You two boys will get the job done in no time," Paige said. They'd both been standing behind me—for who knew how long.

I gave Brett the role of designated washer. Paige helped him fill a bucket of warm water and several rags while I put on my lined windbreaker.

"Why do I do I have to wear a winter coat when Dad doesn't?" Brett asked.

Paige was fast. "Because your father's wearing a sweatshirt under his jacket."

Brett paused, but couldn't counter his mom on that. A winter coat it would be.

"Let's do it!" I said—more enthusiastically than I felt. I grabbed the superglue from the Eckerd's sack. The quicker we got started, the sooner we'd be done.

"Let's do it!" Brett parroted.

We walked out the door like a construction crew embarking on a major project.

Paige was more than eager to point this out as she followed us to the door. "This is one for the movies. You two need an agent."

"Thanks."

We weren't two steps out the door before Brett tired of carrying his tools and handed them over to me. "Time to get to work," he said excitedly, dashing ahead. Paige and I exchanged glances and shook our heads at Brett's enthusiasm. I estimated having his help would triple the length of the job.

I wasn't far off. There was a lot more splashing than cleaning. And a lot more gluing than sticking. The window trim was as easy to manage as Brett. Time after time, it looked like we'd succeeded in joining trim and car body together, but no sooner had we exchanged congratulations than our work came undone. Then there would be some more splashing. Brett was having a great time, while I congratulated myself for not resorting to profanity. At least out loud.

At the seventh attempt, the glue held. Brett and I went back into the house thoroughly soaked. Paige gave Brett a warm bath and changed him into dry clothes. "I hope you don't get the flu like your grandmother," I heard her say as I went to change into dry clothes.

"Let's get ready to go," she called down the hallway.

"Please remind me of why you have to go to UNC today," I called back.

"Good to hear from you. I thought we had lost you there for a while," Paige said as she walked into the room. She was trying to lighten my mood.

"I have to go to the library to work on my thesis. Jack, you know very well UNC doesn't give away second Master's degrees." Paige was sometimes so sarcastic she reminded me of Joan Rivers.

We were almost out the door when Paige decided to give Mom a call.

I was distracted getting Brett ready to walk out the door, and caught only bits and pieces of their brief chat.

"No better than yesterday," Paige said, hanging up.

She didn't seem troubled. I was.

This wasn't the update I expected. "I'll call her again a little later when we get back. If she's not better, you should plan to take her to the doctor tomorrow morning. Probably no need, but we should play it safe."

Brett and I occupied ourselves for the three or so hours Paige needed at the Davis Library. We walked around campus. We had lunch at Spanky's before hanging out on Franklin Street, then a cherry coke at Jeff's.

Cherry coke was Brett's favorite treat, regardless of where we picked it up. "I *need* a cherry coke," he said. It was a family tradition.

Brett and I sat on a bench, savoring every sip. We glanced over at Julien's across the street, Paige's favorite clothing store.

Brett's noisy slurping at the bottom of his drink was starting to annoy me when Paige showed up.

I drove back to home as fast as I could get without getting a ticket. I was driving faster than usual, and Paige kept looking over at me, clearly wondering why.

Mom's phone rang four times. I grew more apprehensive with each ring. Finally, she answered with "Hello?" on the fourth.

There was an edge in her voice. She clearly had not improved.

"How are you feeling?" I asked.

"My cough is worse," she said, quietly. It seemed like she was choosing her words carefully.

"Have you been taking your cough medicine?"

"Yes, I have."

Why is she sounding this way—there's no reason for her to be sorry for being sick.

"How much is left?"

"None."

Too much. The bottle was nearly full when I gave it to her .

"Paige had better take you to see the doctor tomorrow morning."

"Fine. What time should I be ready?"

"Early. Paige will call you when she's had a chance to call the receptionist."

"All right, my dear, talk to you later."

"Good night, Mom. I'll drive over to see you after work tomorrow," I volunteered before hanging up.

After his big day, Brett was asleep, and Paige was in another part of the house, so I had some time alone. I decided to go into my study and work on my play.

My play—*Three Missing Fathers.* My attempt to explore the loss of my dad, and the two uncles who had tried to stand in for him. My attempt to deal with my feelings, and to find a way to share them with my mom. Only a week ago, it seemed like I'd been on a roll, halfway through. But I'd made little progress since December started.

I *had* to write. Despite my fatigue, I truly felt compelled to jot down the next several pages I had already formed in my mind. I looked at where I had stopped five days earlier.

I scanned the last couple of pages. One passage from page 59 jumped out:

"The universe is totally devoid of hope. We're benighted by an immensity of nothingness. Our lives are the most tenuous of our possessions. We desperately cling to them with all our tenacity, only to lose hold at the least propitious moment. If they only meant something. If—they—only—meant—something. A fear of annihilation drives us all."

I read that. And sat there. Didn't put paper in the typewriter. Didn't write a word. Sat there, with echoes of that passage in my mind.

For a while. Stuck on page 59.

My mom is 59.

Working on my play, thinking about the issues it dealt with, wasn't what I needed right now. It wasn't what I should be thinking about. I needed to be where I *am*, not where I *was*. Christmas, Paige, Brett, Mom, North Carolina. Not three people I've lost in Indiana.

CHAPTER 8

December 8th

Ten in the morning and I'm watching the clock. It seemed like I'd been watching the clock since I walked into my office, and I really hadn't managed to get anything done. There was no reason to be so worried about Mom. It was just the flu.

No reason whatsoever to be distracted with worry, but when I looked at the clock again, it showed 10:15. It felt like someone hit my "pause" button, I couldn't think or work, my stomach was in a knot, and my chest was tight enough that I checked my desk drawer to make sure there was an asthma inhaler in it.

This is not like me—I never have problems focusing at work. I enjoy the challenges of this job—petty politics aside—it's fascinating, and frankly I'm good at it. The number of times I've sat at this desk for more than a few minutes and not been doing productive work, you could count on one hand. Maybe one finger.

Focus. Get something done. Anything. Quit watching the damn clock. I reached out and turned my desk clock to face away from me. That will help me focus. Or if I get my boss to add "Worry incessantly" to my job description, I can call this being productive. Not funny. Get to work.

Mom's appointment at the doctor's was scheduled for ten. Barry was punctual, so he should be finished with her at 10:45.

She should be home by 11 a.m. Eleven at the absolute latest.

I'd been thinking about Mom's flu since I was halfway to work. I had it all planned out.

Barry Winthrop listens to her lungs and reassures her that things will clear in a couple days. No more prescriptions needed. Straightforward and uncomplicated. He doesn't even mention to her that in the highly unlikely event things get worse, the medical care here is among the best in the country—with both UNC and Duke nearby—I've lectured at both…

Stop with the hubris—focus on the vision. He'll just smile, and send her home, reassured and on the mend.

It was an excellent plan. And it was helping me get a lot of work done. I looked at the phone. And turned the clock back around. Thirty minutes after ten.

Paige and I agreed she'd call me when she got back from taking Mom to the doctor. Like it was a routine visit. Normal. But today suddenly didn't feel normal. I didn't either. I decided to call Mom directly, starting at 11 a.m.

My eyes started a tennis match between the phone and my clock. No matter how hard I tried to focus on the piles of work sitting in between, nothing was getting done. I kept looking from one to the other.

How could I get my mind back on a positive track? Christmas. I closed my eyes and built a picture.

The tree. Fire in the fireplace. Brett's Christmas list. What's on it? A John Deere tractor and Star Wars figures… Visualize Brett ripping open presents and shouting with glee as he tears into the boxes…

His voice and the image faded.

I opened one eye and looked at the clock. Then the other and looked at the phone.

No sooner had the minute hand on the clock made contact with "11" than I picked up the phone and dialed. Eight unanswered rings informed me she wasn't home. I decided to call again in thirty minutes. Right before I left for lunch.

Damn telephone. Damn clock.

At 11:30, on the sixth ring, it became apparent I was calling an empty apartment.

I tightened my grip on the receiver and listened in vain for Mother's voice. All I heard was tinny rings from across town. Thirty excruciating seconds—then forty-five elapsed. Still no answer. I glared at the receiver in my hands and resisted the temptation to throw it against the wall. My thoughts took an ominous turn.

Something might be wrong.

Something—might—be—wrong—this thought was unacceptable. There were a hundred explanations for what was occurring. More than a hundred.

Winthrop had an unexpected emergency and was late to the office. Paige and Mother went to lunch rather than going straight home. They took Brett Christmas shopping. They went to the pharmacy...

I'd lost track of where I was. The faint sound of the phone in my hand, ringing endlessly across town in my mother's apartment, called me back. I hung up, looking around to make sure I was still alone.

I'm not the kind of person who listens to phones ringing in empty apartments.

What is going on with me?

I had only begun to explore the possibilities when the sounds of my colleagues in the hallway summoned me for what I knew would be a truly miserable lunch. I knew I'd spend the whole time wishing it was over, and my stomach was in a knot so the thought of food was repellent.

All I had to do to get out of it was tell them my mom was sick, that I was worrying about it. But all these folks dealt with clinical medicine and research. They knew the flu was just the flu. Just like I did. And of course that bastard Drake would wind up needling me about it.

And they'd wonder why I was so obsessive about it. Just like I did. All those thoughts Paige asked me to push from my mind. Which didn't work. I was trying to shove them neatly into my play. The one in my study drawer at home. In a stack, in a drawer. Not in my head, unwanted, where I couldn't control them.

Going to see Dad in the hospital, walking through St. Joseph's in Kokomo, tortured depictions of the Crucifixion on the walls, nuns in habits...

Walking down the hallway to join the lunch group, I couldn't stop my eye looking for pictures of a bleeding Jesus on the corridor walls.

The damned telephone was sitting on my desk like an accusation when I got back from lunch. The time frame for normal delays had long since expired. If Mom didn't answer this call, something was definitely wrong. I would be entering a place of which I wanted no part—the parts of life where things were out of control. Out of my control. That thought frightened me. I felt it gathering around me, eager to envelope me as it had in the past.

My old nemesis.

The uncontrolled.

I dialed Mother's number slowly, deliberately. Afraid of discovering what loomed on the other end? There was a brief hiatus before the phone started to ring. My mind sped ahead like a race car.

If mother was home she would be anticipating my call—she would pick up early—she—

One, two, three rings and no answer. *The race car approached the first turn at Indy and had to slow.*

Mom made fried chicken for the last Indy 500 we went to—1974— Am I catching her at an inconvenient time? Making her rush to the phone? A long day spent whipping your neck around, trying to follow the cars.

Four, five, six rings—no answer.

Damn phone.

The race car had strayed too close to the wall and was courting disaster.

Mother's standing outside her apartment—having difficulties with her keys—this couldn't be happening in another December—couldn't— but was!

With the seventh through tenth rings, the race car began to careen off the track.

It's only the flu.

Mom's visit to the doctor likely hadn't gone well. I quit any pretense of working and gave in to what was starting to feel like panic. My hands began to perspire, and the temperature in the room rose as I tried to reach Paige at home. Tried but failed in this as well. Increasingly frustrated, I call Dr. Winthrop's office. A woman's voice—the receptionist—answered.

I was talking without hearing my own voice. Whatever I said, it worked.

A second voice replaced the first. Winthrop's nurse—whose name I knew but couldn't recall. I identified myself and she filled me in. Her voice was businesslike and didn't falter once. Not a single time while mentioning the examination had been as straightforward as anticipated. Mother was being sent to Durham County General hospital for an x-ray.

The small blemish found on her lung, which resulted in Mom's immediate admission to the hospital.

This all led up to, "I'll put you through to Dr. Winthrop."

I sat frozen, and it took a while for my brain to catch up with my ears.

"Thank you," I was vaguely aware of saying. Disoriented, having entered unwelcome territory. The uncontrolled. Passing through its borders made me feel strange.

I live in this world. All of these problems have solutions. Some of which which I've worked on.

How bad could it be? A blemish on the lung—possible pneumonia.

It's still small.

Antibiotics should nip it in the bud and prevent it from getting worse, *unless it was viral.*

"Hi, Jack." Barry Winthrop was talking to me. He was short of breath—as though he had been sprinting from one exam room to another. He elaborated in short bursts: "Admitted your mother—precautionary measure more than anything—small blemish on her left lung—knock it out with standard therapy—could have sent her home—but wanted to play it safe."

Play it safe—yes! Play it more than safe—yes!

"How long do you think she'll be in the hospital?" I asked.

"Barring any unforeseen complications, three days. Four days at most."

Winthrop's voice had returned to normal. I also detected a tone of confidence in his prognosis. This was like an instant tonic for me.

The situation appeared under control.

As soon as I hung up, I called Mom at the hospital.

She sounded normal. "I just needed a rest for the holidays," she joked.

I laughed. "Make sure you take advantage of the spa," I joked in return. "How do you feel?" I added.

"I don't feel too bad. About the same as yesterday. Truthfully—I don't even know why they admitted me."

"Paige and I are coming to see you tonight. Is there anything you need?"

"Only my denture cleaner. I didn't expect to go to the hospital when I left this morning," she replied. Back to comedy.

That was a bad joke, and I wasn't going to give her a laugh. "We'll see you tonight."

I called Paige at home. Her voice seemed stressed. Tired, frustrated, and clearly worried that I would be upset with her. Needing my reassurance that she had done the right thing in agreeing to Mother's admission to the hospital.

She had it. "I already talked to Mom. She sounds fine, everything seems to be under control—you handled the situation beautifully," I said.

Paige was surprised. "You have? And thank you."

"I phoned Winthrop, and he told me she was there. Nothing to be concerned about. Erring on the side of caution and all that. Just like you did by agreeing to Mom's admission."

Without warning, the tone of the conversation changed. Paige's voice dripped with tension as she told me, "It was really awful. Brett was with me. I thought I would be taking your mother to the doctor's office and bringing her right back home to her apartment. Winthrop examined her. Then she needed to go to the hospital for an x-ray. We didn't have time to get any of her things."

"*No!*"

"I had to call Natalie to pick up Brett and she was late. Your mother cried as she hugged him goodbye and that upset him. She was scared in the emergency room and wanted me to go back with her."

Natalie, our neighbor? What the hell—why was Brett there in the first place? He shouldn't be exposed to Mom's flu.

Two choices confronted me. Let this grow into the real argument about to happen, or get off the phone. I never won arguments with Paige, so I quickly chose the second.

"I can leave work early—what time should I pick you up?" I asked.

"Four."

"See you then. And Paige?"

"What?"

"I love you."

Pause. "I love you, too."

My head and office were both filled with fog the rest of the day. I couldn't say what I accomplished—if anything.

I left work early so that we wouldn't be rushed before going to the hospital. I'd left the radio on in the morning—it was annoying—but I didn't have the energy to turn it off. On the way home, I heard Blondie's "The Tide is High" and Abba's "The Winner Takes it All" in succession.

We stopped off at Mom's apartment to pick up her denture cleaner. Paige held a bouquet of flowers she had picked up for her. Durham County General Hospital soon loomed in the distance. It was definitely different than St. Joseph's in Kokomo. Much more massive and modern. Taller. It was a dark night, and the stark lighting gave the white concrete exterior of the building an eerie appearance.

Not exactly a welcoming place. In my personal life, I hate hospitals.

I hate hospitals. People I love die in them. Focus. It's not all bad. Brett came from a hospital.

During the work day, it was completely different. Not only were hospitals the source of my livelihood—they're where I did my best work.

Heavy glass doors opened automatically. A large lobby, dominated by a receptionist's area in the center. Behind it was a large Christmas tree. I looked around for nuns and crucifixes.

Wait—this isn't a Catholic hospital like St. Joseph's. No. Definitely not.

The lobby was expansive and bright. It felt so new, like the hospital had just been opened. Secular hospitals feel right to me. Religious hospitals—especially the Catholic ones, seem half like churches. I believe in science and medicine. My vestments are white coats and the medicines we make to heal people. Really heal people, not like what they do in churches.

All that talk about the spirit—mine is the church of the real world, of research and data.

The receptionist was a woman in her mid-thirties. No doubt with a name and appearance, but I wasn't focussing and it all failed to register. Paige was asking questions and getting answers.

The rectangular visitor's pass shook a bit as I read Mom's name typed prominently on the front, along with, "Surgical floor, room 6224."

Why is someone with a respiratory ailment given a room on the surgical floor?

I was trapped in the elevator with a bunch of strangers and Paige. Everyone seemed to be holding flowers. Mom's room was on the sixth floor, and every button was pushed, so we kept getting crowded farther to the back of the large car. Pressed closer together like cattle. I choked on the cloying scent of flowers.

The sickly sweet smell of flowers. Dad's memorial service—not being able to get away from them. Not being able to get the scent out of my clothes afterwards. What makes people think that flowers help?

I'd had trouble my whole life going into a florist shop. The simplest damn thing—buying flowers for your wife—turned out to be an issue. Something else I could never talk about with her.

Paige looked at me as we got out of the elevator. I could tell she knew something was going on, but wasn't sure what. I wasn't going to tell her.

We passed the nurse's station. The sounds of beeping monitors vied with snippets of television shows as we passed room after room.

The linoleum floor was shiny, spotless. Like it was cleaned every two hours. I knew there was a floor buffer hiding somewhere. The art on the wall seemed to be mostly prints of North Carolina mountain scenes and Piedmont landscapes.

Fighting off uninvited memories of visiting Dad years ago, I restricted my eyes to the pass in my hand, looking from it to the room number next to each door.

6224—the door to Mom's room.

The six o'clock news wafted through the partially open door. I was encouraged that she felt well enough to be watching television.

Mom gave us a large smile as we entered the room. Other than the vaporizer attached to her nose, she looked the same as she had on Saturday.

A red shopping bag with a white Santa on its side sat in the corner of the room, striking a discordantly festive note.

Paige set the flowers by the window and handed Mom her denture cleaner. Quite a combination.

"You sure go to great lengths for a bouquet of flowers," I cracked.

That got a laugh from Mom, and a look from Paige.

"Your room is certainly cheerful," remarked Paige.

"It is, but they need to turn the thermostat down a little," Mom said.

I noticed the room did feel warm as I moved the two chairs closer to the bed. This was a nervous habit of mine, acquired throughout the years. When I visited someone in the hospital, I never quite knew what to do with myself.

You know you need to be there, but you don't know what to do.

A complete contrast to my day job. When I worked in a hospital—I knew exactly why I was there and what I needed to be doing.

There was an awkward silence.

"Move the chairs closer to the bed," said Mom.

"You got it," I said. After the chairs were re-arranged, Paige and I sat down facing Mom.

Mother was smiling at us from the bed. "How's my grandson? I miss him already."

"Just fine," Paige said. "He's with a teenager in the neighborhood, and mad because he wanted to come along."

Behind us, the newscaster announced the weather would be coming up after a commercial.

"Any good storms brewing, Jack?" asked Mom. She and Paige both were well aware of my passion for storms—particularly tornadoes. I watched the weather reports on TV like some people watch sports highlights.

Storms—only in my head!

"No. The weather map I saw last night was boring."

"Has the doctor been in to see you?" I asked.

Mother nodded as she spoke: "Yes. Barry came in about a half hour ago. He said everything appears to be okay. I could just as easily be at home, but he thinks it's better I'm here. A couple of days should do it, and then I can leave."

"That means you'll have to watch the Notre Dame game from here tomorrow night. It's in South Bend, so the Hoosiers will have a tough time. We *can't* lose two in a row," I heard myself say.

With mock anger, Paige interjected, "Can't you two talk about anything except basketball? In case you haven't noticed, there's also a major holiday coming up."

Mother motioned to her Santa bag. "I know, dear, I've been busy. I have lots left to do though. Especially for Brett." Not forgetting my allusion to Indiana's next game, she said "And I now have to make a special batch of fudge for the North Carolina game to make up for missing Kentucky's."

We bantered for a while, until finally I glanced at my watch. It was time to go.

Paige promised to check in the next morning, and I said I'd drop in after work. I kissed Mom on the forehead and was surprised she wasn't hot. The antibiotics were already working.

CHAPTER 9

December 9th

The mysteries of the mind sometimes defy understanding.

The morning of December 9th was one of those occasions. I woke at 5:55 a.m., the exact time I had received a terrible phone call four years earlier. It was a day of great pain, when I began hearing of the death of my surrogate father—my Uncle Norman, and also a few short hours later, included one of the greatest joys of my life. That was the day Paige discovered she was pregnant, and shared the news I would soon be a father.

What a day that was—I can't take many more like it in my life. I spent much of that day, four years ago, feeling like I was being torn in two. Experiencing the pain of losing my uncle who, for all his terrible faults, had also done so much good—standing in for my dad during his illness and after his death. Later that day, in the midst of dealing with my feelings, and trying to make arrangements to get back to Kokomo, Paige came back from the doctor with the news that we were having a baby.

Not only was Brett the source of so much happiness for Paige and I, his happiness was also our major focus. Christmas this year in the Lewis household would be a huge production, as if brought to us by Cecil B. DeMille. The only complication so far was the illness of a cast member—Mary in the role of Mother— who Brett called "Mar-Mar." But I was sure she'd be back on the set shortly.

Careful to not disturb Paige, I quietly climbed out of bed and walked to the study. I retrieved *Three Missing Fathers* from my desk drawer. I sat for a few minutes, the manuscript in my hands.

That day four years ago, Norman, Brett, my promise to Paige to try and be happy this Christmas…

Paige is right, this play isn't going to raise my spirits right now. I need to write this—just not right now. Now is not the right time to write this. That's almost funny. But I will finish this—that's a promise to me.

I returned the play to the drawer before walking to Brett's room. He was awake, and his little voice asked, "Is Mar-Mar still in the hospital?"

I was stunned but had to say something—*anything*. "She needs to rest up for Christmas, but will be getting out in a couple days, and sends you a kiss."

Brett grinned.

I was quickly hit by one of those pre-coffee morning fugue states—Brett kept babbling questions, Paige called from the bedroom, and my mind kept trying to take me down the shadowed path of thinking about the unfortunate coincidence of Mother being in the hospital on this day.

Paige's repeated calls from the bedroom snapped me out of it—wanting to go over the day's schedule; all the ducks that we had meticulously lined up in a row. Mom's illness made everything more complicated—nursery school, babysitters, and hospital visits. We agreed that she'd call me at ten o'clock from the hospital to fill me in on Mother's condition.

"Please call me on time," I said. Paige promised.

On my drive to work did I as much thinking as driving, irritating several fellow motorists by sitting too long at several lights. I mulled over Mother's unexpected hospitalization.

"Today should good," I said to myself. With good reason. The antibiotics should have really kicked in by now. If what I'd seen last night was predictive of what Paige would encounter this morning. No reason to think it wouldn't. None whatsoever.

It's time to start talking about rounding up her possessions and heading home. Which home? Her apartment or the house? Most likely a couple days at our place—but better to let Paige have that be her idea.

We'll also celebrate—throw a big party, down a round or two of vodka martinis. Maybe skip the party, but not the martinis.

At the office, I was able to work without interruption until my secretary walked in, carrying a medical report that she dropped on my work table. I thanked her, but she left quickly without smiling. Clearly, whatever problem she'd had with my boss was still bothering her. When I had some focus, this was something I would need to deal with.

One of the advantages of my job was being surrounded by medical references. I pulled out the closest standard medical text and reread the section on pneumonia. Scanning through. The half-dollar-sized blemish on Mother's lung meant the disease had been caught early and was amenable to treatment—the treatment I had overseen from the beginning. I was on top of it.

I liked Barry, but I really didn't trust anyone but myself. Experience had been a devastating teacher.

The phone rang punctually at ten o'clock. I leaned back and relaxed in my chair, anticipating good news as I lifted the receiver to my ear.

"It's me," Paige said. The tone of her voice made me sit up in alarm.

"How's Mom?" I asked with forced calmness. My mind was seized by an all-too-familiar sense of dread.

Not again—not again!

My free hand was clenched in a fist as a reaction to the absurdity of the situation. I was strangling the telephone.

"Not good, not good, your mother is worse than she was last night."

Confirmation of my fears.

Anger and frustration joined the dread. I sought quantitation by inquiring sharply, "How *much* worse?" As soon as the words escaped from my mouth, I realized I was taking my work voice into my personal life—never a good idea, especially with Paige.

She instantly became defensive and responded, "I don't know. I don't know. Just worse."

The room began to contract around me. I fought against my emotions and tried to be more pleasant as I asked, "Has Winthrop been in yet?"

"No, they said he would be checking in later in the morning," she said.

"Has the nurse seen her?" I mumbled. It was all I could do to speak.

"Yes, but she didn't say anything to me." An ominous pause followed. Stress tainted each and every word: "Jack—*listen to me*—I think your mother is sicker than anyone here *realizes*."

I was slow on the uptake. "Why don't you go home and get some rest. I could come out earlier if you think it's necessary," I said. I had difficulty reconciling the image of my mother as I had seen her the previous evening with what I had just heard.

"I really think I should stay here," Paige said. "You can relieve me sometime in the afternoon."

This was good from my standpoint. It gave me an opportunity to reach a stopping point in my work. "Are you sure?" I asked.

"Positive."

"Could you touch base with me at 12:30 so we can discuss what we do next?"

"I'll try," Paige said.

And that was that. Paige went back to mother, and I began pondering a jumble of reordered work priorities, as well as whether Christmas would be affected by Mother's longer hospital stay. This relapse was likely minor; at its very worst, a temporary setback.

Such was the illusion under which I labored with occasional misgivings until shortly after lunch, when I received a nightmare call from Barry Winthrop's nurse.

"Your mother is being transferred to Intensive Care. You're needed at the hospital immediately," she said. Her voice was mechanical and easily could have been coming from an alien.

She must have hung up—the line was dead before I had a chance to ask a question. I didn't even stop to explain my departure to anyone. I just left.

Shit—I thought I had things under control. I've been calling the shots since Mom got sick. Everything was under control—everything was under control.

I've been playing god in the absence of one.

That shook me.

On my way to the hospital I became disoriented. A prominent sign at the side of the road informed me that I was leaving Research Triangle Park. Shortly thereafter, the odd and unmistakable conglomeration of buildings comprising downtown Durham came into full view. Through the passenger's window, I could see the U-Haul agency where Mom and I returned her trailer after her move from Kokomo. I was headed in the right direction.

The aroma of tobacco wafting through the closed car windows is a rich reminder that I'm living in tobacco country. The farms are mostly gone now, but there's plenty of plants and warehouses—though a number of the warehouses now stand empty.

I exited at North Duke Street, skirting the downtown area past Rutledge Business College.

Durham County General Hospital loomed ahead.

"The Tide is High" played on the radio as I pulled into the parking lot.

Why do I keep hearing this damned song?

I rushed through the doors of Intensive Care thinking I would find Mom there. But Paige greeted me outside the waiting room. She seemed exasperated. Her explanation of the situation was beyond troubling.

Mother had not yet been moved from her room on the sixth floor. No one had said anything about what was happening. Absolutely zilch. Not a word to her about why any of this was being done in the first place. Paige was completely in the dark.

I nodded my head reflexively without speaking. "Still in her room" provided the impetus for me to retrace my steps in a rush. Seeing my mother had suddenly become the single most important thing in the world to me. The elevator kept me waiting for several minutes. Then it inched its way upward, and stopped on every intermediate floor until I reached the sixth floor.

Nothing was making sense. My brain craved just the opposite during the elevator's agonizingly slow ascent—*a couple of days in Intensive Care and Mom will back where she was—a slight setback—*

I arrived in time to see Mom being carted from her room on a gurney.

She looked me with a mix of inquisitiveness and shock, confirming she was as confused as me. "What's happening?" she asked. She was asking her brilliant son, who was supposed to have all the answers.

I DON'T HAVE THE SLIGHTEST CLUE ABOUT ANY OF THIS.

My face broke into the most difficult smile I ever remember. I tried to say everything would be fine, but had only partially completed the sentence before the gurney was wheeled past me. It was that quick.

She was gone when I was in mid-sentence. My words floated unheard, as empty as they truly were.

I literally ran to Intensive Care. Barry Winthrop barely avoided colliding with me in the hallway outside of the waiting room. The physician was hurrying to the treatment area. He was rushing and didn't stop, saying in passing, "Your mother has developed sepsis. I'll fill you in later." He then disappeared behind the doors leading to Mom's new room.

This was one of those unpleasant intersections between my work and personal lives—I had just reviewed a clinical protocol involving a new drug for the treatment of sepsis, and I knew exactly what this meant.

Bacteria were in her bloodstream. This was serious. This could kill her.

Paige was in the waiting room and motioned for me to me to sit beside her. I glanced around the room for the first time as I walked over. Chairs lined the three walls closest to the entrance, two tables holding magazines were in the middle of the room, and a small Christmas tree was along the fourth wall. Above the Christmas tree, a portable black and white television set was anchored into the wall. A soap opera played with the volume turned down below hearing level. The vertical hold required adjusting. The show looked how I felt.

I sat beside Paige and noticed we were being closely watched by a room full of people. They were all speaking in hushed voices. Suddenly, I felt as though I had been slapped.

I've entered a world of dreadfully sick people—without my white coat and name badge. No one is calling me "doctor." I feel like a knight without his armor. Or horse.

This was a place and situation that required immediate action. Paige went to the cafeteria where the phone was located to arrange babysitting for Brett and to call Mom's boss, Vince, to share what had befallen his favorite employee. "Two weeks' absence," she told him. Two weeks to play it safe.

I used the pay phone on the wall outside Intensive Care to call Mike and Ann. In my mind, Ann needed to come, Mike didn't. He would only complicate things.

Privacy of any sort wasn't to be had. I was increasingly uneasy as I searched in my pants pocket for Mike's office number in Kokomo that Paige had given me.

"Hello, Mike Baker." My uncle's voice sounded distant. Intermittent static crackled over the line.

"Mike, this is your nephew Jack," I replied, deceptively calm.

A short pause followed, ending with a tentative, "Jack, how are you?" Mike was trying to figure out why I had called.

He provided me with the opening I needed. "Not too good at the moment, I'm afraid. I'm at the hospital with Mom"

An even longer pause began, during which the static enjoyed free play. Mike's faint "What's wrong?" finally interrupted the noise.

The critical moment had arrived. What I said next would determine whether my uncle decided to drive down or not. "She has bronchial pneumonia that's developed into sepsis." For good measure, I threw in, "They just transferred her into Intensive Care." As soon as the words escaped my mouth, I regretted them.

More static overrode silence. "Is there anything I can do?" At least he wasn't planning to drive down as yet.

"No, not now. Sit tight and I'll keep you informed. A day or two in Intensive Care and she'll be clamoring to get out." The static had cleared.

Mike sounded eager to end the conversation. "Okay, I'll wait to hear from you. Give my regards to everyone."

One mission accomplished. Another one to go.

I began pondering the best approach for the upcoming talk with my sister. I needed her to understand Mom was sufficiently ill to warrant her coming.

This was one call I really wished that Paige would make. My sister and my mom had become increasingly distant over the years. Their visits, few and far between, seemed more like duties than anything else.

Dialing her office number, my discomfort at making the call made me more conscious of my lack of privacy than I had been previously. Perhaps it was my tension that made strangers seem overly eager to pry into my business.

Her secretary's stilted voice announced, "Ann Thompson's office." I was somewhat taken aback by not hearing Ann's voice as I had Mike's. I recovered sufficiently to ask, "Is Ann in, please?"

The formal tone persisted, even more pronounced than before. "I'm sorry, sir," it said. "She's in a meeting at the moment. Can I take a message and have her call you?"

Tension about my uncertainty and the lack of privacy triggered frustration and anger, and I almost seethed, "This is her brother, Dr. Lewis, and I need to talk to her immediately. It's an emergency."

The secretary's voice manner softened somewhat. "I'll see what I can do." The sound of a receiver being hastily dropped on a desktop followed. Two couples eying me warily communicated to me that I had already monopolized the phone for an excessive period of time. I decided not to care.

After an interval of several minutes that seemed like hours, Ann's tense voice asked, "What's wrong?

I was equally tense. "It's Mom," I responded, "She's in the hospital, in Intensive Care."

Ann fired back, "With what?"

"Sepsis—an infection in her bloodstream. She was admitted to the hospital yesterday with a slight case of pneumonia that suddenly gotten much worse. She was fine last night," I replied defensively—*there's no other way for me to be because it feels like it's all my damned fault.*

"Damn! That's all I need!" Ann gasped. "How sick is she?"

"Very sick. You should consider flying up."

A silence of indecision followed. This happened to coincide with Paige's return, and she quickly affirmed babysitting had been arranged. When Paige realized I was talking to her sister-in-law, she seized the receiver.

"You *need* to be here," Paige said. I hadn't a clue as to what was being said from Tampa.

Eventually, Ann said she would come. After checking flights on another line, she told Paige she would arrive at the airport at 1:20 the next morning.

Paige and I planned to remain at the hospital for however long we were needed. The table in the middle of the waiting room had various inspirational magazines, a Bible, and an assortment of *Reader's Digests* at least six months old. Religious literature held even less interest for me than stale *Reader's Digests*, so I left them on the table.

Our uncomfortable stint in the waiting room was soon ended by a beeping sound at the top of the hour. This announced the hourly ten-minute window for visitation. It was time to see Mom. As we walked down the hallway, Paige put put her arm out, turned to look me in the eye, and said, "I think I should call everyone and tell them we won't be hosting Christmas."

"That sounds like a wise decision." I started to walk away—but her arm held me, insistent.

"Jack—look at me. Jack—this isn't your fault."

She wouldn't let go of me until I nodded.

Room 10. Third door on the right. This was where the receptionist by the name of Mrs. Forbes directed us.

I briefly stopped, taking in all I observed. The upper half of the wall or partition consisted of a glass window covered by a brown curtain. The door was partially ajar. On its surface, at eye level, was a small white card with "Mary Lewis" inscribed in black ink.

I motioned for Paige to follow me into the room. Mom appeared to be a prisoner, tied up with intravenous tubing, monitoring electrodes, and wiring from various other electronic gadgetry.

Her face showed a mix of gratitude that we were there and fear of what she was experiencing. I tried to bolster her spirits with the best smile I could muster. Then I glibly asked, "Why have you changed rooms?"

This elicited a faint smile from Mom. "I wanted to get closer to the ground floor."

I tried my best to laugh but found I couldn't.

Mother's smile became more pronounced when Paige said, "Ann is flying in tonight."

"What time?" Mother asked.

"Early morning. You'll probably be asleep," I said.

"I hope I'm awake to see her," Mom said impassively.

In the short time remaining, Paige and I were as positive as we could be for Mom. We told her we expected her to be as good as new before Christmas. Her face lit up as it hadn't since we initially walked into the room.

Paige excused herself, saying she "had those calls to make" without being specific enough to upset Mom.

After she left, Mom said, "Jack."

"What, Mom?"

"I want you to know how proud of you I am. Of the son you've always been, of the man you've become. And that—whatever happens—I trust you."

"I try my best." The beeping sound marking the end of the visiting interlude cut off any more. I gave Mom my customary kiss on the forehead as a gesture of farewell, and she squeezed my hand. Her strength encouraged me.

I went looking for Paige, found her by the phone, and stood next to her until she gave her last brief, "I'll call back when I have more news."

As she hung up, I saw Barry Winthrop's partner approaching—Dr. George Comstock. He was a stiff-necked Yankee and coldly formal to the point of being pretentious—I had instantly disliked him the only time we'd met. I often get frustrated with Southerners—they can take forever to get to the point—but at least they give you the time of day. Not this guy.

Comstock motioned for Paige and I to join him in a small room I hadn't noticed before. He started talking in vague generalities, forcing me to ask direct, probing questions. I sensed his discomfort. We had gotten off on bad footing, and it would only go downhill from there.

The nature of my questions revealed my familiarity with respiratory medicine. This surprised Comstock, but didn't penetrate his detachment.

Comstock didn't divulge much, holding back vital information that we needed to know. As this continued, I became increasingly aware he was being intentionally vague about the gravity of my mother's condition.

"How sick is she, Doctor?" I bluntly asked. Paige shifted her weight nervously from foot to foot.

Comstock continued to reply with platitude. "The prognosis is far from good." He paused. "Your mother is a very sick lady. The septic shock has caused organ shutdown—there's no way of knowing if it will cause permanent damage even if she pulls through."

Even if she pulls through?

This is getting us nowhere. I inhaled deeply and demanded, "What are my mother's chances of surviving the night?"

Irritation flashed in his eyes, but this didn't stop him. Looking directly at me, he didn't bat a goddam eyelash as he told me that my mother would most likely be dead by morning. That the odds in favor of her surviving the night were roughly one in three.

"YOUR MOTHER MOST LIKELY WILL BE DEAD BY MORNING. THE ODDS IN FAVOR OF HER SURVIVING THE NIGHT ARE ROUGHLY ONE IN THREE."

His exact words.

Then he was finished. There it was. THERE IT WAS. All laid out for me in no uncertain terms—*most likely will be dead by morning*—DEAD—*mother had told me about her dream—the same dream she had with Steve and Norman except this time it had been SHE who was going to die.*

Dead by morning.

Paige had been right earlier. Mom was sicker than anyone here had known. *How could I have let this happen—HOW?*

"Thank you, Dr. Comstock."

"You're welcome."

The physician was gone. I looked at Paige, who was just as stunned as I. Nothing could have been said that would have consoled either of us. There was nothing to do but sit and wait. Wait for the beeper, or a hurried call to my mother's room to witness her final breaths. The outcome was totally beyond our control.

She has to make it. The woman who was my responsibility, who entrusted her life to me, lay not more than fifteen yards away.

Afternoon passed into early evening and eventually night, in spirit-crushing monotony. The "beep-beep-beep" punctuated the hours. Paige and I were never able to relax, waiting for a more urgent summons. Mother was aware of our periodic presence, although barely conscious amidst the tubes and machines. Her hand returned a slight pressure as I held it in mine.

She has to make it.

After twelve years of marriage, Paige knew me well enough there was never a discussion of going home. As the hours passed,

Paige and I ran out of things to say to one another. I was alone with my thoughts. And I had a lot of thinking to do.

Mom is one of the two women who are the cornerstones of my life.

Working on the play, I've been spending too much time thinking about the loss of important men in my life. I should never take these two women for granted—and I have.

We'd only be going home tonight if Mom had a fatal crisis. However uncomfortable the waiting room, I was thankful we still had cause to be here. As the clock on the wall crawled toward midnight, it seemed there might be cause for hope.

CHAPTER 10

December 10th

The clock finally crept past midnight. It was tomorrow. The long night wasn't over, but shortly I'd have to leave to go pick up Ann from the airport.

People were little more than shadows to Paige and me as we awaited the next hourly summons to see Mom. Neither magazines nor television served as distractions. Each minute we weren't called shortened the interval Mom had to survive.

After the last hourly visit before I had to leave for the airport, I sought a moment's solitude in room full of vending machines on the first floor. It was empty except for cups that had missed the waste basket or been left on the tables.

I sat down facing the wall at the table farthest from the door. The tears began slowly. I started coughing, which meant an appearance by my asthma as well.

Tears and asthma. An infrequent but bitter combination in my life. The first time, twenty-five years ago, almost this very day, was still fresh in my mind. Actually, it might have been this very day. The day I read my mother's letter from the Mayo Clinic when Dad was there for surgery. I'd read it so many times, I could almost quote it from memory.

"I've sure been a busy gal this week. I've been over at the hospital so many times they think I'm a patient. Why, just today I was strapped on the operating table and half way under before they realized I had just come to visit dad! (If you believe that- you're nuttier than I am.)"

I realized the tone of false cheerfulness she'd used in the letter was the same tone Paige and I had used with her the night before last. *Oh, damn.* I was surprised by the tear's warmth on my cheeks before I tasted salt on my tongue. They began falling on my shirt and suit coat like rain. I had never experienced this before.

My coughing was joined by a sound I had not emitted since childhood. The sound of my sobbing. I was weeping unashamedly, uncontrollably, for the first time since I vowed not to cry at my father's funeral.

They say crying is good for you, but not this time. A feeling of emptiness overwhelmed me after I managed to regain my composure. I glanced around the room. Fortunately, it remained empty except for me. No one had witnessed my temporary lapse. Maintaining the appearance of strength still possessed a measure of importance for me. How much longer it would last was anyone's guess.

This whole thing had lasted less than fifteen minutes. I was tempted to remain sitting here, but knew I'd have to leave for the airport shortly. I had to get back to the waiting room.

My body hurt as I stood, and I felt prematurely old. Before walking out, I tried to pull myself together, and I noticed the tears had evaporated from my suit. It happened to be my favorite. After the long night, it had the acrid stink of sweaty desperation and fear.

The waiting room and its occupants appeared the same as when I had left. I was immediately scrutinized by all eyes, but was dismissed as quickly. I was one of them—a fellow victim suspended in uncertainty and anticipation while a few of the community slept.

What an odd group we were. A motley assembly which otherwise never would have met. White, black, Hispanic, whatever. A soiled mechanic's outfit, a business suit, and rollers in uncombed hair were each indicative of a hurried exit from workplace or home. The television had long since been quieted.

The Christmas tree lights cast an eerie glow against the walls. Whatever our differences, the seconds seemed to pass equally slow for all of us.

My chair had become more uncomfortable than ever. I wouldn't miss it while on the airport run. My only worry about leaving was that Mom would die while I was gone. With considerable misgivings, I walked out the door. If Ann's plane was on time, I would miss only one visit with Mom.

The parking lot was completely deserted. A thin layer of ice covered the windows of my car. A light wind made the cold worse.

As I scraped the windows, I realized my suit coat provided little protection against the cold. Shivering didn't help much. For the life of me, I couldn't remember what I had done with my trench coat, not to mention winter hat and gloves. Normally that would bother me—not tonight.

There was little warmth inside the car. After starting the engine, I fumbled with the controls on the dashboard to crank up the heat . My hands were numb. Ice crystals appeared suspended in my breath.

I made the mistake of turning on the radio. John Lennon had been gunned down near his apartment in New York. Apparently with neither rhyme nor reason. And Indiana had lost their second straight basketball game to Notre Dame.

That was enough radio—my thoughts were dark, but this wasn't helping.

This was Ann's first visit to North Carolina since her surprise trip July 4th for Mother's birthday. The whole thing was a real bummer—didn't go well at all. Ann hardly talked the whole time. Mother didn't have much to say either.

Neither Paige nor I had ever told Ann about what happened after we dropped her off at the airport to fly home. Mom started crying in the back seat, big sobs that didn't stop. I asked her what was wrong, but she wouldn't say. Paige's hand on my arm was a caution that I should let her be.

The closest Paige and I came to passing this along was our frequent hinting to Ann that she should come see Mother more often.

The airport, which locals called RDU, was virtually deserted upon my arrival. I pulled right up to the door of the terminal. If my timing was right, Ann's plane should have just landed.

Inside, I encountered a small gathering of people. Those waiting milled among arriving travelers. Ann was among them—impatiently looking for me.

Younger by two years, Ann looked like a female executive on a business trip. Petite and carefully groomed, her outfit consisted of a short fur jacket with slacks. I thought she was going to freeze. She carried a travel bag and suitcase.

We greeted each other with our usual reserved embrace—we'd never been close. Ann fled Kokomo at the first opportunity, and had literally washed her hands of everyone and everything there. I hadn't been nearly as fortunate.

We walked rapidly to the car with very little conversation.

"Just to make sure I didn't miss anything, please start at the beginning and tell me what's going on with Mom."

I went through the whole story from first flu symptoms, to the medicine I gave Mom, to the doctor visit, to the x-ray, to being admitted to the hospital, "to play it safe." Things looking up, planning to bring her home. Then sepsis and intensive care.

All Ann had done up to this point was nod her head.

Ann paused. "I get that because of your work, you know this area of medicine, and you were just trying to play it safe, and take care of Mom. I'm not blaming you when I ask what I'm about to ask, just trying to understand. Did the septic thing come from her being in the hospital, rather than at home?"

"Sepsis, which sometimes causes septic shock."

"Damn it, Jack—I don't need a dictionary, I need to *understand*."

"Did it come from the hospital or would it have happened anyway? Probably not, but there's no way to be *sure*. And sepsis means there was bacteria in her bloodstream. Septic shock is where the bacteria release toxins into the blood which lead to a cascade of organs shutting down. That's what happened. Now she's in Intensive Care with—with—"

"One in three chance of surviving until morning" was on the tip of my tongue. It stalled there. But not for long. Seemingly with a life of their own, the words escaped from my mouth with a quiver.

"Mom has a one in three chance of surviving until morning."

Ann emitted a loud gasp. She reached out to touch my arm, saying, "Jack, I'm so sorry. Please don't blame yourself for this."

Talking was impossible—we made the rest of the drive in silence.

Mom was still alive when we got to Intensive Care. She managed a slight smile when Ann walked into her room. "Mom, I'm here," Ann said. Our mother immediately lost consciousness.

Mom was barely was able to acknowledge our presence during each of our ten-minute visits at the top of every hour. When she did, her hands were totally limp. We continued to reassure her of our support, to encourage her.

She looked like she could die any moment. It appeared that the only thing keeping her alive were the IV tubes with their slow drip drip drip. Something to fight the infection, something to keep up her blood pressure, glucose. Even with all of this, there was no visible sign of improvement, just survival.

At the end of each brief hourly visit, we departed her room reluctantly, knowing she might not make it to the next hour.

I couldn't face going back to the waiting room and being surrounded by so many gray, hopeless faces. When not in Mom's room, I paced alone by the Christmas tree in the reception area— until it was time to return. Darkness pressed against the windows. An apt metaphor for my thoughts.

"Don't blame yourself," Ann had said. Hearing her say it had the exact opposite effect from what she intended. Because I had been doing my best not to hear those voices of doubt, and blame had been calling from the edges of my hearing ever since Mom got sick. I blamed myself the whole time while trying not to admit it.

Mother was my responsibility. She trusted me, in this, as in all else. Trusted her son, the scientist, the expert in the treatment she was receiving.

My work mind began looking for benchmarks. If she made it till sunrise, she'd beaten the odds. It was just past 2 a.m.—how many hourly interludes until sunrise? Call it five.

There weren't many people coming and going through the hospital's main reception this time of night. The only sounds were those of my footsteps, and my echoing self-doubts.

One after another, the hours passed. Nothing changed but the clock. Mother survived.

The first hints of dawn gave me hope this dreadful night was finally yielding to the hope of this new day. Mother had not died. The most important round had been won, and I said as much to Ann and Paige. Their tension eased ever so slightly.

With daylight, the rest of the world joined us in wakefulness. Concerns of dailiness required our attention. Our son, my work.

Paige arranged Brett's continued care with Natalie, our neighbor who was being so helpful. And I called my boss Herb to inform him of the ongoing situation. Both were stunned, and neither could think of anything to say except, "My prayers are with you." For once I let this pass without comment.

Later that morning, I sat alone at mother's bedside. She lay in a semi-comatose state with no improvement. Her hand was as limp as before. I searched her face for a smile, however slight it might have been, but there was none. She lay unmoving, and I had to look closely to see if she was still breathing.

As the "beep-beep-beep" sounded for me to leave, I realized that while Mom had survived, she hadn't improved. She was the same as before. Comatose with closed, leaden eyelids directed to-

ward the ceiling. I had been wrong to think her crisis was over—
and made a huge mistake in sharing that thought with Ann and
Paige. Mom continued to hover on the outskirts of death.

Toward late morning, an exhausted Barry Winthrop came
into the waiting room for a brief conference. Aware of what we
wanted to hear, he began with, "Mary survived the night because
of an unbelievably strong constitution. She has a long way to go
before she's out of the woods."

"How's her blood pressure?" I asked.

"Stable," he replied. And paused at length. "But that's because
of the drug we are using to support it. We hope to be able to begin tapering off in a day or so." Winthrop massaged his forehead
as if each word was painful.

"When will we know she's made it?"

"It's too soon to tell. We're dealing with a very difficult disease
process."

"How are her kidneys?" I finally thought to ask.

"Not good. We hope they start to crank up again."

*Which clearly meant that they weren't working at this instant. Kidney
function provides the mile markers on the road to real recovery. Urinary output, pure and simple.*

My eyes strayed to the volume of urine in the plastic bag
hanging at the side of the bed. "Could they come back today?"
I asked.

"Not likely. Hopefully tomorrow," Winthrop said. He was becoming visibly antsy to disengage himself from the conversation.

Still nothing from Paige or Ann.

"Thank you for your candor. Please let us know if there is
anything we can do," I added as an afterthought.

"There's nothing any of you can do except go home and get
some rest." After saying this, he walked away without another
word.

We ignored his advice without discussion, acting on some unspoken belief that our presence was somehow keeping Mom alive.

She survived the afternoon in a state of limbo. Not getting better, not getting worse. The day turned into a test of endurance on everyone's part. We became increasingly fatigued. The time we spent with Mom became indistinguishable from the time we were in the waiting room. By early evening, rest was even more overdue, a fact we all tacitly ignored.

Winthrop came into the waiting room as we were discussing plans to stay a second night at the hospital. Overhearing us, he shook his head and said, "Please go home and get some rest." No one moved, which resulted in a frazzled, "Her condition is stable enough for you to go. We will call you if anything changes." We reluctantly agreed.

I experienced a pang of guilt as I stood over Mom's bed alongside Paige and Ann. I was the first to say anything, and I promised we would be seeing her in the morning. She somehow mustered the strength to squeeze my hand while opening her eyes for what must have been a full second. Mother fully understood what she had just heard. I struggled to maintain my composure as Paige and Ann said their goodbyes.

Paige went to get Brett, and I barely had time get into the house and switch on the lights before hearing the phone ring. Running to answer, while Ann followed behind, I was relieved it wasn't the hospital, but Mom's boss, Vince. "I've been calling the hospital since last evening. She was listed as critical for the longest time, but now they say she's guarded. How's she doing?"

"Not good. But getting through the night was a good sign," I said. Covering the mouthpiece, I whispered "Mom's boss" to Ann, who looked concerned.

Vince's voice was tinged with relief. "Is there anything Pamela and I can do?" he asked.

"Not at the moment, but thanks for your offer."

"Tell Mary I'm saving her last paycheck for her," he said.

"I shall. Thanks for your concern."

Another "I'll pray for her" made me wince.

I took a moment to call Uncle Mike. It was pretty much the same conversation. The same words. They seemed to work. Somehow. After hearing them, Mike decided not to drive down, and I promised to update him every day.

No sooner had I hung up the phone than Paige came in with Brett. He ran to me as if he hadn't seen me for weeks. He had a huge smile. I picked him up and hugged him tightly. *This* is what I needed.

The first words out of his mouth were "Auntie Ann—did you come for Christmas already?"

Despite her exhaustion, Ann replied smoothly, "No—I came down to find out what you want. But I'm tired from my trip, and we have plenty of time to talk about it. So why don't you put your thinking cap on, so you can be ready to have a good long talk about presents. Presuming, of course, you've been a good boy."

Brett's look was priceless—"Oh, I have, I really have." He paused. "Has Mar-Mar come home from the hospital?"

"Grandma has decided to stay in the hospital. That way she'll be rested up for Christmas. She asked us to hug you for her.," I said.

"This is going to be the best Christmas *ever*, she better really rest up," Brett responded.

CHAPTER 11

December 11th

I awoke in a darkened room feeling so tired—as if I hadn't slept at all.

What day is it? Why am so tired?

Mom. The hospital. Picking up Ann from the airport. The odds against Mom. Being up straight through two days. This is Thursday. The phone didn't ring after I went to bed. Mom survived the night. She'd made it till Thursday. Thursday the 11th.

I managed to squint my tired eyes into reading the lighted clock across the room—5:45 a.m. I could sleep a whole extra night.

Thursday. Exactly a week from when she first told me she was "coming down with the flu."

The dim glow of the clock gave shadowy hints of the painting hanging above it. It was a very sad painting of a very sad clown that had hung in my Uncle Norman's bedroom over the years. It was one of the few things salvageable from his estate.

Paige hates that painting—says it gives her the creeps, and keeps threatening to throw it away.

I had matured to manhood under the painting's shadow. Along the way, I'd developed a gut sense the clown exemplified Norman, with its sorrowful expression symbolic of his despair.

It's the 11th. December 11th. Four years ago today, we buried Norman. What a strange time to be thinking about this. I need to keep my mind on Mom, Paige, Brett, work—and not get lost in the past.

Mom. At Norman's gravesite, standing beside me looking more fragile than I had ever seen her, clasping my hand as if needing reassurance she was still among the living. While we were standing there, a friend came up and asked me, "How can you keep going—when you believe in nothing?"

As I replied, "You just do," I squeezed Mom's hand.

Six o'clock passed without a sound from Brett. I lay in bed, watching the second hand crawl through the next several minutes. I remained in bed before Brett stirred.

The house was quiet, but my mind was full of sound...a disorganized chorus of three voices overlapping and intertwining— *Ann's voice saying, "Don't blame yourself," Paige's calling out, "It's not your fault," and Mom's quiet voice repeating, "I trust you."*

The litany seemed endless—I tried, but I couldn't mute it.

The more they told me not to blame myself, that I wasn't responsible—that it wasn't my fault—the more responsible I felt for Mom, for all of this.

Mom often called me "Mr. Spock"—teasing me about my devotion to logic. That logic was failing me now. I knew I'd made the right, prudent, safe decisions. Logically, I shouldn't blame myself.

But I do.

Brett suddenly sang out, "Da-ad, I'm u-up!" Paige reached over and touched me on the shoulder. She was wide awake. We are going to start the new day together, Brett's happy voice babbling away in his room. No sound came from the study where Ann was, so she was somehow sleeping through it.

Brett was very glad to see us for the first second two. But this soon evaporated into a half pout, followed by, "Do you have to go back to the hospital with Mar-Mar?"

Paige immediately replied, "Yes. We need to go back to the hospital to help Grandma get better."

Left unexpressed was the fact Mom's illness had necessitated canceling of all plans for Christmas. Nor at this point was there any guarantee that there would even be one for the three of us.

"The doctors want to make sure Mar-Mar gets well, and we are acting as her assistants," I told him.

Brett was practically glaring at me. Either we had missed the boat entirely in satisfying him, or there was something else wrong.

Paige was clearly ahead of me in sensing what was wrong. "What did you do over the last two days while we were at the hospital?" she asked.

Brett stared at the floor, which was not like him. Something was definitely not right. But he wasn't going to get straight to the point—we were going to hear the whole story.

Nursery school was great, and preparations for Christmas included making pipe-cleaner stars, construction paper chains, and macaroni trees. The party was only a week away, and Paige and I *had* to attend. Brett had so much fun with Natalie and her four-year-old son, Dale.

"Dale is my new best friend," he said.

That's when Brett began shifting his weight from foot to foot. That's when he brought up the teenaged boy we'd used as a baby-sitter on many occasions without a problem. And what the boy did when he stayed overnight. Which was vague.

What?!

After much prodding and evasion, Brett finally told us the boy had exposed himself. Brett persisted in this story to such a degree that Paige and I were forced to believe him.

For a second, I was sufficiently angry to deck the kid, if he'd been there. But fortunately he wasn't. There wasn't anything for me to do except go along with Paige and agree not ever to use him again. This, and do our best to downplay the importance of the episode in Brett's mind and concentrate on the immediate future.

The future was today. The future was now. Another morning at nursery school for Brett, followed by an afternoon at Natalie's with his new best friend Dale. We used happy talk about Brett's day to take his mind off the chat we'd just had, and to distract him from thoughts of Grandma.

If all went as planned, we would be able to pick Brett up that evening— *If all went as hoped and Grandma didn't relapse or die.*

When we arrived at the hospital, we found two families were sleeping on chairs in the Intensive Care waiting room. The room appeared unchanged compared to when we had seen it last. The unoccupied furniture and magazines remained frozen in disarray, ash trays held roughly the same number of cigarette butts, and the Christmas tree lights blinked with the same monotonous frequency. A few minutes after we arrived, the beeper sounded to announce visiting time.

Mother was surprisingly alert. She greeted us with open eyes and the slightest hint of a smile. She appeared better. Ever so slightly better. In a barely audible whisper, she inquired, "How is my grandson?"

"He misses his Mar-Mar," Paige replied.

There was no question Mom was alert and able to follow everything we said. But she wasn't moving, and she hadn't moved since our arrival in the room. She seemed riveted to the pillow.

Paige, Ann, and I were as cheerful as we could be for the entire ten-minute visit. Mother's eyes registered occasional approval, but little else. A menu with wine and cognac was devised for her recovery dinner. It would be held at Bakatsias, a Greek restaurant

Mom wanted to try. We all had different theories on how to pronounce its name. Finally, Christmas lists were discussed with a special emphasis on gifts Mom had mentioned wanting.

Things seem to be looking up. Am I sure? This time I better wait before saying anything.

As we were leaving Mom's room, Dr. Winthrop came looking for us. We adjourned to the same vending area where I had cried the night before. Or had it been two nights? I was starting to have trouble keeping track of days—they all blurred together. He dispensed with small talk and launched into an update—

"Not good in spite of stabilizing—"

"Remains gravely ill—"

"Body has not started recovering from the effects of the bacterial toxin—"

And there was something new. Something really important. Mother's blood gases indicated she wasn't receiving sufficient oxygen by normal breathing. Without pausing, the physician told us this would have to be remedied by placing her on a respirator. Hopefully for a short interval.

"Are there any questions?" he asked.

He sounded stressed.

A silence ensued. I was on a rollercoaster. The emotional high brought on by thinking Mom was better had now become a definite low. She wasn't better. At best, she was holding her own. And one really had to stretch to believe that.

Paige and Ann stared down at the table as they waited for me to speak. I thought my mind was playing tricks on me. Led my eyes to believe what they had seen was an improvement compared to yesterday. This hadn't been so. This hadn't been so according to Barry Winthrop—who was in the best position to know. Mother's life continued to hang in the balance. She had made little, if any, progress since this nightmare had started. Now she needed a respirator to breathe. A breathing tube was not a sign of progress.

"Can I see my mother alone for a few minutes before you hook her up?" I asked.

I didn't know how I would have reacted if my request had been denied. Or if Paige or Ann wanted to accompany me. Fortunately, neither occurred. Winthrop asked only that I allow him several minutes to inform the staff of what was happening.

Paige and Ann glared at me. In bewilderment and frustration. I tried my very best to be encouraging. Tried to emphasize Mom's tenacity and the quality of care she was receiving. Tried as hard as I could possibly try. Then I left them, unable to believe anything I had said.

Mom was awake and smiled when I walked back in. She had expected me to return by myself. On the right side of her bed, a space had already been cleared to accommodate the respirator. I walked to her side and gently took her hand.

More than anything, I wanted to tell her how much she meant to me. To plead with her to fight, to live. *This is what I should say—but can't.* Instead, I pressed her hand and said, "You'll be getting better soon."

I'm stuck in this sad place where I can't seem to say or do the right thing.

"The respirator is only a temporary measure to help you breathe. They'll take you off it in a couple of days."

For the first time, uncertainty was an unwelcome visitor to Mother's eyes. She looked sad, and I could feel her doubts. She was in a place she didn't want to be, and my empty reassurances weren't helping.

After all, many years ago, she'd made them herself to me about Dad. In the letters from the Mayo Clinic that I still had.

"Daddy sat up in the chair for two hours or more today, and also walked down the hall. Maybe that doesn't sound like much to you darlings, but believe me, it was.

"Still don't like it here, you know. Not complaining—just making a statement. It's a sad town to me. Such sick people come here. I suppose some of it is interesting. One learns a lot, maybe too much for their own good. I've spent all my time this last week walking to and from the hospital. I want to get downtown maybe tomorrow, but I've been saying that ever since I got here, and haven't made it yet. Don't know exactly why I even want to go. (Don't care much for this town, you know.)"

Maybe Mom knew where I'd gone, maybe not. Either way, her touch brought me back. Her hand clasping mine—as if we were sealing an agreement. Its strength surprised me.

Her grip began to weaken, clearly indicating it was time for me to leave.

"I'll see you soon." Her hand became limp. Thinking this meant she had fallen asleep, I turned and walked to the door. Before leaving, I turned for a final glance at her.

She wasn't asleep—instead she was looking at me with an intense stare. She raised her head up from the pillow and said, "I love you."

"I love you, too," I responded, which brought a faint smile from her and a surrender to sleep.

Paige and Ann were waiting in the corridor. We stayed there and spoke in subdued voices.

Paige and Ann clung to my opening—"Stronger," and "Raised up in bed," but they wanted more in the way of explanation. Paige's hesitant "What about the respirator?" caught me by surprise.

"A couple of days should do it," I said.

Ann quickly asked, "But why?"

My work self seemed to answer this one. I wove a verbal maze of alveolar space, oxygen tension, and the systemic ravages of septic shock. I finished in plain English: "She's not getting enough oxygen, and the respirator will help. The problem could be a carryover from the pneumonia." I sounded confident. Yes. I did.

Paige looked at Ann with a puzzled expression on her face. "And for how long?" she asked.

"A couple of days," I repeated. Pulled the estimate out of the air before proceeding with, "Of course, Mom won't be able to talk during that time."

"She won't!?" An emotional emission in unison from the two women.

"No, the tube on her windpipe will interfere with her voice box," I explained.

Ann and Paige shook their heads in response. They weren't happy, but there weren't any more questions.

Mother was sleeping soundly when we saw her again in late morning. A nurse told us she had been sedated and wouldn't awaken for at least several hours. Off to the side, the respirator gave a resonant gasp at the end of each respiration. Protruding from the machine like tentacles were more tubes, joining the assortment of plastic conduits from other sources. Mother was oblivious to her surroundings.

Now began a time of counting. For six hours, nothing changed except the clock. Increasingly exhausted, we stood silent and motionless at the foot of the bed during each ten minute visit. Rhythmic risings and fallings of a diminutive chest cavity met our gazes. Twelve breaths per minute, a hundred and twenty during each visit, each concluding with a resonant gasp. She was breathing. She was breathing and wasn't dead.

She regained consciousness only once. During our last visit, she smiled when she saw us, and promptly returned to a deep sleep or coma. For this reason we were surprised shortly thereafter when Barry Winthrop interrupted his rounds to provide us with an encouraging report.

"We have begun to wean Mary from her medicines a little bit at a time—"

"She's showing signs of getting stronger—"

"The respirator shouldn't be needed for much longer—"

"If her condition continues to improve in a like manner, a transfer from intensive care soon."

He managed a weak smile as he finished. He pleaded with us for a second time to go home and get some rest. "Vitally important for your own well-being," he emphasized as he had done previously. "This is what Mary would want you to do," was thrown in for good measure, which resulted in Paige and me agreeing to follow his advice. Ann, by contrast, decided to stay over until the next morning.

The drive home gave me a chance to think.

We're not out of the woods as yet, but at least we're pointed in the right direction. Once Mom's out of Intensive Care, she'll need a couple days before being released. Maybe a week of rest at our house before going home to her apartment. If all goes well, Mom could be close to normal by Christmas. First things first, though. Her kidneys have to start working. Hopefully today.

After dinner, we sat in the family room watching television. The Christmas tree had a few presents under it already, all of which Brett had carefully massaged, shaken, weighed, and inventoried.

Apparently much of his day at nursery school had been taken up with discussion of the fact Christmas was exactly two weeks away. All the kids in his class understood two weeks meant Santa was just around the corner.

Yawning as Paige led him up to bed, Brett reminded us Santa needed to deliver on that John Deere tractor.

For the first time since Mom went into Intensive Care, this seemed possible—even real. The fear that been holding my chest in a vise finally let go.

I made plans to go tractor shopping.

CHAPTER 12

December 12th

Friday dawned with a feeling of strangeness. It took me a while to figure out why. The sense of dread that had been with me for weeks was gone, like a weight off my chest. For a moment I even had the fleeting hint of a smile at the corners of my mouth. This was the day—to use one of Mom's favorite clichés—we'd be getting out of the woods. That thought brought energy like a patent medicine tonic. Rather than lying in the dark as I had so often lately, I got right up, leaving Paige asleep. As yet, there was no sound from Brett.

Flipping on the bathroom light, I impatiently squinted at the face in the mirror while my eyes adjusted to the glare. Aside from a stubble of whiskers and subtle etchings of stress, it showed an eagerness for the rest of the world to awaken so my day could begin in earnest.

The warmth of the water on my cheeks was the first pleasant sensation that had registered with me in nearly a week. That realization made me stop rushing, and slow down. Brett still asleep meant I could savor this feeling for a moment before applying the shaving cream. This day would be better. Water droplets ran down my cheek where tears had been the rule of thumb.

I squirted sufficient shaving cream in my hand to include Brett before realizing he wasn't by my side. I half expected him to rush in at the last minute to claim his share, but I heard only a faint stirring from his room.

She's going to make it. She's got twenty or more years left. Maybe a lot more. Happy, productive years. This is going to be one of those things we can laugh about over several scotches. Like one of those great Hoosier comebacks. Mom is from Indiana, so I guess that's exactly what it is.

I realized I'd lost track of things when I found a strange man looking back at me from the mirror, his face half-covered in dried shaving cream, razor still in hand. *It's a good thing Brett didn't come in.*

I finished up and went downstairs, walking into the family room. I looked out the window. I could barely see the outlines of the newspaper at the end of the driveway. Yesterday and its news had flown by unnoticed, including the score of Indiana's latest basketball game against Texas Tech.

Placing a coat over my pajamas, I went out for the newspaper, hoping to read about an easy IU victory in the Hoosier Holiday Classic. Mom would be glad to hear about a win, even if it was over a weak opponent.

Mom is really interested in Indiana's upcoming game North Carolina in Chapel Hill. Only eight days away now. No point in getting tickets, going to the game in person will tire her out. We'll watch it on television. Crap—she's probably not going to be up to cooking fudge. I'll have to wait a few games.

Pulling out the Sports section, I found Indiana beat Texas Tech by thirty-six points. Ted Kitchel, a forward from Galveston, had scored forty two of those. Kitchel was Mom's favorite player, so that would make her happy. I couldn't wait to pass along the news.

Footsteps overhead distracted me from the box score. Joining them was the faint sound of a piping voice. It sounded like Brett was conducting a room-to-room search for me upstairs, calling out "Da-ad" repeatedly. He was headed for the bedroom, which meant he'd wake Paige, so I headed upstairs.

By the time I got there, Brett had jumped on the bed, and they were engaged in conversation. When I walked in, they stopped talking and smiled at me.

I wondered why everyone was so happy until I realized they were responding to me. I was actually grinning. Smiling for the first time since Mom had gone to the hospital. For the moment, we had returned to something approaching normalcy.

I laid down next to Brett and we all relaxed. We talked about everything, we talked about nothing. Christmas lists, Carolina basketball, and nursery school art projects and playgrounds.

Much better than talking about blood pressure and bacterial toxins.

My great mood carried over to the hospital, where Paige and I revived a sleeping Ann in the waiting room with our cheerful dispositions. Ann's night had been filled with short naps on uncomfortable chairs, interspersed between intervals of watching Mother sleep. I was trying to convince her she was in need of a good rest when Barry Winthrop walked into the room.

We huddled together in a corner of the room like we were on a football field. Winthrop's voice was different from the onset. Calmer and relieved. He was finally able to share some good news about what had been an exceedingly difficult case. His gaze alternated between the three of us as he carefully chose his words. He led off with, "Mary is resting peacefully and showing signs of responding to her medication. We have been able to reduce the dose of dopamine for the first time since she went into septic shock."

Blood pressure on the rise. Exactly like it should be happening if she were getting better.

"She still has a long way to go, but we're headed in the right direction." He paused before asking, "Do you have any questions?"

"What should we expect now, assuming a steady, slow rate of improvement?" I asked.

We hung on every word as the physician outlined the three milestones required for recovery.

"Increase in urinary output—"

"Weaning from dopamine we've been using to keep her blood pressure up—"

"Plenty of rest."

He concluded with, "In any event, you need to be patient since all this could take some time." An uncomfortable silence ensued, which Paige ended by saying, "Is there anything we can do to make Mary more comfortable?"

Winthrop inhaled deeply before replying. "You can't do anything other than what's currently being done. But there's something else. Please take care of yourselves. The stress you're dealing with could easily make you sick. And we don't want her exposed to anything she doesn't already have."

Before he left, I thanked him. "We appreciate you being straight with us. That hasn't always been the case in our family." As he walked away, Ann and I exchanged the kind of look that made me believe she was thinking of the same letter from Mom. We'd read it over and over.

"Darling Jack—I can't do as you ask about asking the doctor when we can come home. You see, dear, it's a big mess up here as you could ever find. Daddy doesn't have just one doctor, but three or four. You ask them nothing; they tell you when they are good and ready. Daddy's coming along fine, sweet, but it's too soon yet for them to say when he can leave. He must heal before we can. Try to understand, please. It's terribly hard for me to stay—I want you kids so badly. But each morning when you get up, do as I do—just think it's another day nearer the time. Try it, honey—it'll help just a little."

Mother was perceptively stronger during the next visiting interval. The tubing and the respirator remained very real presences in the room, but somehow seemed less imposing than they had yesterday. All signs clearly showed she was getting better.

Through the day, Mom's face gradually became more animated—with occasional smiles that reached all the way to her eyes. Her grip was more forceful, and she could sit up.

The ventilator prevented her from speaking, but the nurses had brought her a notepad, and she was using it. Her handwriting was shaky, but what she wrote made sense. She was much more responsive and seemed to be thinking clearly.

Mom smiled when I told her of Kitchel's stellar performance in Indiana's victory. Ann and Paige's eyes started to glaze over at this discussion.

Instead of taking pity on them, I doubled down and gave an extended monologue about the glories of Hoosier basketball. Mom's brightest smile of the day came when I described a game I took her to at Assembly Hall on my birthday. We sat up in the rafters and watched Indiana beat a heavily favored Ohio State team. When we finally returned home, an exploding flashbulb captured our expressions as we walked through the door. It turned out Paige had used the opportunity to set up a surprise birthday party.

Ann laughed and said she'd love to see the photo. Paige volunteered to find it. Ann had relaxed, an unusual thing when she was around Mom.

Odd—but this might be the most comfortable I've seen Ann and Mom be together since we were kids.

Mom's strength appeared steady throughout the day. There were times she seemed tired or less attentive than others, but that was understandable. She really cheered up when we told her that we'd bring Brett to see her the next day.

We had no concerns about leaving her overnight, and we expected her to be even stronger in the morning. Mom smiled as I kissed her on the forehead before leaving. In the hospital parking lot, Ann told us she intended to fly back to Tampa on Sunday.

On the way home, we stopped to pick up Brett from Natalie's.

Brett babbled about his day, then peppered Ann with questions about me when I was little. He laughed at some of her stories.

But the real joy came when we told him he was going to see his Grandma tomorrow.

CHAPTER 13

December 13

I woke up looking forward to the day, which promised to be even better than yesterday. Mom was now in good enough shape that Brett was finally able to see her. Probably only a quick wave from the doorway, but it would cheer both of them up. Brett missed his grandma as much as she missed him.

We were going to check in on Mom before running errands the rest of the day. Basic shopping and household errands had mounted up over the course of the week. And Christmas quickly loomed.

Plans were finalized at breakfast. Ann was thinking about flying home to Tampa the next day. It was clear she was experiencing pangs of guilt about leaving. Paige and I remained silent while Ann rationalized her decision. The start of a new work week came up several times as she talked it through with herself. It wasn't altogether clear that Ann was convincing herself she was doing the right thing. Neither Paige nor I wanted to step in as Ann wrestled through things.

Ignoring everything his aunt had said, Brett asked, "Why do you have to leave?" He wanted her to stay. Paige had to explain as best she could as Ann excused herself from the table to call the airlines for flight reservations. She seemed on the verge of tears.

Ann returned shortly to announce she was successful in securing reservations on a 3 p.m. flight on Sunday afternoon. She also announced her intention to buy Brett a present before her departure. We decided to stop at a store called Monkey Business on the way to the hospital.

Brett was excited about receiving a gift before Christmas. We left in a better mood than any time since Ann's arrival.

Arrival at Monkey Business coincided with the owner unlocking the door for business. She was surprised to see customers so early in the morning. Chimes heralded our entry through the small doorway, rendered even tighter by the bulk of winter coats. Brett led the procession.

The owner retreated behind the counter, giving us free reign to roam the aisles in search of Brett's present. Thirty or so seconds was all he needed to see that neither *Star Wars* figures nor toy guns were on the shelves. Clothes were all the store had, and this was what Ann was buying him. In no time, a frown registered his disappointment.

Arms crossed in comic toddler anger, Brett fumed silently while Ann and Paige chose an outfit for him. Normally it wouldn't have taken much to put him in a better mood, but this hadn't been a normal week. My promise of a treat got nowhere.

I was reaching for other bribes when our little kid grenade went off, right there in public. Brett threw a tantrum. Tantrum is a small word—he threw a toddler tornado. Yells, screams, and shouted protestations came out of his mouth in ear-piercing volume. He had been pushed well beyond his limits and was communicating this fact in the only way he knew how. Ann's shocked reaction reminded me she hadn't spent a lot of time around kids. The store owner barely blinked.

I turned to Paige and asked if there was anything she could do to quiet him. The expression on her face communicated everything that needed to be said. It was up to me to remove Brett from the store while Ann completed the transaction of buying the outfit. Her look said *now*. So *now* it was.

We hadn't been outside for more than two minutes before Brett calmed down. He surprised me by asking, "Is Mar-Mar going to be all right?"

I was caught off guard. "She's still very sick," I said before I could catch myself.

Brett persisted in staring at me. He expected reassurance. Suddenly I concocted the word "brittle" to describe my mother's condition. It was the best I could do under the circumstance.

Brett didn't really understand "brittle," but at least it sounded like "better" to him. His aunt and mother came out of the store carrying a moderately sized package. Normally this would be a cause for excitement since it was his, but Brett hardly paid it any heed. Clearly, in a three-year-old's gift rankings, clothes were lower than nothing.

There was little conversation in the car between Monkey Business and the hospital. The drab scenery of a typically gray December morning passed by rapidly.

My mind changed focus as we drove. First it shifted to taking Ann back to the airport, and then to getting back to work in the coming week. The big puzzle was the night featuring both Brett's nursery school Christmas party and the goodbye party for a colleague at work. By the time we pulled into the parking lot, I had begun to think about Christmas.

Brett and I waited in the lobby while Paige and Ann went to Intensive Care to check on Mom. This patience was my acknowledgement of yesterday's improvements in her condition. I guessed they would return in about fifteen minutes with good news. Then I would take Brett in for a brief visit with his grandma.

We stood in the lobby by the enormous Christmas tree. Brett gave careful attention to the ornaments, and was disappointed to hear the carefully wrapped boxes beneath the tree were empty.

"When can I see Mar-Mar?" asked Brett.

"Shortly," I said.

Strangers stopped and asked Brett what Santa Claus was bringing him. I was again caught off guard when he replied, "My grandmother coming home from the hospital to be with us."

They were genuinely touched. It was like a line from a movie. The Lewis family Christmas, starring Tiny Brett.

A few more minutes passed. Brett became impatient.

"Aunt Ann and your Mom will be back any minute," I said. Any minute and I would briefly see Mom to reaffirm that she continued to improve. Then we could leave the hospital and get on with the day. But I made the mistake of looking at my watch for a second time. Twenty minutes had elapsed since Paige and Ann's departure.

Twenty minutes, when I had given them fifteen minutes to return.

Time started to weigh on me like it did on the toddler beside me. We shifted our weight from foot to foot, crossed and un-crossed our arms, and gave a fair amount of loud sighs.

Why am I so anxious? There are at least a hundred explanations for this slight delay. But where are they?

My back was facing the direction of Paige and Ann's approach, so I had to rely on Brett's beaming face to inform me they were finally coming. I reached out to grab him, but he was too quick and ran to them.

I was watching Brett run as Paige and Ann entered my field of vision. They were in a hurry and looked frantic. Brett was running towards them with his arms outstretched. But they were ignoring him, desperately seeking me.

Something was wrong. Something was terribly wrong.

Paige rushed up to me, out of breath, and fought to get the words out. Horrific words that hit hard. "Heart attack. Relapse. Winthrop. They don't know. Worse."

I wanted to cry, scream, but didn't. This couldn't be happening. But it was.

The doors leading to Intensive Care were directly in front of me. This was where Mother was worse than yesterday. She had lost precious ground. A voice was speaking to me. Paige's. Her voice telling me Barry Winthrop was waiting for me there.

My feet started moving.

Winthrop stood in the corner of the waiting room, stethoscope in hand. He immediately vented his frustration. "We were weaning her off her medications. Now this," he said, diverting his eyes from me. Looking at the floor, he added, "We think it's a heart attack, but won't know for sure until the enzymes come back from the lab."

His voice showed real concern. Mom was a real person to hm. With the concern was something else much more unsettling to me: uncertainty.

He didn't know what had happened. A heart attack was only one possibility. One among many—all of them bad. Only the lab results would tell if the heart had been involved. Enzyme levels indicative of tissue damage. But there was a lab value already known indicative of something else—kidneys.

"How are her creatinine levels?" I asked.

Winthrop's head moved from side to side. "About the same," he mumbled. A bad sign. A very bad sign. Mother's kidneys essentially remained shut down.

My mind raced ahead. The frustration of being told my mother had slipped from the brink of recovery was overwhelming. On the edge of my consciousness, I heard, "Several days' setback." He was trying to reassure me. If only it seemed true. It didn't.

Nothing remained to be said.

"We'll do our best to pull her through," Winthrop said.

"Thanks again," I replied.

I stood there for a while after he left.

Where were the flaws in my decision-making? Given the same facts, I'd make the same decisions again. The choices were obvious. Always err on the side of doing more than required. Play it safe to assure a speedy recovery. This is what I did every step of the way. It was a simple case of the flu. The damned flu. Nothing more.

Paige and Ann were right. I'm not to blame for this. All of my decisions were right. There's nothing wrong with anything I did. But something's wrong with my mindset. I was playing god. There is no god, not even me.

When the beeping called me for my next visit, I could barely find my way to Mom's room.

I heard the resonant gasp of the respirator as soon as I reached the door.

She can't die. I can't even let myself think this might be a possibility. It's just a setback. She'll make the ground back up in a couple of days. We'll be back on track to recovery.

We'd brought Brett with us today, expecting this to be a cheerful morning.

Through the catheters and electronic monitors I could barely see Mom. She seemed to be sleeping. On a small table by the foot of her bed was a clinical chart. I picked it up and read. Prothrombin time, complete blood count, urinalysis, blood gases—the numbers weren't where they were supposed to be. I put the clipboard down and walked to her side.

Mother's eyes opened. She looked bewildered, clearly wondering what was happening to her. I smiled, hoping she wouldn't notice I was on the verge of tears. I knew instantly she had slipped much further than I had feared.

With seeming confidence, I echoed Winthrop's narrative of a temporary setback. But while my voice said one thing, my mind betrayed it, screaming, *Please don't die! Please don't die!*

All the while, my mother's eyes strained, seeking an answer to what had gone wrong. As if I were omniscient.

Reassure her, I said to myself, on the verge of losing it. "They're running tests and will have results in no time. Nothing to fret about," I said. Or words to that effect.

Intravenous fluids dripped ever so slowly. The respirator persisted in its irritating "gasp-gasp-gasp." Her urine bag remained unfortunately empty.

Don't lose control.

I repeatedly squeezed my mother's limp and lifeless hand, fully aware my palms were sweaty. No response. A continuous stream of words came from me like a giant run-on sentence. Empty talk about *anything* to avoid the issue facing us. It wasn't just that Mom had relapsed, it was that no one was sure why. That the best possibility was a heart attack offered little comfort.

I built sandcastles of words. None of them took the fear from Mom's eyes.

Out of nowhere, a nurse tapped me on the shoulder. Visiting time was over—leaving this time felt like an escape. Mother blinked farewell as I kissed her on the forehead. I told her to keep fighting. Those were the only words I could find in parting.

Please don't die. Please don't die, continued to haunt me as I walked from mother's room. This was a terrible setback. My family was expecting me in the lobby with an explanation for what had happened. *What am I going to tell them?*

I needed to provide them the illusion everything was under control when, in actuality, not even the doctors knew. The clinical picture would be fuzzy until the tests come back and the enzyme levels were known.

Hopefully they will be only mildly elevated, indicating a small heart attack. That's the best we can hope for. Mother's recovery would be delayed, but she'll survive. On the other hand, it would be much worse if the enzyme tests are negative. That would mean dealing with the unknown.

Quit thinking. Couch everything in the most positive terms. Ignore uncertainty.

Please don't die. Please don't die.

Regroup. Maintain control.

In the lobby, my family approached me. When we had clustered together, we were like an island that others had to detour around. Bits of conversation followed. Questions and answers: "Conscious?" "Yes, but weak." "Heart attack." "Maybe, we'll know for sure later."

More significant were the questions which were not posed: "Do you think she'll pull through?" "How much longer before all of this is over?" Brett sullenly followed our exchange without speaking. He didn't miss a word.

An undercurrent of disbelief surrounded us. This couldn't be real. Tense and troubled, we tried to console one another, refocusing our attention on the problems of the moment. Restructure the day was the first thing e had to do. Errands were postponed indefinitely. We planned out the rest of the day.

Ann decided not to change her plans about returning to Tampa the next day, but to spend the night with our mother before she left. Paige would drive Brett and Ann to the house while I remained at the hospital. After arranging the next round of babysitters, Paige would rejoin me in early afternoon. Ann would relieve us both toward evening.

As he was leaving, Brett looked at me and asked, "Why aren't you coming with us?"

I was out of answers. Paige rescued me with a fiction about his grandma wanting me to keep her company for a while. Her answer seemed to work but set me on edge.

I was left alone to call Vince and Mike. Vince first. He knew this time that something was wrong.

I made a point of not being too negative. Gentle. "Resting comfortably after a difficult morning. Probably a heart attack. Several days' setback."

Vince's voice was tinged with disappointment. "Anything we can do, please ask. Our prayers are with you."

"Thank you for your concern. Keep you posted."

One call remained—to my uncle. Misdialed twice. Called the old number of my grandparent's house by mistake. Memories. *Last two digits different. Have to concentrate better.*

"Hello. Hello." Bad connection. "Mike, is that you?"

His stepson Clyde answered. "Just a minute."

Over the static, I gave the same contrived explanation I had given Vince.

"Should we come?"

"Not yet. Wait until she's stronger."

"Okay."

Whew. "Give my regards to Barbara." All over for now. I wouldn't have to talk for him for at least a couple of days. Maybe.

I was met in the waiting room with looks of empathy and compassion. Everyone had heard of my mother's relapse. I sat and visited Mom when summonsed by the beeping. The sameness of the hours was even worse than the underlying tension.

Endurance was the name of the game. A series of fifty minute waits in anticipation of the ten I would have with Mom. There was no change in her condition when they finally came. The blinking of the Christmas tree lights in the waiting room mocked me the same as the gasp- gasp-gasping of the respirator in her room.

Diversions were few and far between. An occasional trip to the vending area for a coke and candy bar. Several more to the bathroom. Feeble attempts at conversation with my cohorts in the waiting room. Sit. Sit. Walk. Walk. Talk. Talk. Minute upon minute. Hour upon excruciating hour. Caged in an arena that seemed progressively smaller and more threatening. From morning to late afternoon, Mom lay immobile, sometimes in a coma, sometimes with open eyes that pleaded, "Help me. Help me. Don't let me die."

By late afternoon, when Ann returned, I was ready to leave.

Farewells had always been difficult for Mom and I. Ever since Dad died, we both had an awareness that when you say goodbye to someone, you can never be certain you'll see them again. But today I was so exhausted, it was easy to say goodbye.

CHAPTER 14

December 14

Sunday morning, I stood in the family room delaying my departure for the hospital for as long as possible. Paige was entertaining Brett upstairs. I heard the occasional buzzing of their voices.

Normally, my mother would have been just arriving for breakfast. The faint thud of a car door would herald her arrival, signaling Brett to rush to the window. Looking in the breakfast nook, I half expected the table to be set for four. No places had been set. The pile of presents under the tree, on the other hand, continued to grow.

Scenes of my life right now are starting to feel like something out of Dickens' *Christmas Carol,* with the pages scrambled or like a deck of cards being shuffled. The ghosts of Christmas Past, Present, and Yet to Come, all jousting for preeminence.

Playing in the Kokomo snow with Ann—Brett tearing packages open—scattering ashes in Duke Forest—Dad showing how me to play with Lincoln logs—Mom with Brett and her great-grandkids—Paige at our first married Christmas when we were in grad school—Brett not remembering his grandmother—getting my first bike—putting out eggnog for Santa—teaching Brett his first Christmas carols

Echoing laughter from Brett and Paige upstairs made it sound like they were having a good time. Given my funky mood, I thought it better to leave them undisturbed, and walked out the door into the December cold.

The window trim on my car had come loose again. My Super Glue fix had held briefly, but then came undone. *What a metaphor for life right now.* Like some of my Southern friends say—sometimes the simplest things in life are what trip you up. I can't even get Super Glue to work. As another friend would say, what a complete and total PhD move.

Backing out of the driveway, something else caught my eye. We'd moved Mom's station wagon from her apartment to across the street for safety. But a large dent in the rear of the car showed this plan hadn't quite worked out as intended. Paige must have hit it backing out of the driveway. Being distracted wasn't something I was going to blame her for right now.

The backlog of my work at the office began to creep into my mind as I drove through our neighborhood, past neat houses, some with Christmas lights that had been on all night.

Pine trees sometimes intruded in my peripheral vision as I drove.

Given the amount of time I'd lost since Mom got sick, and how much I was likely to miss moving forward, I needed to do a little mental triage. With the FDA submission deadline, and our internal political rivalries, dropping the ball was the one thing that could kill me. Whatever time was left over could be spent on reports and publications. Finally I was out of the neighborhood, if not out of the weeds.

Heading north on Garrett Road, I found that thinking about work deadlines had me so tense I was strangling the steering wheel. I turned on the radio hoping to find some music. The radio had nothing but church services. *What else should I expect, given it's Sunday morning in the South?* Mostly evangelicals. I'd pause at each station long enough to catch a few words, before turning the dial. The snippets formed an appropriate soundtrack for my drive, given the number of churches I was passing, each with a sign out front, either citing a Bible verse or providing a call to the faithful—or faithless. Praise Jesus. Trust in Him and have everlasting life. John 3:16.

I continued to scan. Organ music and talk about pearly gates with streets of gold. Choruses of hallelujahs in the background. Requests for money. Hellfire and damnation the only alternative to heaven. Money. Salvation.

I finally found an alternative as I reached the bypass. Advertisements for Christmas sales. A different kind of salvation—available at the Church of the Mall. *What to buy Brett and Paige for Christmas, and when?* There was little time for shopping with Christmas less than two weeks away. Clearly, the ads worked better than the radio preachers.

Crossing Cornwallis Road, the road I was on straddled the city limits. The city of Durham was to the east; the county to the west. Away from the city, green pine trees contrasted sharply with the drab grayness of dirty snow covering the ground.

Hillsborough Road came up without warning. For a brief moment, habit triggered the impulse to turn onto the street leading to Mom's apartment. *She's not home—she's in the hospital.* That thought put a knot in my stomach as the radio served up Blondie's "The Tide Is High."

This song had been chasing me around all week, bits here, bits there. But this time it finally played from the beginning. It seemed like the theme song of an awful week. Mom always had the radio on around the house when we were growing up. I'd forgotten that.

I listened the same as I had done that August when my father was dying. Listened while I recalled my mother ironing in the living room while I repeatedly heard "Twinkle, Twinkle, Little Star" and "Born Too Late" on an altogether different radio that seemed the same in that instant.

Mom ironing in the living room—"Twinkle, Twinkle, Little Star" and "Born Too Late" on the radio—ironing and spraying starch endlessly—obsessively, as if getting every crease out of Dad's shirt could help him get better.

Veritable threnodies.

I actually thought that. If my friends at work weren't teasing me about cliches, they were giving me a hard time about being verbose.

Veritable threnodies.

I laughed at myself. Laughed for the first time in days.

I turned off the radio. Songs from the present—songs from the past. Tears streamed down both cheeks. It would have been great if this was making me feel better, but instead I felt sick to my stomach.

Tobacco warehouses flanked me as I drove down Guess Road. This area had been at the center of an industry—tobacco—whose products had killed more people than guns ever had. How odd it was now a center of medical research and healing.

What am I going to find when I get to the hospital? She has to be better.

I was only feeling sicker as I got close. Almost to the point of gagging when I saw the Duke Street exit sign. I was almost there.

She has to be better. Her creatinine levels have to be lower. Her kidneys have to be showing signs of recovery. The enzyme tests have to show she's had a mild heart attack. She has to be better.

Any hopes I had about Mom being better seemed to evaporate when I walked into the hospital. It felt like Mom was somehow telepathically warning me to stay away. The hospital seemed unusually empty, and the emptiness was threatening. The corridors leading to Intensive Care were silent—staff and visitors were inexplicably absent. Although on familiar turf, I became disoriented—like I was caught in a bad dream.

My pace quickened. I clenched my fists. The few people I encountered threw glances at me as if I were an interloper. The waiting area was deserted except for the presence of a solitary, forlorn individual—Ann.

She rose wearily from her chair. Yesterday's makeup was stained by dried tears. The erosion of her usual professional neatness gave stark testimony to the nature of the ordeal she had endured over-night. Several packs of discarded cigarette butts in the ashtray at her side were icing on the cake. She sighed deeply before em-barking on a tense monologue: "Mother's condition hasn't really changed since you left yesterday. Most of the night, I watched her sleep. The few times she was awake, she barely recognized me."

We stood facing one another as I struggled to collect my thoughts. I managed to ask, "Have you talked to Dr. Winthrop?"

Ann's answer was a straightforward, "No." She went on to say she had seen him several times, but he seemed always to be rush-ing to emergencies.

I nodded. I needed to find a nurse or resident who could brief me on Mom's condition. But practicalities first—

"Are you still planning to fly back to Tampa this afternoon?" I reluctantly asked Ann. I dreaded her answer.

Guilt flashed her face. I knew the answer before she gave me a subdued, "Yes." I'd known the answer before I asked the ques-tion. As she spoke, her eyes had avoided my gaze like Barry Win-throp's.

"Why don't you go back to the house and get some rest before you leave?" This felt as awkward as it could get.

"No, I'm staying here until I leave," Ann half-croaked in a voice wrecked by exhaustion, stress, cigarettes, and crying.

"Then why don't you go to the cafeteria for a break?" I asked.

Her reply was barely audible—"Sounds like a good idea." Ann seemingly couldn't wait to get away from me. Nor I, she.

Why did it feel so awkward? This was Ann's fifth day here. And she had four nights with little or no sleep. She showed up and let Mom and me know she cared, even though the two of them haven't been close for a long time. Give thanks for that—and forget the rest.

I went looking for an update and almost collided with an Intensive Care nurse in the hallway outside the waiting room. The white letters of "Ms. Bryce, RN" were prominently displayed on a blue nametag pinned to her chest. I introduced myself as Mary Lewis' son.

"Oh, yes, I've just been reading her charts," she said in one of those gently beautiful Southern voices—all smoothness and no edges.

There was a tense pause before I blurted out, "What are my mother's enzyme levels?" My Yankee bluntness, which I immediately regretted, caught her by surprise. Clearly this woman actually cared about what happened with my mom—and I needed to treat her like she did.

Before she could answer, still taken aback, I added, "Sorry for being curt—I'm exhausted."

Ms. Bryce smiled, shifted her weight from one foot to another, and reached out to gently touch my arm as if to soften bad news. "Your mother's CPK and LDH are not elevated, which means it wasn't a heart attack. Creatinine levels, as well as urinary output, remain unchanged. She had a really rough night. I'm so sorry—we're doing all we can."

I stood there, fighting to keep control of my emotions. It was touch and go, but I did. She kept her hand on my arm until I managed to say, "Thank you." Some people belong in healing, and she was one of them.

After the nurse had gone, another blue nametag approached—"Dr. Appleton."

"Are you Mary Lewis's son?" When I nodded, he continued, "Does your mother have a history of exotic infections?"

"No," I replied. "Like what—and why?"

"I was thinking in terms of Q fever."

"The most exotic thing my mom has had are periodic bouts with the flu."

Dr. Appleton reacted to this with a puzzled expression, no closer to solving the mystery of my mother's illness—but clearly thinking *hard*. He reached out and distractedly shook my hand before walking away without another word. He was so evidently giving his full attention to the mystery of my mom's illness that I excused his bad manners instantly.

I considered not telling Ann, but she needed to know before she got on the plane. I was as matter-of-fact as possible when she returned from the cafeteria. "The enzyme levels indicate Mom didn't have a heart attack. Her kidneys are still shut down. They just don't know what's wrong with her."

At first, Ann showed no visible sign of emotion. Then she looked at me directly in the eyes and said, "I have to be at the airport at 2:30." The tone of her voice made clear her decision was firm.

All I could do was nod. I glanced at my watch; Ann needed to leave in less than two hours. That was not something I looked forward to. "It's that time—we can go see Mom," I said. Ann sighed, but walked alongside me.

Mom's condition was so grave we were permitted to stay with her until it was time for Ann to leave. Mom lay speechless because of the respirator, occasionally lapsing into unconsciousness. Sometimes we sat, sometimes we stood. There wasn't any place comfortable to be.

When awake, Mom couldn't talk—silent tears streamed down her face as she looked at us.

Ann and I made feeble attempts to cheer her up. With stories about Brett. About her friends at work. Her eyes made clear that our efforts were failing. Our pauses stretched longer. Words were increasingly difficult to find, and after a while we stopped talking.

Mom had often told me that if things were past the point of a real recovery, she would want to die quickly. But when she was conscious, she was demonstrating gritty determination, so even though she couldn't talk—clearly she still had hope and wanted to live. But she was also clearly upset.

Ann abruptly stood, and I realized it was time for her to leave. She went to Mom's side and held her hand while I sat—wishing I was someplace—anyplace—else. Mother's hand seemed lifeless.

Ann's voice was soft and calm as she talked about work and personal matters awaiting her in Tampa. She was building up to what needed to be said. She was building up to what she needed to say.

As she continued talking, she gained momentum and spoke more rapidly. Like she was mustering the courage to say something greatly troubling her. She was leaving.

This was followed by a promise to return during Christmas. Ann started to cry, quietly, shoulders shaking.

Mother could neither talk nor write in response, but she kept crying.

Ann didn't say goodbye, but she squeezed Mom's hand and kissed her on the cheek before walking out of the room.

On Ann's departure, Mom's eyes turned to me. I tried to be cheerful. "She'll be back. The next time you see her will be a much happier occasion."

I lapsed into awkward silence, not knowing what else to say. Fortunately, Paige interrupted us.

This freed me to to take Ann to catch her plane. We said almost nothing to one another on the drive home to get Ann's luggage, and likewise on the drive to the airport. Ann insisted I not wait with her at the airport. There was a brief hug at the curbside.

"Give Brett a kiss for me," she said in parting. I told her I would and watched her walk away.

When I got back to the hospital, Mom was asleep. She didn't awaken.

By early evening, Paige and I knew it was time to get Brett and spend some real time at home.

This was our Christmas for the present. No ghosts played in my mind as they had hours earlier. There was only the now as we experienced it—being together, turning on music and the Christmas tree lights; finding whatever food we still had in the house and sharing a simple meal; talking about the Christmas party at Brett's school. Guessing what Santa was doing at the North Pole.

Paige and I pretended, as best we could, that things were normal.

After a while, Brett fell asleep. I carried him upstairs and tucked him into bed.

CHAPTER 15

December 15

The morning of the 15th was one of those Mondays where everything was out of sorts. As Paige and I reviewed our schedules over a hurried breakfast, Brett's eyes followed our discussion like a tennis match. His face was sullen. He knew something was wrong. And that it had to do with his grandma being sick in the hospital.

That wasn't the only thing bothering Brett. He was about to be picked up and dropped off at nursery school by Natalie, and after school would be spending the afternoon at her house. Normally, he would have been delighted by this, but the novelty had long since worn thin. Not even the news he was going to have a sleepover at a friend's house tonight was sufficient to cheer him up. I even tried mentioning Santa, and school parties. Nothing worked.

Paige and I sorted out our day. She would spend the morning reading poetry to Mother, while I was at the office. I would relieve her immediately after lunch, which would give her some time to catch up on her Master's thesis. We lingered at the table for a few minutes after finishing, gathering a little strength for the day.

With Brett there, we hadn't been able to go into it in depth, but it had quickly become clear both of us were aware Mom's recovery would not be swift. It would be slow, and incremental, and she was going to need a great deal of our care.

Brett was aware during this, that his parents were communicating without talking, and became even more frustrated.

Knowing the time for a perfect exit, I gallantly left Paige to deal with him and headed off for work. This was the first time I felt I was really letting Brett down, and I spent some serious time beating myself up about that. I promised myself I'd do better.

The drive gave me a chance to think things through. Mom was far too sick to recover rapidly.

Improvement would be in miniscule steps. First would come a slow rise in oxygen levels, which would allow removing the respirator. Next, she would be moved from Intensive Care to a normal room. Finally, discharge from the hospital would be followed by an extended convalescence at our house. A simple path to recovery. I hoped there weren't too many turns.

Cornwallis Pharmaceuticals appeared on the horizon. In less than ten minutes, I was forced to begin updating friends and colleagues on my mother's condition. Update with "There's been no change," or "Mother's holding her own." Update when I myself didn't have a clue as to what was happening. Nor did anyone else, beginning with Barry Winthrop.

It would have been far better all around if I had been invisible. The updates left a lot to be desired, but everyone was kind to me, and they let whatever I said ride. I don't know what I would have done if they hadn't. "Let us know if we can be of help," many offered. Nothing more could be said.

My office felt strange to me. I stared vacantly out the window for a few minutes before sitting down at my desk. Mountains of paper demanded my attention. I thought of the deadlines they represented, and the fact they all would have to be pushed back indefinitely. New dates were beyond my ability to estimate.

As I sorted through the stacks of folders, envelopes, memos, and loose pages, one definitely unpleasant thing caught my eye. An envelope from Personnel. Only rarely does anything good come from Personnel.

Thinking about it, I hadn't seen or heard from my secretary

Crystal in quite a while, and she wasn't sitting outside my door. Hmmm.

Given everything, I didn't have time to look into the matter of her disappearance. The envelope sitting in front of me seemed likely to provide a solution to this particular mystery.

I looked at it for a while. Picked it up, turned it over a few times. Put my finger under the flap and started to open it. Stopped when I'd torn about an inch. Put the envelope back down on my desk. *I can't deal with this today. Maybe tomorrow.*

I did a quick sort through the mounds, looking for the easy stuff. Whatever it was, if my signature could get it off my desk, I signed it—otherwise I put it aside. Each time, I felt strangely detached from my signature once I saw it on the page. I was not myself.

Next I resisted the temptation to call Paige at the hospital. Instead I called Ann, Vince, and Mike. Each was readily available, yet seemed eager to get off the phone. There wasn't much to take away from our brief chats.

Ann's allusion to the cost of another ticket implied a return trip was unlikely. Vince again expressed his concerns and repeated his intention to invoke the deity's aid in curing Mary's illness. Mike almost decided to drive down to North Carolina with his wife—but didn't, to my relief.

The balance of my time in the office was spent answering work-related questions from staff and colleagues. Any answer I could give that would end the conversation was the one they got. Everyone seemed uncomfortable in my office.

I wasn't getting much done, and wasn't winning myself any friends by being at work. I left for the hospital at lunch.

Anxiety gripped me more tightly the closer I got to the hospital. As I rushed into the waiting room, I almost collided with Paige.

I could always tell when Paige was on the edge, because she spoke rapidly, in sentences that come out in volleys of rapid fire.

As we stood in the middle of a room unmindful of onlookers, I had to struggle to keep up. She had spent the three hours reading poetry aloud to Mom—Teasdale, Browning, Millay. The whole time, Mom had lain in bed unmoving.

"And listen, Jack, this is critical. When I say unmoving, I mean—really unmoving. Your mom didn't move at all for three hours."

That took me a moment to digest.

Up to this point, Paige had avoided talking about Mom's condition. I could tell she was about to share something she was uncomfortable about. Her words slowed down, and then stopped altogether. She sighed sigh, paused uncomfortably, then, "Not as alert as yesterday," and "Slightly swollen."

Combined, this confirmed my gut sense that Mother had lost ground over night. I also realized Paige was not only trying to soften the blow for me, but was also having difficulty expressing what she had witnessed.

Dr. Winthrop suddenly tapped me on the shoulder. Someone else was standing beside him—a total stranger.

"This is Dr. Bryant," Winthrop said. "He's a cardiologist; a consultant I've brought into the case." Bryant was in his mid-forties, a bit corpulent, with a limp, damp handshake and what sounded like a Georgia accent. He plucked his eyebrows, and his eyes never joined in when his mouth smiled.

The two doctors motioned for Paige and I to follow them to a small room located a short distance from Intensive Care. I clasped Paige's hand out of habit. Her palm was wet with perspiration and cold as ice.

The room was small and claustrophobic, packed with a table and chairs. Four unforgiving walls confined us. Paige and I sat facing the two physicians. Dr. Winthrop began forthrightly. "The nature of Mary's problem remains somewhat of a puzzle to us. We only know that she is dreadfully sick and hasn't had a heart attack," he said. His eyes darted around the room, as if there wasn't a comfortable place for them to settle.

Paige looked at me. Her face was incredibly sad.

We were still completely in the dark. All I could think to ask was, "What's my mother's clinical status now?"

Winthrop's voice was monotone as he said, "Her kidneys are shut down, with no sign of recovery." His tone changed. "She has generalized edema, which is a new development." That was a discouraging note.

"Edema" echoed in my ears. Swelling. A retention of fluids. A reflection of problems, which in turn cause more problems. Edema makes everything harder for the body. Paige's "slightly swollen" sounded like it might be an understatement.

Winthrop went on to truly confuse me, saying, "She continues to be alert in spite of the fact she should be in a coma given her overall condition."

Should be in a coma? What the hell is going on?

"What additional tests are you running?"

"Tests for exotic infections," Winthrop replied.

Exotic infections? They're grasping at straws!

"What next?" I asked, my voice dry.

"There's nothing we can do except wait and see," Winthrop said. His voice was sympathetic. He cleared his throat and shifted uncomfortably in his chair before adding, "But there's something else."

Oh. "What?"

"A complication has arisen which Dr. Bryant has come to discuss."

Bryant had been slouching back, but at the sound of his name pompously sat up in his chair. Looking first at me and then at

Paige, he began to speak as if lecturing: "Mrs. Lewis is experiencing decreasing cardiac output. I find this anomalous since there are no signs of a heart attack, but it is a real effect nonetheless."

Anomalous?

His phrasing irritated me—I disliked the man immensely. At least now I knew the reason he was present. What I had just heard was unexpected and unwelcome, forcing an exchange of shocked glances with Paige. "What does this mean?" I asked.

"It means that any clinical improvement is contingent upon a reversal of this trend. Unfortunately, this is not likely to happen spontaneously, and will depend upon the underlying cause being identified and treated."

"I see. I see." But I didn't. I could barely listen as he kept talking.

"You and your wife must be patient as best you can under these difficult circumstances. I suggest you take care of the rest of your family as well as you are obviously able to take care of yourself," he had the effrontery to say.

Then there was silence.

Then Winthrop said, "Call me at any hour. Here's my home telephone number."

He and Bryant left. Paige and I sat for a while without speaking, still holding hands.

Tears came. They lasted for a while. I tried at first to regain control of myself, was only partially successful, so just let them come. Eventually they dried up. Paige sat silently, her hand soft and gentle in mine, and never said a word. When I was done, she gave a tiny squeeze to my hand, and stood up.

I knew I needed to see Mom, and that it wasn't going to be easy. We started walking—a few scant yards separated me from—whatever I would find.

I paused outside the door without looking in. I was afraid of what I would find, and feeling sick to my stomach at the thought of it.

Reality. It hit me as soon as I passed through the door. The reality that Paige had trouble expressing, that the physicians had attempted to explain. A reality far different than the one I had encountered the previous day. Much worse.

Mother lay amidst the usual jungle of tubes, next to the same ventilator. That much hadn't changed. But there was something else.

Her body was grotesquely swollen.

I couldn't tell if she was sleeping or unconscious. Or if she were aware of how she looked. She was horribly bloated, unlike anything I had ever seen. I had no idea what had caused this, but knew something was terribly wrong.

Without warning, she looked me right in the eyes, holding me in a gaze I couldn't escape.

She had been waiting for me. My face tried to smile to reassure her, but failed. Failed because it dawned on me we were losing. We were losing. She was worse. She'd slipped further, and she knew it. She knew.

I held my mother's hand which remained as limp as before, but now much larger in size, her fingers like pickles.

I had never felt so beaten in my lifetime. With the respirator doing all the talking for both of us, I saw what should have been obvious since I walked through the door. She didn't even look like herself—she looked like someone else. Someone dead for years. Norman.

It was Norman staring up at me from the bed. The swelling had distorted Mom's features to such an extent that the resemblance was unmistakable. Norman's fleshy face had returned to ridicule my efforts to save mother. My uncle had had been the one who had charged me to protect her after Dad's death; only he could hold me accountable for my failure.

My mind began playing tricks on me. Norman was dead, yet here he was. My accuser. Holding me accountable. Mother's first complaint of flu had occurred on the anniversary date of his choking on a pork chop; her septic shock had appeared on the anniversary of his death. What awful coincidence.

I was unable to get Norman out of my mind all day. Every time I looked at Mom, his face looked back at me. Throughout the afternoon, her eyes were always on me, clutching at every move I made and every word I said. But I had difficulty looking back at her.

So I did things. I retrieved chipped ice for her chapped lips, read poetry from the books Paige had left, and made every effort to divert her attention from her suffering.

All the while, Mom's eyes never let go. These were the same eyes that had showed their love for me my whole life. Love, and trust.

She trusted me when she got sick. She trusted me when we put her in the hospital. She trusted me all along.

Now her eyes showed love. But her trust had drowned in helplessness and fear.

CHAPTER 16

December 16

Suddenly I'm awake unable to sleep and all wrapped up just like I was as a kid—just like when I used blankets and pillows to protect me against a world of hurt after Dad died—I'm wanting it to be the same now as it was back then—wanting it to be that way as much as I've ever wanted anything—

When I carefully arranged the blankets and pillows all the same way after Mom kissed me good night—as many of them as I could get around—stack on top of me—so that I was totally insulated—buffered against more pain—many times when it wasn't even winter—

Arrangement of the pillows beneath the blankets was absolutely critical—a normal-sized feather at the foot of the bed and a double-sized one positioned at my back—then two large foam rubber pillows allowing me to sandwich my head in between them—and finally a third feather pillow that I held to my stomach—

With the pillows in place I carefully layered the blankets over and around myself—first was the sheet—for optimal effect I tucked it under the double pillow at my back so I would have a seal—next came two middle weight blankets, mounted by a heavier third—this was my inner core capped by my first bedspread—

A bulkier outer core was to follow—an old, cordless, heavy electric blanket—two more moderate-weight blankets capped by two woolen army blankets—and a second bedspread on top—

I lay inside and under them all in a fetal position as if in a womb—I had to burrow a small tunnel in order to breathe— every morning Mom made the bed with a single pillow, a sheet, blanket, and bedspread—the rest she carefully fluffed, folded, and stacked ever so neatly in the closet so I could get at them the following night.

With Paige beside me and Brett at a friend's house, a terrible thought began to take shape in my mind. I immediately assumed a fetal position, hoping not to bother my spouse.

The thought grew stronger and I placed a pillow over my head in an attempt to suppress it. My effort was futile. The thought was becoming fully formed and too horrible to contemplate. Then it was upon me, rushing into my consciousness like a raging torrent.

Mom isn't going to make it.

That thought snuck in; I chased it away like a stray cat.

Mom isn't going to make it.

It came back. I chased it away again. Again and again, like a cartoon from the 1950s.

Novelty quickly wore thin with repetition. Paige broke the loop, startling me by shifting position. The thought came back—*Mom isn't going to make it*—but this time I couldn't chase it away. The battle was lost. Mom wasn't going to recover. I thought about waking Paige, but decided my need to be held was less important than her exhausted sleep.

Mom isn't going to make it.

I couldn't imagine life without my Mom. But I couldn't save her. No one could. Absence. Death. Nothingness—awful truth so terrifying most people have to deny them by embracing the delusion of an afterlife for their loved ones—for themselves.

If I was ever going to embrace that lie, it was here and now. It would be so easy, so safe, like my fort made of blankets and pillows.

I tried—I reached for hope. *No—I can't do it.*

I glanced at the clock. It was time to enter a new world—the one my mom was exiting. I reluctantly freed myself from the knot of sheets and blankets, and carefully sat up on the edge of the bed.

The room was so dark I had to navigate by braille. Inching hands and feet through the inky blackness, touching furniture, then wall—I found my way to the doorway.

Stepping into the even deeper darkness of the hallway, I ran my finger along the wall, counting doorways for the short distance to the bathroom. It was located exactly where I expected it to be. As was the light I switched on after I had closed the door. The light startled my eyes, and they had trouble adjusting.

Mom isn't going to make it.

There it was again, shaking me like an earthquake. *There's nothing I can do. I can't save her.*

Looking in the mirror, I was shocked by the haggard face staring back at me. If she was here, Mom would tell me to get some rest. Or say I was working too hard.

Mom isn't going to make it.

I repeated the words softly to myself. No hope.

Paige was calling me from the bedroom. I couldn't make out the words—her voice sounded strained.

Mom isn't going to make it.

Walking into the bedroom, I found Paige looking at me with an expectant gaze. Her face was illuminated by the small lamp near the phone. Her face was etched in a composite of uncertainty and doubt.

"Jack, what's going to happen?" she asked. Her voice had a raw edge I'd seldom heard in the almost twenty years we'd been a couple. Her eyes pleaded with me to provide an answer other than the one she was expecting. They stayed fixed on me like I was a lighthouse in the midst of a raging storm.

I paused—deciding what to say. Finally, I told her, "Mother's in a difficult phase. It's too early to tell."

I stood by the bed, waiting for the inevitable, "Is your mother going to live?" It never came. I saw the beginning of the question several times in Paige's eyes, and once she took a deep breath and started to ask it. But a hasty retreat quickly followed on each occasion. Rather, I heard, "I wish I could crawl in your pocket until this is over."

I suppressed a wince and carefully chose my words in replying. "Don't worry, we haven't much longer," I said. "Things will get better soon," I added.

No, they wouldn't.

"Do you have to go in to work?" Paige asked.

"Yes—my desk is buried, and there are things that can't wait."

"I might as well get up," Paige said. We talked about wishing Brett were with us, but agreed it was better he wasn't.

I paused as I pulled out of the driveway. Mom's car still sat where I'd parked it, unmoving.

Mom isn't going to make it.

Pulling into the parking lot at work, I realized I was about to become an orphan. The thought ignited a powerful sense of loss and disorientation. I was thirty-five years old—but this was affecting me as if I were a child.

Looking around, I was glad I was early, and—for the moment—alone. Work was the last place I'd want to have people see me distressed. There were sharks in these waters; it wasn't safe to let anyone see me bleed.

Getting from the car to my office was much harder than usual. My legs felt like I had weights attached to them—every step was leaden.

Mom is going to die.

Why did I lie about this to Paige? No, it wasn't really a lie—she didn't actually ask the question.

No one intercepted me between my car and the office. No one walked into my office. It seemed as if people were intentionally avoiding me. Looking out the window, I ruefully considered the task at hand.

Mom is going to die. I need to arrange for her cremation.

Mom is going to die. If I can't save her, I need to take care of her the best way I can. However impossible it seems right now, I have to make arrangements. And better now than later—there's no way of knowing what kind of shape I'm going to be in then.

Mom and I had not talked about her wishes at length. But we had agreed that the ordeal of Dad's funeral would never be repeated, and I knew cremation was her general wish. I knew from other conversations over the years that Ann and Paige were comfortable with it as well.

The urge to "preserve" lost loved ones can be strong. Some of Mom's family from Indiana might object, but they're distant relations in more ways from one. And if we buried her—what then? I thought of of my father's companionless grave that I had never visited since his burial. Steve's remains in Indianapolis, the grave of Norman next to my grandparents near Galveston.

All properly memorialized. Each with their own plot, their own dignified marble headstone. But their bones were alone. Unvisited not just by their surviving loved ones, but by their own *life* essence, now long gone. Just bones, a small plot of earth, and a carved rock.

This was the sum total of it all. The end result.

My hands were shaking as I pulled out the phone book from my desk drawer. What an unpleasant heading to search for. Death? Leafing through the yellow pages, it took me a while to find Triangle Crematorium. Dialing, I hoped no one would answer.

I was startled when a voice introduced itself as "Mr. Weathers."

I heard myself responding with a distant and forced voice. "Arrangements…Mother passing away shortly…cremation."

Mr. Weather's response was delivered in a voice steeped in routine—

"Triangle Crematorium provides for picking up the body at the hospital. The actual cremation, and nothing more—"

"The family has to decide how they wish to dispense with the ashes, whether it be in an urn or otherwise—"

"If a memorial service is desired, it needs to be arranged by an outside agency—"

"What are your plans for the ashes and a memorial, if any?" The question caught me by surprise.

My shoulders wilted toward my desk.

Ashes. A harvest of ashes.

A harvest of ashes after all we have sown.

Barren—another futile episode in a world empty of meaning.

Plans. I had to make plans. How could I have forgotten that?

There was an embarrassing silence as I struggled with myself. The realization that I couldn't save her had occasioned the impulse to do *something*.

But I couldn't even do that. I wasn't thinking things through. She had friends, coworkers, family who'd want a chance to share their grief at her loss. We needed a memorial service.

I should have thought of that—I shouldn't trust myself right now. I was thinking about things in a disconnected way. Even dealing with her body was beyond me. I couldn't even think about the rest of it.

Mom is going to die. Having the man from crematorium on the other end of the line underscored the fact it would be happening soon.

My voice deserted me. I couldn't talk and wanted nothing more than to rid myself of the conversation. Instead, Mr. Weathers was waiting for me to answer his question.

"I'll call you later," I finally mumbled into the phone.

Each passing second brought my mother's approaching death that much closer. The thought of this paralyzed me in my office so that I couldn't even make a pretense of working; immobilized me so that I was frozen behind my desk for as long as I remained at work.

Toward late morning, I felt my body jerk into motion. I felt myself rising rising from my chair.

Mom is going to die. But she's not gone yet. Be with her while she's here.

Up—and—out the door—I walked out of the building. No one talked to me or stopped me as I left work.

I found myself in my car—moving. Moving faster and faster and faster—

To the hospital—faster—faster—faster—get there before something happens. Don't let her be gone before I get there!

A man dressed as Santa Claus was performing for the families in the waiting room when I arrived. No children were present, so oddly he was playing to an adult audience. I hesitated at the door, feeling like an interloper. Lights were flickering on the small tree. "Ho-ho-ho, and merry Christmas!" Santa boomed.

A smattering of embarrassed laughs came from the audience. Everyone seemed confused. But this soon changed, and the laughter steadily increased as people forgot where they were and why they were there.

Santa pulled neatly wrapped presents from his bag and began to distribute them. The hospital had gone to the trouble of inscribing names on the small white tags. Each gift was received with the glee of a child.

I heard my name being called. I tried to smile as Santa handed over my own neatly wrapped package. My mouth felt like papier mâché.

"Thank you," I muttered awkwardly before I retreated from the room. *I just can't do Christmas right now.* In the corridor, I slipped my present into the pocket of my coat without looking at it.

As I neared Mom's room, I heard Paige's voice reading poetry, letting me know Mom was still alive. That, and the wheeze of the respirator. The two sounds were merging together. I didn't want to enter, but I couldn't hide in the corridor.

Paige was the first to notice my presence. She looked up at me with a face I didn't want to see. Paige knew. She knew what I hadn't told her earlier in the day. Mother was going to die. She was going to die, and there was no safe haven to which Paige could escape—in my pocket or otherwise. I placed my hands on her shoulders, peeking at the book to see it was Teasdale's "Winter Dusk"—she was almost at the end:

> *"I think of the mother who bore me*
> *And thank her that I was born."*

As Paige finished, she said, "Mary—Jack's here to see you."

Mother's body was still swollen, swollen beyond description. She opened her eyes in greeting. They were lucid, as if defying her illness.

Paige hastily departed. "Thank you for staying with Mom. Drive safely," was all I managed to say to her before she left.

Mom and I were alone.

I sat at my mother's bedside. Her eyes never left me. I took her hand as I had yesterday, hoping for the smallest sign she was regaining strength. It was the same. Completely limp. Limp, despite my exerting increasing amounts of pressure, as if trying to squeeze some of my life energy into her. So much pressure that her fingernails began to cut into my skin. But she continued to lose ground.

Mom is going to die.

The respirator provided the only sound in the room. I noticed her parched lips seemed worse than they had been yesterday. I needed to do something. Chipped ice. It hadn't done much good when I tried it before, but it was all I had. Chipped ice in a washcloth.

The urge to do something, anything, was overwhelming. I immersed myself in the task of getting Mom chipped ice, to the exclusion of everything else. I absorbed myself with the minutest detail of walking to get the washcloth and ice, then retracing my steps in returning to apply them to her lips.

Mother's eyes stayed with me. But when I finished, it was clear nothing I was doing was relieving her suffering in the least.

Empty gestures. Devoid of meaning or result.

As always, the clipboard with Mom's charts hung at the foot of the bed. Each day I made a habit of checking them, and today was no exception.

Rising creatinine levels—

No urinary output—

Mother's kidneys were still shut down, and getting worse. This was particularly troubling. The longer her kidneys remained shut down, the less likely it became they would crank back up. Cardiac output is also declining, caused by her still mysterious illness.

What does she have?

I wasn't making any sense. Knowing she was going to die, calling the crematorium…yet still looking for hope on her chart. I lapsed into old thought patterns, logic fighting with hope, scientist's mind wrestling with a son's heart.

I couldn't pretend to look at the chart any longer. The numbers and prognosis were staring me right in the face, and I could do nothing about them. Nothing, save that of carefully replacing the clipboard on the hook at the end of the bed, and returning to Mom's bedside. Her eyes still followed my every move.

Words tumbling, I started to ramble. I babbled about the number of times she had attended to me when I was sick as a child: fevers, flu, allergies, asthma, poison ivy; too many to count; too many to reconstruct from memory.

As I talked, her eyes became distraught. I'd never seen eyes like these. They pleaded to continue living. Pleaded for something I was powerless to give. I could only try to comfort her with a stream of prattle—

About her course at Duke in January—

About our trip to the beach in October—

Using my empty words to try and soothe her—and myself. Using them to try and drown out the shouts coming from deep inside in endless repetition.

Please don't go—please don't leave me—

So it went until I finally exhausted my useless prattling. A sullen silence commenced.

After all we had shared together as mother and son, it had come down to this: silence. With Mom's eyes becoming more and more fatigued as the minutes expired. Finally, her eyelids became as lead and began to close. They didn't reopen in response to my goodbye, or my kiss to her forehead.

How many more partings would there be, before the last?

Walking into the house, I noticed for the first time how things in our little family were starting to fall apart. Half-finished fast food lay on plates awaiting disposal; a week's unopened mail sat on the kitchen counter. Evidence our family was unraveling under the stress was everywhere. Our entire routine had come apart. Paige, Brett, and I were all in the house—but we weren't together—something was keeping us apart.

There was a silence echoing through the house. It was the talk we were avoiding. The lights from the Christmas tree did little in the way of relieving our gloomy mood.

The moment of truth came when we were sitting in the family room, when Brett asked about his grandma. Paige and I tried to explain to Brett that his grandmother was still very sick. So sick that he couldn't visit her at the hospital. So sick it was highly likely he wouldn't be seeing her on Christmas.

Brett listened patiently, sad eyes alternating between Paige and me. He was trying to take all this in, but seemed puzzled. His grandma's absence was a new experience. In his brief lifetime no one had gotten seriously ill. This was Christmas, and his Grandma needed to be a part of it. After all, they'd made plans.

Brett's eyes looked from us to the tree, and then around the room. What we were telling him didn't make sense. She wasn't coming to our house, and he even couldn't go see her at the hospital.

"Will Mar-Mar be coming over for Christmas like she did last year?" Brett suddenly asked, ignoring what we had just told him. "It's just over a week away." Brett knew this because he was marking the days off on a calendar.

Paige and I exchanged quick glances. Out of the corner of my eye, I could see Brett sitting anxiously and awaiting a response.

I was trying to think of what I could possibly say.

Paige was direct and calm. "Your grandmother won't be able to be here on Christmas."

To try and distract him, I asked about his current Christmas list.

Brett half-heartedly reviewed his list for Santa before going to bed. *Star Wars* figures and a John Deere tractor were still at the top.

I have to make time for shopping before the stores run out.

A telltale yawn heralded Brett's bedtime. We got him cleaned up, and went to his room for his customary reading of a goodnight story. I turned the pages of the same *Green Eggs and Ham* we'd read so many times.

I looked up from the book. Brett was staring a hole through me. His little fists were clenched, and his face was red. It might have been a second that elapsed. Perhaps two. Three seconds at most before the screaming started. Before the tears.

I hugged him, held him close, not letting go. His sleep came before my tears arrived.

CHAPTER 17

December 17

The sound of Brett's voice, calling out from down the hall, woke me. I glanced at the clock, thinking it must be the middle of the night. Guessed wrong. Almost time to get up anyway.

At Brett's door, I groped in the dark for several seconds to find the light switch. In the light, I saw Brett sitting upright in bed—his arms stretched out toward me. He was frightened. I sat beside him and he whimpered, "I had a bad dream."

I'd heard from a number of friends over the years that for their kids, bad dreams were a matter of routine. Not for Brett, though. This was the first bad dream I could recall him having.

Brett clutched me around my neck. I was surprised at his strength and felt the fear radiating from his body. He told me the story of his nightmare in exasperated gasps. In his dream, he awoke to a silent house. When he called out, no one answered. He thought we were playing a trick on him, that we were playing hide-and-go-seek. But he couldn't find anyone as hard as he looked. He looked in every room of the house, over and over. Then he remembered. Grandma was sick and in the hospital and that was why she wasn't there. But Mom and Dad weren't sick. We had to be playing a trick on him. Except we weren't answering him. He called over and over, searched everywhere. We were nowhere to be found.

Brett had awoken from this nightmare feeling more alone and afraid than he had ever felt. He was afraid we weren't coming back, the same as Grandma.

I hugged Brett and tried to reassure him it was a bad dream and nothing more. Paige was in the bedroom sleeping, and neither of us were sick. Brett asked if his Mom could stay home with him like before Grandma became sick. I tried to think of a way to make that work today, and couldn't. I couldn't tell him the day was going to be a non-stop juggling act between babysitters and the hospital. Or that I needed to drive over to Grandma's apartment to search for her personal papers. I couldn't tell him these things—but I also couldn't lie to him.

"Be patient. Things will be back to normal soon."

I knew this was wasn't good enough. The bitter truth was that things would never be normal again. I could guide Brett away from his nightmare, but no one could return the favor for me.

In that wonderful way little kids have, Brett switched the topic to *Star Wars* figurines. He hoped Santa would bring him some to complete his set, even though he hadn't put on them his list. And the Christmas program at nursery school was tomorrow! I was informed sternly that we *had* to be there.

I had completely forgotten the Christmas program at Brett's school. But one thing I was certain of in my marriage was that my wife *never* missed things like this. We heard her stir in the next room, and Brett rushed to her. He babbled about the Christmas program, but didn't mention his scary dream.

Brett's excitement carried us through breakfast. We heard all about his skit as we sat around the table.

We couldn't sustain things past breakfast. Paige's eyes clouded over with preoccupation, and I glanced at my watch. It was time that the family disperse: Paige to the hospital, Brett to Natalie's, me to Mom's apartment. I felt torn between wanting to leave and wanting to stay with them.

My eye sought for and found the familiar—Mom's neighborhood. Mom's street. Mom's apartment. Although I knew her car was at my house, I felt a twinge of disappointment when it wasn't parked in its usual space. Though she wasn't there and would almost certainly never be returning home again, it still felt like I was paying her a visit.

The winter wind hit me as soon as I stepped from the car, looking for the crevices of my coat at neck and sleeves. I was surrounded by gray—sky, street, sidewalk. Unraked leaves scooted along the ground, as if in a hurry to get away from me. The landscape felt lifeless, hopeless, fraught with futility and ravished aspirations, full of questions to which I no longer had answers.

I looked up and brushed away a tear. Mother was not standing on the front porch waiting for me. As soon as I stepped inside and closed the front door behind me, I heard Mrs. Weston approach. She wore a housecoat of the kind I'd seen at J. C. Penney, short gray hair pinned back, no makeup. Arthritis had given her a slight hitch in her gait, and the foyer was sizzling in the dry heat that she preferred in her advanced years.

Aware that a conversation with her was unavoidable, I managed a fractured smile.

Her face creased with concern, she asked, "How's your mother?"

I opened my mouth to speak, once, twice, but nothing came out. On the third attempt, I managed a weak, "She's holding her own." *A damn lie.*

"I'm so glad," Mrs. Weston said. "I've been so worried."

Claustrophobic heat unnerved me. I felt trapped—in so many ways. Fortunately, the old woman saw fit to release me. "Please let me know if I can do anything and tell your mother hello for me," she said.

"I will," I assured her.

Walking away, it took all I had to make it to the landing of the stairway and turn the corner, out of her sight. I had to grab hold of the bannister to avoid falling on my face, but managed to keep moving. Each stair brought me closer to the rooms Mom would never see again.

The South is full of odd places and things. Faulkner's writings had set a high bar on quirky and strange, but I would regularly encounter things that struck me as so far from normal, they could only happen in the South.

Mrs. Weston's apartment house was one of those places. In addition to the inferno-like temperature in which she kept the interior, the doors of each room weren't secured by either a lock or a deadbolt. Instead, the doors were locked by clasps and padlocks. Like your bicycle chain, or the door to the old shed where you keep your crazy uncle, on the old family tobacco farm out on the Johnson County line.

Finally, I stood in front of the miniature Santa Claus Mom had hung on her front door. My hands shook as I fumbled with the small padlock key. At least the key was within my grasp, a small consolation. But then it fell on the carpet, and I was forced to bend down and reach out to pick it up. It was like a little blob of mercury; it scooted away from me. Scoot scoot scoot, until I snagged the son-of-a-bitch and finally unlocked the door.

Not that I was really looking forward to going inside. Slowly, ever so slowly, I nudged the door until it opened to a hesitant slit. I stared through it until I felt compelled to throw it open in a rush and get on with it. Get in, get what I needed, and get out.

Once inside, my express train became a local, meandering with frequent stops. Mom's apartment already seemed stale. She hadn't ever wanted to live here, she wanted to live with us. But no matter how she felt about being here, she had made it a home, not a cell.

Everywhere showed signs of her life. Her time in Kokomo was well represented—a classic photo of Ann as prom queen, my barometer from science class, my little league team picture, Norman's wooden chest, and a poem she had written for my grandmother at age 13, titled, "To Mother."

But in just over a year there was evidence of the life she'd built here in Durham. Her work schedule and some joke cards from coworkers stuck to the fridge with Feed Store magnets, right next to one of Brett's more colorful crayon drawings, a nice photo of

Duke Forest I couldn't place, a photo of Brett in a standing frame on top of the television, from about a year back, wearing a goofy blue shirt and a huge grin.

Her home was stale but not sterile. It was clear Mom had expected to return when she left for the doctor's. The bed was half made. A few unwashed dishes in the sink, a blouse over the chair in her bedroom, moldy food in the fridge.

I suddenly felt uncomfortable, and stood, listening. An eerie silence surrounded me—and I realized that was what bothered me. My ears had been straining for Mom's footsteps—or her voice. Two things that would never be here again.

Mom is going to die. She'll never be coming home—never be happy here again. I couldn't believe I was admitting it. Happiness was nonexistent where she was headed—there was no existence after death.

Important things needed to be done about the unimportant. I couldn't save Mom, but I had to do something—even if that something was only paperwork. Something in preparation for nothing.

I didn't expect to find her papers in the closet, but I was drawn there nonetheless. It was awkward. I felt like I was invading her privacy, rummaging through her personal items. And I was ensnared by malaise. It pressed at me from all sides. I saw an assortment of hats and packages that I would have to contend with later. A row of Mom's clothes poised in pointless readiness for new days that would never come. On the floor was a box I knew contained my childhood memorabilia: my little league uniform, my Hopalong Cassidy drinking glass, a picture I had drawn in the first grade... Next to the box rested a large sack of packages in Christmas wrapping paper. It must be her Christmas presents for this year. Christmas presents she wouldn't be able to give on a holiday she likely wouldn't see.

This was too much. I had to look away, but tears blurred my vision so I couldn't see anything anyway. After I squeezed them out of my eyes, I angrily shut the closet door and went to Mom's chest of drawers. I opened the bottom drawer. On top was a manila folder—sitting there as if it was waiting for me.

My hands trembled, causing the folder and its contents to shake. I pulled out an old sheet of folded paper; as it unfolded, I found it full of Mom's penciled writing. With the creases to the paper, I strained to make out what she had written—which turned out to be a poem.

The domino building you built so tall
Your precious finger marks on the wall
Your cowboy guns and your cowboy hats
Your crumpled pajamas and mud on the mat
I look at these and think of you

Your swing standing still beneath the trees
The birds, the flowers, the bugs, and the bees
A wad of chewing gum left on the sink
A half of an R.C. I wouldn't let you drink
I look at these and think of you

The grass that's worn on the hill out back
And all the toys you keep in a sack
Your army men standing neatly in a row
Your castle in the sand made just so
I look at these and think of you

My darling, my sweet, you'll never know
How lonesome and lost I am when you go
I watch the clock and hope and pray
You'll come home to me safe at the end of the day

I must have been six or seven when Mom wrote this. I reread it three times before turning to the next.

This one seemed more recent, more neatly written; it was only folded once, and had a title.

LITTLE BOY LOST

It seems I've lost a little boy
No need to sound alarms
I know he's gone forever
Must get used to open arms

I tucked him in bed as usual one night
And with the break of dawn
In his place I found a tall young man
My little boy was gone

I must accept this drastic change
I'll need strength I know
How swiftly the time did pass
How swiftly he did grow

I've always known the time would come
When boy and Mom must part
But I'm eternally grateful
For the memories I have in my heart

Now he's learning to fly alone
Give me courage to let him go
He must never see the tears
My loss he must never know

He must be strong to face the world
And courageous to decide what is right
It won't be hard if the young man now
Is the boy I lost last night

I don't know how long I spent reading and rereading the second poem. Did it date from high school, when I went off to college, or…probably the latter.

There was a manila envelope in the drawer labeled "Important Papers" in Mom's hand. This was what I was looking for. I opened it to make sure, and found Mom's insurance papers and her last will and testament. I put the folder of poems back in, closed the drawer, and stood up with a sense of relief. I couldn't take being in here any more.

Leaving Mom's apartment was like being in a waking nightmare. I was relieved not to find Mrs. Weston in the oven-like foyer, which was stifling and silent as I opened the door to make a furtive exit. Attempting betrayal, the door creaked loudly anyway. I left without looking back.

I tried hard not to think about anything until I was parked in the hospital lot. Everything was a blur between my car and Intensive Care.

I was stopped in the corridor outside the waiting room by Mr. Franklin—I recognized him from Santa's gift-giving yesterday—who motioned that we needed to talk. Franklin's father was dying from emphysema, and he was showing the strain. He hadn't shaved in a few days, and his strong frame—he was a diesel mechanic or something—looked worn at the edges and was starting to fold in on itself a bit.

We walked into a corner. I could tell he was nervous because he was fidgeting with his calloused hands, still showing traces of grit from his work. I shifted my weight from one foot to another. He didn't say a word for an eternity. Finally he sighed and began talking in spurts that were difficult to understand at first—more from his exhaustion and discomfort than from his raspy voice—like a rusty old truck engine run too long without oil, combined with a heavy Tar Heel accent. I had trouble looking away from the spit at the corners of his mouth.

Finally I caught on to what he was saying. Paige. Paige had lost her composure while in the waiting room. She had been sobbing, saying, "I don't want Mary to die."

I tried to reconstruct the image but failed—I needed to disengage from the conversation and get to Mom. I reached out, put my hand on his arm, and told him, "Thank you, I hope things go better with your dad."

I hadn't even taken a step when Dr. Winthrop appeared out of nowhere, and grabbed me by the arm. Dressed in his doctor's coat, he was muttering over and over, "Not good. Not good. Not good," and oddly reminded me of Alice's White Rabbit. Winthrop motioned for me to join him farther down the corridor. I felt my chest tighten for what must be bad news.

"We had to give your mother a tracheotomy. You weren't here, so Paige signed the consent form," he said.

I'm never here when I should be.

"Her condition has deteriorated?" I felt like a dumbass, asking the obvious.

Winthrop winced. "Yes. Her blood gases and creatinine levels are worse."

I shouldn't have been surprised. "Have you figured out what's wrong?"

Winthrop shifted his gaze to the floor. "No. Her disease still defies diagnosis, but we're trying to sort it out." His voice was a frustrated, fatigued whisper. They didn't know what was killing her.

"Do you think she'll survive?"

"Yes, I do."

Bullshit. "What quality of life will she have if she survives?"

"That one's tougher," Winthrop said quietly. He avoided eye contact. He cleared his throat. "I expect she might have some difficulty in climbing stairs because of a loss in pulmonary capacity. But I expect nothing more."

Bullshit. It didn't stop me from a brief moment of fantasy, though. I envisioned Mom walking again. Shortness of breath was a small price to pay for survival. But no. She was going to die. I knew it in my gut. I knew it in my head. Further discussion was a waste of time. "Thank you. That's comforting," I said.

Bullshit.

In the absence of additional questions, Dr. Winthrop emphasized Mom was lucid, in spite of her sickness. He was grasping at straws to come up with good news. He excused himself to attend to another patient.

Each step toward Mom's room was more difficult than the last. I did my best to put on a cheerful face, but knew I had failed. I heard Paige shakily reading poetry, but she stopped upon my arrival. She offered no words of greeting. Her eyes were red, and she was pale, strained, exhausted. She wanted me to do something. Anything to make it all go away.

As if I could.

The fact I was here, and she could leave, seemed to give Paige's spirits a boost. She turned to Mom and read a few final verses from Teasdale to finish the poem. Squeezing Mom's hand, she promised to return soon, then fled out the door.

Mom was clearly sicker than when I had seen her last. I saw the new incision in her neck, and the tube connecting the incision to a gasping respirator sitting at the side of the bed. The tracheotomy was firmly in place.

Her eyes never left me. Not long after I arrived, she started crying, and didn't stop. Tears ran down both cheeks. The only sounds were the respirator, and the beeping and pinging of the various machines keeping Mom alive—if you could call this alive.

I don't want you to die.

Hour after hour, I alternated between sitting and standing. When sitting, I held Mom's hand in mine. I paced her room like a caged animal. One then the other, over and over. Both options were exhausting and exhausted. Day waned into dusk.

Dusk passed and the blackness outside edged closer. Outside the window—darkness. Nothingness. The void. The godless void. All poised to engulf her. If it didn't come tonight, then tomorrow, or the day after. My stillness, my movement, my words were all empty of meaning or impact. They were all for naught.

I said goodbye, promised to return tomorrow, told her I loved her, and kissed her on the forehead. Then I walked out the door.

If Mom was going to leave this life tonight, I wanted her last memory of me to be a warm one.

CHAPTER 18

December 18

Brett was excited—we were on our way to his nursery school's Christmas party. It was St. Stephen's last day before the holiday break—no class, just a party. Brett talked nonstop about it the whole drive from home. Santa's arrival was only one week away, and he was in top form.

This is the Christmas I've wanted for him.

The parking lot was full of his classmates, and their parents carrying cameras and wrapped presents. Each student had drawn a name from a hat and brought a gift for that student. Brett had drawn a girl's name, and Paige had helped him pick out something crafty—which seemed to involve glitter.

Brett could hardly wait to get out of the car and once he did, ran to join the parade of children headed toward the school. He was soon out front, looking like he had in the front seat of the mall's miniature train, which seemed like forever ago, even though it was less than two weeks.

A large Christmas tree covered much of the back wall of Brett's classroom, decorated almost entirely with student art projects. Brett's teacher—Mrs. Simpson—acted as its sentinel. She was from a founding family of Durham and didn't have to work, but seemed to really enjoy children, with whom she was sweet but very firm. With parents, she had perfect manners and paid precise attention to social niceties. Every conversation reflected her firm conviction that "God was in his heaven and all was right with the world." And manners seemed to have something to do with god. It was clear she couldn't even imagine anyone believing differently. I always expected her to be wearing white gloves.

Mrs. Simpson granted each child permission to run to the tree and deposit their gifts beneath its neatly trimmed branches. She gave frequent reminders to them to return to their desks rather than remain gathered around the tree.

Mrs. Simpson greeted us and let us know Brett was "a dear," "very well behaved," and "extremely smart." She paused and sighed deeply. "Brett has told me about the situation with his grandmother. My prayers are with all of you." Paige hastened to thank her. I managed a weak smile.

I stood at the back while Paige mingled with parents and Brett's classmates. She was definitely in her element—both as a parent and former schoolteacher. Her white blouse, navy cashmere sweater, and matching pleated skirt made her look like a mom from Hope Valley—Durham's toniest neighborhood. Smiling, charming, seemingly at ease, she could have been president of the Junior League—only I knew her poise and easy grace covered a deep layer of anxiety. I was proud of her anyway, but knowing how hard she had to work at this made me even prouder.

I need to remember to tell her that tonight when we're alone.

Most of the time I stood at the back, leaning against the wall, exchanging an occasional comment with one of the other dads. I wasn't always the observer in large social situations, but being at a religious school to mark a religious holiday accentuated my feeling of being an outsider, out of step with those around me. Before we enrolled Brett, Paige had extracted from me a promise not to mention my atheism to fellow parents or anyone connected with the school, or this feeling would have been even more marked.

I watched the kids snacking on punch and cookies, eyes wide and cheeks red with excitement. Some of the parents managed to sit at undersized desks, which was an entertaining miracle in itself. The slim curves and easy flow of Paige's skirt kept catching my eye, and she flitted from one chat to the next. Seeing her mingle, mopping up the occasional spilled drink, reminded me of my grade school years back in Kokomo, when my mom had been room mother to our class. Mom too had been able to conceal her innate shyness, dispensing punch, treats, and conversation like a natural.

In the middle of this bustle and chatter, Mrs. Simpson raised her arms like a choirmaster, palms upright, and the whole room went expectantly quiet. She directed the children to stand in two rows for the opening of the Christmas program. At her quiet command, girls adjusted bows and boys tucked in shirttails. The shuffling of their feet was punctuated by furtive giggling.

At this cue, moms retrieved cameras from their purses. The children sang "Away in a Manger" and "Jingle Bells." Cameras clicked, catching Mrs. Simpson smiling like a queen of old. Each child—even those who strained to remember the lyrics—basked in the subsequent applause.

Mrs. Simpson thanked the children for their performances and asked them to go to their desks. Those few parents who had squeezed into these managed to extricate themselves, and moved to the back and sides of the room.

The air bristled with toddler energy—the time had finally come to distribute gifts. Mrs. Simpson signaled for the children to reach into their desks and pull out the presents they had made for their parents.

Mothers and fathers beamed at this ritual lesson of the value of giving over receiving. Paige and I struggled not to smile as Brett presented us with a drawing constructed haphazardly from multihued paper and colored unevenly in crayon. A vaguely Cubist Santa staring at us from a wintry background. Black letters appeared to read *Christmas 1980.*

Mrs. Simpson congratulated us on having the good taste to be Christian and to send our children to St. Stephen's. After my promise to Paige, my lack of faith had never come up in conversation with her, and I wasn't sure Mrs. Simpson would have heard if it had. She read the obligatory Christmas story. Mary, Joseph, the manger, and the birth of the son of god. The star in the east, and the wise men bearing gold, frankincense, and myrrh. The children beamed, content with the miracle and the hope for all mankind—and many presents to come.

The student gift exchange occurred amidst chaotic merriment, and then—right about the time the sugar wore off—the party was over. A cheerful chorus of "Merry Christmas!" came from the kids as they donned their coats.

On the drive home, Paige explained to Brett that she would spend the day with him while I went to the hospital "for a while."

"Will I see Grandma today?" Brett asked.

The question shouldn't have caught us off guard, but it did. "Not today, darling. Not today," Paige told him.

Brett was quiet, seemingly deep in thought, clinging to his gift like a life-saver. He had received a holiday coloring book. "I'm going to put my present under our tree with the present I got for Grandma," he said. With this decisive statement, his brows unfurrowed.

"That's nice," Paige and I replied in chorus. The rest of the drive home took place in silence. Brett was crashing, coming down from his sugar high, his singing, and presents-giving. I suspected Paige would soon have him down for a nap after I dropped them off at home.

Winthrop was anxiously awaiting me at the hospital. We adjourned to the familiar corner of the waiting room. "She's deteriorating further…about as sick as a person can be…"

I couldn't follow. It had been just the flu. That was less than two weeks ago. Now, Mom was dying not more than forty feet away.

I was so distracted I barely heard Winthrop say, "My wife and I will be heading back to the Midwest for the holidays. To Kokomo—where your family is from, if I recall correctly."

"I hope you have a great Kokomo Christmas," I replied, meaning every word. I couldn't believe it. He was going to my hometown, the scene of my best Christmases ever.

"We might need to consider moving her to Duke if she doesn't show any improvement soon," Winthrop said. I nodded. We shook hands, and he walked away.

Mom lay semi-comatose in her jungle of tubes. The swelling of her face and neck had diminished somewhat, but still she resembled Norman, which made me shiver. She was so motionless she seemed glued to the mattress. An occasional involuntary twitch was her only sign of life. Her mouth was a dentureless cavern. Her once raven-black hair was a solid gray. She used to be so beautiful—now her face looked like a mask. There was no one but me to keep vigil.

I felt dejected. She didn't even know I was there. The respirator chugged away. My head knew she was going to die, but my heart clung to the hope she would somehow survive.

There were phone calls to make. Somehow I had to communicate to Ann, Vince, and Uncle Mike. I decided to be straight with Ann, but more circumspect with the others.

I dialed Ann's number and resolved to be blunt, to tell her she had to come immediately if she ever wanted to see Mom alive again. To my surprise, she seemed to already know Mom was dying. There was an uncomfortable silence.

Was Ann really going to leave me alone with this? But she had already come and gone, back to Tampa.

"You'll never see her again," I said.

Work meetings, personnel problems, the impossibility of finding flights so close to Christmas… "Good luck." Ann sighed and hung up.

I felt awful, standing motionless for several minutes with my hand still on the receiver, wondering how I could have handled the situation differently. It had been a waste of time, and hadn't made anything better for Ann, Mom, or me.

I dialed Vince's number and resolved to speak Southernese, putting a positive spin on everything. Vince was easy, and played the part right back. I informed him her condition remained "guarded." I was relieved I didn't have to lie. Not too much, really.

"I'll keep Mary's paycheck ready for her. Wish her a merry Christmas from all of us," Vince responded.

I paused a moment to collect myself before dialing Uncle Mike's number. But he couldn't be reached at his office, and neither he nor Barbara answered at home. They were probably already headed to North Carolina.

Sure enough, I dialed Paige at home and was told they had called her to surprise us with the news of his arrival. She had already arranged that Brett stay with the neighbors when we were to meet them. Nothing about these arrangements thrilled me.

Paige picked me up at the hospital at mid-afternoon to meet my uncle and Barbara at Howard Johnson's. The orange roof made it famously easy to find.

Uncle Mike and his wife Barbara met us in the lobby. He looked the same as ever with his tawdry gold necklace and polyester shirt, open to show an alder forest of white chest hair. Barbara still stacked her hair in sanctimonious splendor. I hadn't thought of hair spray as a perfume before.

Our handshake was subdued and our hugs constrained. I managed a smile and said, "I hope that your trip wasn't too tiring."

A land yacht of a Cadillac was Uncle Mike's pet status symbol. He was wearing cowboy boots, and I thought he looked one Stetson short of a full fake Texan. "It wasn't too bad. The roads were all clear. I just set the cruise control and let the car do all the work."

A silence followed. I shifted my feet awkwardly and cast my gaze to the floor, wishing these folks hadn't come.

"How's Brett?" asked Barbara, in her usual sharp-edged voice, which grated on me as always.

"Fine, under the circumstances," Paige said. "We've had a lot of help from neighbors and friends."

Conspicuous by its absence was any mention of Mom. No questions about her condition. I waited until we were all seated in Uncle Mike's Cadillac and were halfway to the hospital before I offered the information without being asked.

"Mom is still very sick and isn't showing signs of improvement. Enzymes show she didn't have a heart attack, but beyond that they haven't got a clue about what she has."

A nervous cough jiggled Barbara's hair. The term "enzyme" was something beyond her understanding or that of Uncle Mike. It was a faux pas on my part, and I made a mental note to use smaller words from here on out.

"Is she resting comfortably?" Mike asked.

"She was mostly asleep when I saw her earlier. Hopefully she'll be awake to see you when we get there," I said, keeping it simple.

The hospital came into view. "My, that's a lot bigger than what we got at home," Barbara exclaimed.

"It sure looks modern," added Uncle Mike.

"Not that old," Paige agreed.

Uncle Mike and Barbara nodded their heads. We entered the parking lot silently. Uncle Mike carefully steered the Cadillac into a space, taking great care to park in such a way as to avoid the possibility of a car door on either side being opened and denting his prized possession. "That should do it," Uncle Mike said proudly, as if he had moored a supertanker.

———

We hurried through the lot and walked in silence though the lobby to the elevator. We remained silent as we walked the final yards leading to Intensive Care.

I went in the room to see Mom while Paige, Uncle Mike, and Barbara sat in the oddly deserted waiting room. Surprisingly, Mom greeted me with open eyes. They radiated fear. I told her Mike and Barbara had driven down from Kokomo to see her. Her eyes softened into happiness.

Mom's smiles had been few and far between. I decided that, however much I personally found Mike and Barbara loathsome, I would remember to be thankful for their effort to get here. Even if it killed me. But that didn't mean I was going to close my eyes to who and what they were—family but not my kind of people.

Mom and Mike were the lone surviving representatives of what had once been a close-knit family. Mom had lost her two other brothers—Norman and Steve—and although she had certainly had her issues with Mike, particularly to do with some finagling he apparently engaged in relating to my grandmother's estate, he was the last of her brothers. The last one who knew what it was like to grow up in the big old house in Kokomo. Shared history—that was what mattered to her right now.

I felt Mom's eyes follow me as I left the room to retrieve her visitors. I found myself groping for words to say to them. Mom was ready to see them, but she wouldn't be able to talk because of the tube through her windpipe.

I trailed a step behind Uncle Mike and Barbara as they entered Mom's room. They weren't prepared for the sight greeting them, judging by their reaction. Feigned enthusiasm. The tones in their voice were strained, unintentionally raised in volume. It was as if they were trying to convince themselves the image before them wasn't real.

Mom managed a faint grin upon their entry. I decided to give them some time alone, and went to join Paige in the waiting room. We sat silently, holding hands in the crayon glow of the Christmas tree. What felt like an hour was only ten minutes before Mike and Barbara returned.

Mike and Barbara walked into the waiting room. They seemed happy—smiling as if they had just been to the movies. I couldn't believe my eyes. Mike turned to me and glibly said, "I don't think Mary expects you to come back in." I wasn't surprised by his lack of concern, just repelled.

I went back to Mom's room. She was pretty clearly frosted at me—but I wasn't sure why. Her eyes were hard and angry, glaring into the depths of my soul. I felt like she was trying to communicate with me. But this was as far as I got. When I tried to figure out what she was trying to get across, I hit a brick wall.

In parting, I kissed Mom goodbye on her forehead. I pressed her hand, but received no response.

That could have gone better.

Uncle Mike drove us to the cocktail lounge of Bakatsias, the Greek place where we'd been planning to celebrate Mom's release from the hospital. I ordered a double scotch on the rocks. Paige hesitated for an instant and then requested a single.

Mike and Barbara overcame their reservations and ordered a whiskey sour and piña colada, respectively. "Nice and polite" was how they described their drink choices. I inferred that these were the types of drinks fellow members of their church congregation back in Kokomo might approve of, given the circumstances. I was mystified by this couple. People in the South were often quirky—these two were even stranger.

Our conversation was sparse and tortuous.

"This sure is a nice restaurant," said Uncle Mike.

"It's one of our favorites, but we don't come here often," I replied.

Silence.

"I'll bet Brett's growed a ton since we saw him last year," chirped Barbara.

I cringed, half because of how Barbara had butchered the English language, and half because she was completely unaware of having done so.

Paige tensed, likely suppressing her teacher's instinct to correct bad grammar, and replied, "He certainly has. It seems we're dealing with a different child on a weekly basis."

Barbara's face became even more confused. Her empty stare betrayed that she was struggling with the idea a child could somehow be different every week. Fortunately, we were distracted by the arrival of the drinks.

The waitress asked if we wished to run a tab, and I answered "No!" a bit too eagerly. My appreciation for their coming had worn out faster than expected. I couldn't stand prolonging this any longer than necessary.

The check was discreetly positioned next to my double scotch while Uncle Mike averted his eyes to the next table. My drink tasted like vinegar, but I needed it to get through this.

"Your mother looked better this evening than I thought she would," said Mike.

I exchanged glances with Paige. The conversation had become serious. It had taken long enough. Uncle Mike was trying to determine Mom's prognosis. I had to lay it out in simple layman's terms, but how? I was still hoping they would keep their visit brief. Maybe they'd leave in the morning. I needed to get them the hell out of Durham before Mom died.

"Mom did appear to rally a bit, but she is far from well," I said evenly. "She will need a really long time to recover."

"It's a darned shame she had to get sick," Barbara said. "She always talked about how much she done liked it down here."

"Yes, she does," Paige responded hurriedly. "And—" She faltered. "Mary has become an important part of our family." She inhaled deeply, regained her bearings and continued, "Working part-time at the store has helped."

Uncle Mike nodded. "Mary likes Vince. She's only had good things to say about him. I'd like to meet him."

I nodded and pondered how to discourage such an encounter. There was another uncomfortable silence.

"Jack—we need to pick up Brett," Paige said finally. She conspicuously swallowed the last remnants of her drink.

Uncle Mike and Barbara looked taken aback and looked over to me. I drained my glass in a similar fashion. Uncle Mike stared dejectedly at his half-drained whiskey sour and said, "It appears the youngsters have more practice than we do."

Barbara emitted a loud, nervous laugh. She gulped almost two-thirds of her piña colada in two massive swallows. Uncle Mike followed suit.

They dropped us at our car, and Paige and I left to pick Brett up and go home.

When I tucked him into bed a little while later, he told me my breath smelled funny.

Not funny enough.

CHAPTER 19

December 19

It was mid-morning at the office, and I had just started to make inroads on my backlog of work when the phone rang. The company still hadn't assigned me a new secretary, so all my calls were ringing straight through. My grip tightened as I picked up the receiver and heard Paige's voice. Winthrop wanted to transfer Mom to Duke University Medical Center and needed my consent.

Even though the doctors at Durham County hadn't been able to diagnose what Mom had, her condition had gone beyond the point they could treat her, reaching the point that she needed treatment at Duke. Brett had been born there—the highlight of my marriage.

Mom is going there to die.

My voice sounded like it belonged to another person. "Yes, of course I consent. Do I need to come there to sign anything?"

"No," Paige replied, "I'll sign for you. And you needn't come. I'll ride in the ambulance with her."

I was relieved to not have to be involved in the transfer. "Has anyone told her?"

Paige hesitated. "Yes."

My heart sunk. "How did she react?"

Paige sighed. "She was very angry, and actually tried to slap Dr. Winthrop when he told her."

I imagined Mom being so angry that she had to be restrained. "That's not good. Are you absolutely sure I shouldn't come?"

"There's not enough time. Besides, Mary might be more willing to go to Duke knowing you'll be there to meet her."

I could make it there in a half an hour. "I'll meet you in the intensive care unit at Duke North shortly after lunch. Don't look for me. I'll find you."

"All right, dear."

"How is Mike taking all this?"

Paige sighed again. "He doesn't know what's going on, which is just as well. He's stayed out of the way."

I said, "I'll see you shortly," and hung up.

A new hospital means new nurses and doctors—Winthrop will be off the case—he's going back to Kokomo anyway. I'll likely have limited access to Mom's room. As uncomfortable as the waiting room and Intensive Care at Durham County General are, at least they are familiar.

The time until I left for the hospital felt fragmented. I tried to avoid coworkers, but couldn't. Their mouths moved and they kept making the same sound. "How is your mother doing?" They were a maddening, gray blur. What could I say? *My mom is dying.*

As I rose from my desk, the phone rang again with a call from Human Resources. I could begin interviewing for a new secretary next week. *Next week, when most likely my mother would be dead.*

I managed to make it to my car, by the time I got it started, tears were streaming down my face. I had to get away from the lot of them. I wanted to be anywhere else, but not Duke North.

Halfway to Durham County General, I realized I was driving to the wrong hospital. I pulled over by the side of the road for a minute to collect myself before heading to Duke North.

I turned onto the street leading to the parking garage. Duke North was near the VA hospital, and both were surrounded by older houses, many with signs out front advertising cheap room rates for families of out-of-town patients. I wondered if this was what the Mayo Clinic had looked like when Mom was there.

Entering the garage, I fumbled trying to get a ticket from a dispenser. The only place to park was the last spot in the furthest corner from the exit leading to the hospital, three floors up.

My solitary steps resounded with a cavernous echo at first. Then I encountered company. Friends and relatives of other patients. Many had bouquets of flowers and wrapped presents. Each possessed worried expressions and were rushing rapidly in the same direction as I. My tap-tap-tap had become an echoing river of footsteps.

An icy wind greeted me after I had walked down three flights of stairs and exited from the garage. Signs of newly completed construction surrounded Duke North's main feature—a large glass cylinder extending skyward. The entrance was flanked by a hill of concrete and rock. Midway through the construction work, it wasn't the most welcoming place.

It was freezing outside, but I didn't want to go in.

A funereal scent of flowers immediately assaulted me upon my entry to the hospital proper.

Even since Dad died—cut flowers make me think of death. Mr. Penn and the sickly smell of flowers at his funeral home back in Kokomo.

The sight of a florist inside the doors explained the smell. I held my breath in order not to inhale. Yet the scent persisted as I walked rapidly past the florist to what looked like the information desk.

I looked behind the desk and was taken aback by the man I saw sitting there. It looked like Mr. Penn himself—

Mr. Penn is staring back at me with the same face I saw looking back at me back then—the same face and the same professional sadness—I would never forget for my portion of ever.

I somehow put together words to ask, "What room is Mary Lewis in?"

A moment of typing yielded my answer in a dispassionate voice—"Intensive Care, eighth floor, room A16."

"Thank you," I heard myself say—*in a voice that sounded like mine although my brain didn't want to thank that son of a bitch Mr. Penn and his store-bought sincerity.*

Despite a sudden wave of revulsion over what I might to find on the eighth floor, I almost ran to the elevators. Doors opened for me as if by a prearranged signal; opened to an elevator empty except for a faint whisper of what sounded like my mom's voice:

"Life is a slow malignant disease from which we all eventually die."

Everyone thinks I'm the only one in the family with a dark outlook. But Mom has been saying things like this to me for years. Why am I hearing this now?

Is Mom thinking this at this very moment? Am I tuned in to her brain? Mental telepathy? The scientist part says no! But it's that—or I'm hallucinating.

The elevator stopped and the door opened without warning, to a long corridor with doors opening on either side. Freakishly, it looked like St. Joseph's when I was there to see Dad.

The hair stood up on my neck as I fought off images—*Dad with yellow skin and a bloated belly.*

Numbers with arrows on the wall reminded me of where I was, and pointed to where I needed to go. *Stay grounded—keep it together. You are in North Carolina, going to see Mom, not in Kokomo seeing Dad.*

I wasn't ready for what I found in the intensive care unit. People were literally overflowing into the corridor from the waiting room. A steady stream of nurses filed past them, unmindful of those watching them pass.

Confusion appeared to reign. I searched in vain for a counterpart to Mrs. Forbes. All I could find was a sign reading, "Please be seated until signaled to visit. Maximum of two visitors per patient." Amidst the turmoil, I found Mike and Barbara staring at the wall facing them.

"How did my mom take the ride over from Durham County?"

"I think she done good. Barbara and me rode in the car behind the ambulance," said Mike. Barbara nodded in agreement.

"Have you been to see her yet?"

"Yes ,for a couple of minutes, but I couldn't tell no difference from what I seen at the other hospital."

A ten-minute interval elapsed. I stood against the wall and observed. Strangers leafed uncomfortably through magazines and waited. A television with a blank screen sat on a table in the far corner. Blank—like the faces in the room.

At first I didn't notice the tugging at my left sleeve. But its persistence caused me to glance down. It was Paige. "You're finally here," she said.

Mike and Barbara observed us, unblinking, as if they were watching one of those soap operas set in a hospital. Paige was doing her best to disguise her obvious agitation.

I asked how things were going, when I already knew the answer to the question.

"They're okay," Paige said while trying to avoid my eyes. " It's about time to go back now and see your mother, if you're ready." I could tell something was bothering her. Something she didn't want to tell me.

The signal to visit interrupted us—a soft chime. "We'll be back," I said to Mike and Barbara.

I followed Paige to the room. A16. A blank nameplate guarded the entrance to the door. I decided not to think anything about that.

The familiar sound of the respirator had been joined by the slow pinging beep of a cardiac monitor. Surrounding Mom was another jungle of tubes and probes.

I stood at the foot of my mother's bed. Her eyes immediately opened and flashed at me in anger. Not being able to speak because of the tracheotomy, she silently asked with her lips, "*Where is Ann?*

"Ann's been called out of Tampa for a business meeting," I replied, before adding, "She'll come as soon as she can get here."

Mother's eyes softened a little.

We only had a few minutes left, and Paige filled them, cheerfully describing Brett's Christmas party at school. Her voice was so cheerful as to make as sound as if she were engaged in a normal conversation, rather than what it was. Mother gazed at her wistfully the whole while, until the chime signaled it was time for us to leave.

I kissed Mom on the forehead and told her we would be down the hall. She didn't smile at me. She didn't do much of anything.

Paige and I encountered a young female doctor midway down the corridor. A blue Duke nametag read "Dr. Weinstein." Paige uneasily introduced me as Mary's son.

"Can I talk to you about my mother's condition?" I asked.

"Certainly, Mr. Lewis. I'll be glad to answer your questions." Dr. Weinstein appeared eager to be helpful.

"Are you by chance the physician in charge?" I cautiously asked, knowing this most likely wasn't the case.

"No, that would be Dr. Trapp," she responded. "He's chief of nephrology here."

Nephrology—perhaps this was the clue to what else was going on with Paige—mother's kidneys—dialysis?—but dialysis couldn't be all that was wrong—the whole picture.

"When does Dr. Trapp perform rounds?" I asked.

"He's already been here today," Dr. Weinstein said, "and since it's Friday, he probably won't be back until sometime this weekend."

Paige was nervously wringing her hands. "Maybe I'll be able to meet him then," I said. I knew I'd have to talk to Trapp to find out what was troubling Paige.

"That's very likely. He makes a special point of talking to the family of patients," Dr. Weinstein said.

Paige was still wringing her hands, but I had to forget Trapp for moment and focus on Weinstein while she was available. "Have you been able to determine the full extent of my mother's problem?" I inquired.

"Not yet, but she was only just admitted. Her kidneys are in bad shape, but we're hoping that if we give them a little help, her condition will improve."

"Is there anything we can do?" I asked.

"Yes—we'd like for you to sign a release so that we can put a shunt in her wrist if dialysis becomes necessary."

"Of course."

After she left, Paige asked me, "Jack, why do they tell you everything is going to be all right when they know that's not true?"

"Paige, more than likely she's only a resident. A positive attitude is an important part of the treatment process. She was probably giving her best judgement based on an initial workup. Dr. Trapp will undoubtedly have more definitive information."

"I already talked to him, before you arrived."

Why doesn't she come right out and tell me? "What did he say to you?"

"He said he just reviewed her charts and examined her."

"Get to the point—what did he tell you?"

"He said that your mother is a very sick woman, and—"

"Paige, please tell me the rest."

The next words came out as a whisper. "He said that she wasn't going to live."

I know this—why is it such a shock hearing someone else say it?

We walked back to the waiting room. I told Mike and Barbara Mom was resting comfortably.

The balance of the day was occupied with waiting to see my mother for a few minutes every two hours. Paige and I went in, sometimes alternating with Mike and Barbara.

In our next visit at 3 p.m., Mom was awake, but it looked as though she had grown weary of the struggle. In her eyes I saw the first hint of surrender. Before leaving, I grasped her hand and said, "I love you, Mom."

Her eyes sparkled for a second—then faded almost as rapidly. She was losing ground with every passing second.

Four long hours of waiting followed. All the while, nurses scampered around the intensive care area like a swarm of insects. And although I was hoping to see him, Dr. Trapp played Godot and never appeared.

At 7 p.m., Mom didn't awaken. I watched her sleep for a bit, kissed her, and said quietly, "Good night, Mother."

We gave up on Trapp, said goodbye to Mike and Barbara, and left. Paige had her own car and would stop to pick up Brett on the way. I drove into a darkness that my headlights couldn't seem to penetrate, and felt as alone as I'd ever been.

When Paige got home with Brett, she took him straight up to bed.

Before going to sleep myself, I peeked in Brett's room. He was sprawled, and whatever he and his friend had been running around and doing all day left him out like a light. He was clearly exhausted, but his sleep was bringing him energy for the morning. Very different than Mom, whose exhaustion seemed like a watch spring winding down with no hope of rewinding.

In a way, time really is running down for her.

CHAPTER 20

December 20

I was sitting in my favorite chair in the family room—looking across the room at the lights on the Christmas tree. Paige was upstairs with Brett in his room, playing a mysterious game with *Star Wars* figures that only he understood.

The Indiana–North Carolina basketball game is today—if Mom wasn't in the hospital, she'd be coming over.

Paige and Brett had left me alone to call Dr. Trapp. It was Saturday and his office was closed but the hospital had given me his home number. He answered after two rings, sounding as if he was expecting a call from the hospital.

"Good morning, Dr. Trapp, this is Jack Lewis. I believe you talked to my wife yesterday about my mother's prognosis."

Dr. Trapp's voice softened. "Certainly. I was meaning to contact you today to talk about your mother's case. It's quite complicated. I'll be glad to discuss what little I know at this time. We'll have a better picture of her condition after we've had a chance to run more tests."

It was clear I was being managed, and Trapp wasn't going to be as candid with me as he had been with Paige.

What a total waste of time—there's no point continuing this conversation.

"Thank you, Dr. Trapp, you've been very helpful. I hope to meet you in person soon."

"You're quite welcome. I'd like that, too. All we can do is hope for the best," were Dr. Trapp's parting words.

It's finally over—what a waste of oxygen.

Except it wasn't over. While Paige continued to divert Brett upstairs , I had two more calls to make. Vince and Ann. I had to tell them both about Mom's move to Duke. That, and answer their questions.

Vince was downright cheerful, which caught me off guard. He told me that "Cadillac Mike" had visited his store in a cowboy hat, and made a point of introducing himself as Mary's brother.

I cringed, but Vince wasn't finished. He thought Mike was a real nice fellow. A real nice fellow who went out of his way to meet everyone in the store. This had all the aspects of a true farce. "Well, bless his heart," I said. *I've finally learned to talk like a Southerner. What a complete jackass.*

Mike had already told Vince about Mom's move to Duke, leaving out what he himself didn't know. Vince was satisfied, and I was off the hook. As usual, he closed with, "Of course, we're praying for Mary every day."

One down and one to go. I glared at the lighted Christmas tree and thought hard about Ann. We were never close growing up. I knew this call was going to be difficult—*she knows—she has to know.*

Ann answered immediately. She was expecting my call.

"Hi, Ann. I have an update."

"How is she?" she snapped back at me.

"Not well. She's been moved to Duke."

"Duke? That can't be good," Ann replied—thinking out loud. Then she caught me off guard by throwing in, "And how are you?"

"I'm—I'm fine. All of us are holding up fairly well," I replied—*no one is—least of all me.*

"That's good," Ann responded. Her voice was now shaded with a tinge of doubt.

"There's a lot of news—I'd better start at the beginning."

Ann hesitated before giving me a wary and tense, "Okay."

"Mike and Barbara drove down from Kokomo the day before yesterday—" *It seems like a hell of a lot longer than that.*

"Oh, good grief! That can't be any help."

None—if she only knew. "Not really—" *say something positive—anything—* "At least Mom was glad to see them."

"Are they staying with you?"

"No, at a Howard Johnson's by the hospital—"

"At least you have that going for you."

"That's right. They got here just in time to see Mom transferred to Duke."

"Why was she transferred to Duke?"

"She was getting progressively worse. They have a dialysis machine at Duke."

It's beginning to sink in—this is Norman's birthday—December 20th—"Your mother is your responsibility," he'd said.

"A what?"

"Dialysis machine. Mom's kidneys have been shut down for so long she can't eliminate wastes from her body. The dialysis machine will do that for her. It will filter her blood."

"Oh! How did Mom react to the move?"

"Not terribly well. She tried to slug Winthrop."

Ann gave a short, nervous laugh—then her voice got quieter and more pensive. "Did you ride with her in the ambulance?" she asked.

"No, Paige did. I was at work and got there after they arrived."

"Is she settled in her room now?"

"If you can call it that—"

An uncomfortable silence followed. *I finally have to say it—this—* "Ann, there's something you should know. Mom asked where you were and I told her you were on a business trip."

Ann's voice became defensive. "But that's true—and I have to leave tomorrow for another one. Everything here at work went crazy while I was up there the first time."

"I understand." *—I don't—* "I'll call your secretary if I need to reach you. But I've got to run. Brett is calling from upstairs. Take care."

"You do the same."

The commotion upstairs was Brett asking if his grandma was coming home from the hospital today. "Not today" was our answer.

Mike called from the hospital—Mother was having a shunt inserted, so no visiting would be allowed till much later. This meant we wound up entertaining Mike and Barbara.

The five of us—Brett included—went to lunch at a place called Pyewacket in Chapel Hill. The food was great—Paige loved their lemon tamari dressing, and I liked the trout when they had it—and it seemed like a calm place to eat and talk.

It was easy to find them when we arrived—Cadillac Mike was outlandishly conspicuous in his cowboy hat. Barbara's hair was... remarkable.

Despite the carefully chosen setting, it wasn't a pleasant meal. The endless disruptions to Brett's routine had not left him at his best. He tipped over his water glass. He complained about his food. And about missing his grandmother.

Brett redeemed himself now and forever by asking Barbara, "Is your hair real, or did you buy it at the store?" Paige looked at me—practically turning purple she was trying so hard not to laugh. This was one of those crazy, impossible-to-explain moments that made having our son so special.

A persistent tugging on my sleeve got my attention—I looked up, and was greeted by concerned stares from Paige and Brett.

We were standing in the piercingly cold wind outside Pyewack-et's. Mike and Barbara had left.

Paige and Brett were talking over one another. "Honey, where were you?" and "Dad—Dad—when are we going Christmas shopping for Mom and Grandma?" Paige looked worried, Brett just wanted attention.

"Just thinking," I said.

I shivered—but not from the cold. I'd been hallucinating again, or at least I hope I had been. The thought that what I'd just been hearing might really be Mom's thoughts from the hospital was more than I could bear.

I stared at the pavement as we walked to our car. Trying hard not to remember what I'd heard her think—or say.

"Where is everyone? Ann? Jack? Jack, where are you?—Are you listen-ing—If this is living—I don't want to live! I can't move, I can't do anything. I can't even watch TV.

There's no hope that I'll get better—are you listening? I've endured enough—can't take any more. If I could end this myself now I would—but I can't. I want—I need you to help me end this—I want to die—

Jack—are you listening? You've got to help me end this."

As we walked—even though I knew it wasn't a good idea—I tried to hear Mom's voice again, but couldn't.

I knew the Indiana–North Carolina basketball game was on, so I flipped on the car radio. The announcer on WCHL was be-moaning the fact Indiana was leading North Carolina twenty-three to fourteen in the first half. Brett's moans from the back seat made clear that I'd heard the score correctly.

Frustrated by his team's sad performance, Brett started chant-ing, "Turn it off—turn it off—turn it off!" until I gave in.

We weren't talking. Silence led to more silence. I strained to hear Mom's voice again but was met with silence. It was daylight, but I felt like a premature dusk had descended around me.

Pulling up at our house, as Brett piled out and started running around playing airplane, Paige turned to me, put her hand on my arm and said, "Jack, I know this is an unbearably hard time for you. I love you, and I'm here for you." She waved as I drove away.

The echoes of her quiet voice and calming touch helped kept the voices quiet on the drive to Duke.

Entering the hospital, the harsh light hurt my eyes. Off to the right, the gift shop and its sickly smell of flowers brought me the usual and unwanted memory of Dad's funeral.

Don't get off track. Keep moving. Hit the up button. When the doors open, get on the elevator. Push eight. When the doors open, get off at the eighth floor. Find the waiting room. Sit and wait for the chime and the next visiting session. Walk to Mom's room.

I hoped to find Mom awake, but she was asleep. A bandage was on her left wrist, covering the shunt they just put in. She was shriveled up so she no longer resembled Norman. She looked grotesque amidst the tubes. I knew she wouldn't want to be seen this way. Or remembered this way.

How would she want to be remembered?

Like she looked when she got when all dolled up to take Ann and me to the movies in Kokomo—bundled against the winter's cold and pulling us through the snow on a sled—meeting me at the front door with a plate of peeled and carved apples when I ran home for lunch from school to watch the World Series—and thousands—no, count-less—images of her from when I was growing up and she was the best mom in the world—the absolute best.

"Mom—was that really your voice I heard, or am I going crazy?"

The only answer came from the wheeze of the respirator and the pinging and beeping of the machines.

What had I heard, or imagined I'd heard?

"If this is living—I don't want to live!"

Aside from the action of the respirator, Mom wasn't moving.

Here I am at my mother's deathbed—just she and I—all our days as mother and son come down to this.

The end is near. Hours away, if that. Very close.

I began crying. Crying like I never did over Dad's death—I might never stop crying.

Mother still wasn't moving. Tears flowed down my cheeks onto my shirt. I couldn't control this. I couldn't fix this. All I could do was end this.

I can't—I'm not ready yet. Sorry, Mother—so very, very sorry.

She didn't stir one bit as I kissed her forehead. Said goodbye to her for the day. Perhaps the last. Part of me hoped it was, part that it wasn't. I was torn, and tearing more with each moment.

It wasn't easy, but I managed to pull myself together before walking out of her room. How I got in the car and on the road was a bit of a mystery.

I returned home to Paige's tale of Brett first throwing a tantrum over North Carolina losing, then running around like a madman, screaming, "Go, Carolina!" over and over and waving his arms when they rallied to win.

The excitement of this triumph proved a bit too much for our tiny Tar Heel fan. After climbing up and joining me in my chair, he regaled me with a chattery narrative of the comeback, and promptly fell dead asleep. Instead of carrying him up to bed, I let him sleep there.

When Paige went up to bed, I picked Brett up like a warm, limp sack of potatoes. Carrying him into his room, I decided this was one night I should let him sleep in his UNC sweatshirt. Turning out the light, I paused at the door. Something in his room gave me strength.

I went to the bathroom, and stood there for quite a while—staring at myself in the mirror. If I was looking for answers there, I didn't find them.

Eventually I went to bed, and made myself a cocoon beneath the blankets on my side of the bed. Placing them over my head, I curled into a fetal position. I felt protected as though in a womb. Safe as long as I remained motionless.

CHAPTER 21

December 21

I woke up in my blanket fort, completely bunkered on my side of the bed with pillows covering my head. I felt warm and safe, yet strangely exposed all the same. Peeking out at the clock, I found I'd overslept. Based on the warm mound on the other side of the bed, and the silence in the house, Paige and Brett had as well.

It had been quite a week, so I decided to let them sleep a while longer.

Slipping quietly from under the covers, I went to my study. I hadn't even looked at my play for what seemed like weeks. Instead of reaching for it, I sat down and opened the top drawer, taking out the packet of Mom's letters from the Mayo Clinic. Flipping through the stack, knowing that this was the very last thing I should do, I pulled out the letter from 12/21/1955—twenty-five years ago today. Stifling a small cough, I started to read.

"Received letters from you two again today. I've only read them four times already. Don't want to miss anything, you know. The mail is coming through a lot better now. Hope yours is. Speaking of mail, will you darlings please tell Grandma to tell everyone that I am writing no one but you two—"

I started coughing and had to pause. Damn asthma. Reading these letters was bringing it on. I should probably stop.

"The doctors are doing what is best, but it sure is rough. Daddy feels great, but sometimes after an operation a person has trouble getting

their bladder back in shape. It's nothing serious, but it just takes time. That's our trouble now. Boy, I wish he had mine."

I could hear every word as if she were speaking. My coughing was getting bad, and I started wheezing—I was having serious trouble catching my breath. I needed to stop reading before I got myself into real trouble.

"Wonder if I can get any sleep before the man next door starts snoring. There ought to be a law against it. Good night, my sweets. Meet you in my dreams."

"I love you."

By the time I put the letters back, I was in the middle of a full-fledged asthma attack.

Somehow I found myself in front of the bathroom mirror. Through some miracle, I got there without waking anyone, and I closed the door to make sure it stayed that way. In between long, wracking coughs, I stood there, gazing at a man of thirty-five rather than the boy of ten that Mom had been writing to. A vise constricted my chest. Those letters were a reminder of more than losing Dad. I'd had asthma attacks every day the whole time my parents were at the Mayo Clinic—clearly something about them triggered things even now.

Maturity might not have not given me the ability to help my mom, but at least it helped me to make an association between symptom and cause. Even if it hasn't made me smart enough to avoid triggering the problem. Paige is so right about this.

Luckily, I made it to the toilet before I threw up. Like every serious attack since I was a kid, that took care of things. The vise let go, and the coughing stopped. I could breathe and stand up, and brushed my teeth to get rid of the taste.

Slowly, deliberately, I began preparing to shave. But no sooner had I splashed warm water on my face, than I was distracted by sunlight passing through the window. I lathered up, and started to shave.

This could be Mom's last day.

My hands were so shaky, I was lucky I didn't butcher my face before I was done shaving.

Peeking in both bedrooms, I decided to let everyone keep sleeping, and headed downstairs.

Normally I would have turned the Christmas tree lights on. This morning I couldn't do it.

Mom said moving to North Carolina meant she would never again have to spend Christmas alone. We'd had one good Christmas with her last year. She'd spent months telling folks and laughing about Brett's Christmas Day disinterest in his gifts—and his fascination with the wrapping paper and ribbons. And she'd talked all year about how much she was looking forward to this one.

She's not going to make it.

There was nothing but silence until Paige and Brett stirred and eventually rose from bed.

He sulked when we dropped him off at the babysitter. Brett clearly knew something was wrong—awfully wrong, with his grandmother. This wasn't how Christmas was supposed to be at all. They had made plans to go shopping, and Grandma said she'd take him to see Santa. It was a *promise*.

When he said, "Everyone at school knows that *grandmas* keep promises," Paige looked at me. It was clear we needed to spend some real time with Brett.

At the hospital, walking into Mom's room, I was surprised to see her awake. Desperately groping for something positive to say, I said, "It's a beautiful day outside."

Hearing this, Mom turned her head toward me. What should have been a simple act seemed to require all her energy and cause considerable pain. Her eyes were glaringly disinterested. I drew breath to talk, but no words came out.

Paige came to the rescue and began to talk about Brett. How he was missing his grandmother. Although listening to Paige, Mother's eyes didn't move from me. It was unnerving. And there was something more. She seemed both angry, and determined—and though I had an idea why, I wasn't sure.

Paige ran out of things to say, and I still couldn't find words. So we left. Even before we walked out, Mother turned her back on us. Halfway down the corridor, Paige started crying.

When we got to the waiting room, I told Paige I needed to be alone and was going for a walk. She looked surprised—small wonder, as in all the years we'd known one another, I'd never said anything like this. She nodded as if she understood.

I'd been holding my face like a block of granite. Though this wasn't a new thing for me—I smiled so seldom that Mom called me "Great Stone Face"—the the cause this time was different. It wasn't just not having a reason to smile—I was angry.

A cold, corrosive anger was consuming me. It wasn't a hot, screaming rage, it was the kind that ties you in knots, makes you smaller, consumes your insides and shrivels your heart. It felt like my life force was bleeding out. I could feel my hair turning gray and my bones turning brittle.

I had to walk this off before it killed me, so I got out of the hospital as fast as I could. I just walked, walked past the VA and rows of old houses. Walked alone until I stopped on a corner, finally able to draw a full breath. Standing in the chill winter air on an empty sidewalk that was leading me nowhere. Alone in the face of approaching death. I turned my back on that thought, and turned around.

By the time I got back, I may not have been myself, but I could at least imagine being that guy again sometime, if maybe not soon. I sat down next to Paige and put my arm around her.

Mother was asleep when Paige and I returned to her room. Since it looked like this would continue, I drove Paige home. Throughout the afternoon, I called the nurse's station to check on her. Hearing that she was still sleeping, I decided to visit after dinner. I left word of this with the nurse in case Mom woke up. Mike called in the middle of this to tell us they were heading home in the morning, so Paige invited them to dinner at the house.

There didn't seem to be a right place to be today, at the hospital or anyplace else. We stopped at Winn–Dixie to shop for dinner. Paige was purposeful; I uselessly ambled beside her. When she was in the butcher's department picking up chicken, I found myself mindlessly staring at a display of pork chops. *Never those*—I moved away. Paige had kept moving, so I went to find her, spotting her in the bakery department picking up Christmas cookies as a treat for Brett.

After we picked up Brett at the babysitter, he sat silently staring out the window and refused to talk to either Paige or I.

When we were almost home, he asked Paige, "How's Grandma?"

"Not well," Paige replied, which begged Brett's immediate second and third questions.

"Will I ever see Grandma again? Is she going to die?"

A tense "Yes!" escaped from Paige's lips as we pulled into the driveway.

As I put the car into park, I shifted so I could see Brett in the rearview mirror. He was in his car seat in the back, leaning forward, thinking hard. It looked as though he was about to ask which question the yes was for, when Paige opened his door and unbuckled him.

When we walked into the house, Brett ran upstairs to his room and slammed his door. He stayed there until Mike and Barbara arrived.

Dinner was a knock-off of my favorite, Paige's chicken with noodles. She didn't have time to make the handmade noodles I loved and used store-bought. Good, but neither authentic nor amazing.

While the food was passable, the company and conversation were awful, and the evening seemed to last forever. Brett was quiet and distant, staring out the window into the darkness most of the time. Paige did her best to be pleasant, Mike was himself, and Barbara looked like she'd sucked on a lemon. It was a dismal and depressing sendoff for Mike and Barbara, which somehow seemed appropriate—if not comforting.

After agreeing to keep them posted, and being told by Barbara that "God will make sure it all works out," we said goodbye to my aunt and uncle. The three of us stood waving from the front door as they drove away in their huge Cadillac, Mike at the wheel with his hat on.

They're gone—back to Indiana. And as my neighbors might say, in less-than-fond farewell, god bless their hearts. I'd lived here long enough to use the Southerner's middle finger.

When we went back in the house, Brett went over to inspect the presents under the tree. He knew what his name looked like, and he was able to find and feel and shake a couple of small pack-ages of toys that Paige had wrapped up after our stop at Winn–Dixie. Even this didn't seem to cheer him up.

After putting the last of the presents back, Brett walked over to stand in front of the mantle over the fireplace. He pointed up at the photo in the middle and asked, "Are we going to take a photo with Grandma this Christmas?"

The photo, of Paige, Brett, and I with my mom, all dressed in our Christmas best, had been there since the holidays last year. My eyes had crossed it hundreds of times in the last few weeks, but somehow I'd been willing myself not to see it.

Without thinking, I said sharply, "It won't be happening this year."

Maybe he knew what I was saying, or maybe he thought I was telling him Christmas was being canceled. Whatever the cause, Brett immediately started crying, which quickly morphed into a full blown tantrum—a storm of sobbings, half-formed sentences, and tears that not even Paige could calm. Managing to get him upstairs was all she could do.

Driven by the storm, I headed for the hospital. If I left now, I could make the next visiting time.

Mom was waiting for me. I wasn't expecting a welcome.

It was Sunday night, the last Sunday before Christmas, and Duke North seemed almost deserted. My footsteps echoed on the polished linoleum of the hallway to Mom's room.

There won't be solutions to any of the problems I'm about to find.

I was halfway through the door to Mom's room when her eyes found me. They didn't hold much of a greeting, and were far more intense than in the afternoon. Her look stopped me in my tracks better than a brick wall.

I didn't know what to do. I tried words. "I love you, Mother."

Her look didn't soften.

"I love you more than words can—"

"Jack, pay attention. There's no use of either of us continuing with this—"

Maybe it was her eyes speaking, maybe I really could hear her thoughts.

"I've had enough and can't die. Can't die no matter how hard I try. You're going to have to give me a little help. I'll spell it out for you. Make it perfectly clear so they're won't be any misunderstanding. Sorry to have to do this—sorrier than I've ever been in my life."

I was paralyzed. I tried not to hear, but nothing I tried could block it out.

"Please don't ask…"

Her eyes finally softened.

"There's no other way, dearest, or I wouldn't be doing this—please understand. Please be strong enough to let me go."

Mother sat up in her bed, reached up, grasped the tracheotomy tube leading from the respirator to the incision in her neck. For about a second, she paused.

I was frozen.

Never turning away from me, face set in grim determination, she yanked the tube from her throat.

Alarms started screaming, and a stampede of nurses and doctors immediately rushed around me, shoving me away to get to her. Amidst the mayhem, through the confusion, her eyes found mine.

She'd made her wishes clear. As her look hardened, I gave in and nodded my head.

"All right, Mom. I understand."

The hospital staff engaged in a flurry of frenetic activity, reconnecting the respirator. They made clear I was in the way, and they were still working on her as I rushed out the door to get away.

All that remained was for me to honor her wishes, and let her go.

A task for tomorrow. It would take that long for me to gather the strength.

CHAPTER 22

December 22

Sunday had barely become Monday when the phone rang, short bursts of harsh sound. I answered the phone quietly, trying to not disturb Paige. "Mr. Lewis, you had better come to the hospital immediately," a man's voice said to me. The line went dead.

I rolled out of bed and looked at the clock: 1:07 a.m. Lack of sleep made me dizzy for a moment. December 22nd, Monday. Three days before Christmas. A call unwanted but not unexpected.

Groping in the darkness, I placed the telephone on its receptacle. I missed it twice. Beside me, Paige stirred and asked if anything was wrong.

"I'm leaving for the hospital," I mumbled. She retreated safely back into sleep.

I dressed quickly, not stopping to kiss Paige or Brett goodbye. I walked out the door into a darkness like an abyss. My footsteps echoed briefly on the deck until I reached the stone steps leading to the driveway. A neighbor's dog barked in the distance.

Headlights illuminated each twist and turn of the route to the hospital. On either side of the road, familiar houses and trees were somber shadows as if in stationary mourning. The darkness was unrelieved save for the futility of an occasional street light. I didn't see another car until reaching the hospital parking lot. Every fraction of a mile along the way, I had to remind myself not to think. *Don't think about anything.*

My footsteps resonated through the expanse of a deserted parking lot. The glass doors at the hospital's entrance sprang open with startling suddenness. My pace had increased, but now everything else seemed to slow down. Standing in front of the elevator, I stood fuming as it took forever to descend from the upper floors. Ascent proved no more rapid.

Finally, I was free of the elevator. Stillness surrounded me. I strained to hear Mother's voice as I rushed to her room, but I heard nothing.

When I got to Mom's room, she was comatose, surrounded by two nurses and a doctor too busy to notice my presence. Now I could hear her voice.

"Thank you for coming—you need to see this."

The doctor and nurses were scurrying—frantic. Their strained voices whispered of a heart attack. Or something else not as yet identified. They added medicines to intravenous lines in a last-ditch effort to sustain life. Fluid flows and monitors were frantically adjusted. Finally, they spoke of Mom's heart having a normal rhythm.

They were all so focused on her I might as well have not been in the room. It was like being in one of those nightmares where no one can see you, and you can't do anything while awful things happen to someone you care about.

"You know I love you, and that I've tried my best to stay. I'm so sorry to miss Christmas—you need to make sure Brett knows how much I love him."

The exhausted and frustrated faces of the medical team told the story. Something had gone terribly wrong. As they saw it, they were doing their best for Mom, and I wanted to show the respect of using their names. The nametags read "Ms. Webster," "Ms. Livingston," and "Dr. Ramsey."

A splattering of blood stains covered the front of Dr. Ramsey's coat. They were on Ms. Webster's and Ms. Livingston's uniforms, on the sheet covering mother's upper body, and on the respirator as well.

"I can't endure any more."

Worse was in the offing. An unobstructed view of my mother's face suddenly appeared to me through the shifting movement of the medical team. A hideous, grotesque mask matted with sweat. Grayish eyelids, heavy as lead, embedded in creased, cadaverous skin. Her dentureless mouth gaped, and her hair was a tangled mess—she looked ancient.

"This isn't how I want you to see me—this isn't how I want to be."

I felt myself beginning to reel and grabbed the wall to steady myself. My eyes were drawn to the blood-stained sheet. To my mother's legs and feet, which were uncovered. Her feet were splayed at an oblique angle. Pink nail polish peeled from nails awaiting a fresh coating they would never receive. Her legs were those of a much younger woman and appeared attached to the wrong body.

Forcing myself to look away from this, my eyes ventured to a shelf on the wall by Mom's head, *to something* inconceivable— something out of place. A box of diapers. At first, I thought they had been put there by accident. But I quickly realized I was wrong. Mother needed them like Dad had needed the bag hanging at his side.

I tightened my grip on the wall. The woman who had given birth to me lay swaddled in a diaper. The blood-splattered sheet prevented me from actually seeing the wrapping, but I knew it was there.

"Jack, your mind knows what you need to do. Your heart needs to get to the same place."

Dr. Ramsey's face was suddenly directly in front of me. My head was full of static. His voice competed for my attention in fragments: "Heart attack—out of immediate danger—there's nothing more we can do for her now."

I nodded. Nodded like a moron. And didn't really know why I was nodding. All I could see was my mother's blood splattered everywhere. That and her box of diapers.

More words from Ramsey were trying to break through the static. "Go home and rest—nothing more you can do here—we'll call you if her condition changes." I sensed myself still nodding after he walked away.

I know what I have to do—Paige will want to be here.

I felt dull, almost medicated, on the drive home. The dashboard clock read 3 a.m.—exhaustion called for sleep.

I returned to Duke with Paige just after noon.

Mom was laying in an upright position, covered with a clean sheet. Surrounding her and engrossed in her care was a totally new team: two nurses named Ms. Carter and Ms. Bryce, and a male physician, Dr. Long.

Mom's eyelids were closed, face serene. Her hair had been neatly combed. I hadn't told Paige the details of my earlier visit.

"Now this can finally end."

It took several minutes before our presence in the doorway was acknowledged by the medical team. Totally absent was the frenetic activity I had seen the previous night. In its place was a professional efficiency, and minimal conversation in calm voices.

Dr. Long was the first to notice Paige and me. He motioned us to join his team. I walked to the foot of the bed and stood, Paige by my side.

"Are you Mary's family?" Ms. Bryce asked.

I nodded sadly .

Dr. Long beckoned for me to join him in the corridor. "There's nothing more we can do," he said.

"I know, she tried her best to make it, but couldn't," I said. "She's ready, it's time. What do you suggest?"

"The gentlest way is to stop the the drug we are using to keep her blood pressure up—what we call a pressor."

"Then do it."

I followed him back into the room.

Time seemed suspended in a room getting smaller. Paige and the nurses hadn't moved.

Dr. Long took a few steps and without a word turned a stopcock. It was done.

"Thank you."

Nurse Carter looked around and walked from the room. Paige looked puzzled, so I whispered to her that the end was near.

At this, she held my hand.

At first nothing changed. Then Carter returned.

One of the steady blips missed.

We stood silent amidst all the sounds of equipment…and another blip missed.

A female chaplain entered the room—the result of Carter's handiwork. She walked to the head of the bed and looked at me for a signal to begin praying.

Another blip skipped, and the waves on the heart monitor got smaller. And smaller. It was impossible for me not to see what was happening as Mom started to leave us.

The chaplain was looking at me, puzzled. *There is no god. What was she doing here?* Her presence was a distraction, taking my attention from Mom, where it belonged. She finally got uncomfortable enough to leave the room.

Mother's heartbeats had become infrequent—she was almost gone. Paige's hand squeezed mine.

"Goodbye."

A piercing tone proclaimed the end. Dr. Long turned off the alarms.

She was gone. We'd been at the hospital less than an hour.

Paige and I were both quietly crying.

Mom's eyes were closed, her windows to the world shuttered forever.

When I could move, I went to the side of the bed and kissed my mother goodbye.

That seemed to break the paralysis I'd been feeling, and I rushed out of the room halfway down the corridor. As I leaned against the wall and tried to make myself breathe, Paige caught up with me.

"Do you want me to make arrangements for a memorial, or do you want to handle that yourself?" she asked.

"Could you handle it? And the obituary."

"Of course. Does this Friday—the 26th—work?"

I nodded.

"What are you…"

"I'm going to scatter her ashes in Duke Forest," I said.

Mom is gone. Now all I can do is honor her wishes.

Cremation, and scattering her ashes in a beautiful place she loved. These gestures may feel empty of meaning to me, but she more than earned them.

My responsibilities are almost over, except for remembering.

CHAPTER 23

December 23

I awoke in darkness to the sound of pine trees swirling in the wind.

Mom is gone, and there is a hole in my heart the size of the moon. But I have to think of Brett—it's two days to Christmas.

The swirling wind was truly a reflection of my thoughts.

It was only the flu. This is unimaginable. I have to focus on Brett now—I can grieve later.

I barely noticed Paige's hand on my shoulder. Then a shaking motion, coupled with five or six, "Jacks!" returned me to the present. She was studying me intently.

"How are you?"

An easy question with a hard answer. I resisted the impulse to cry as the silence between us lengthened. I managed, "I'm hurting, but Brett comes first."

An expression of genuine concern registered on Paige's face. In a voice slightly more audible than a whisper, she responded, "I know."

"It won't be easy, but we can still make it a good Christmas for him," I said.

As she started to roll over to get out of bed, I reached out to touch her arm.

She rolled back to look at me.

"I love you, and appreciate you being there for Mom and me more than you'll ever know."

A hot shower and coffee got me started on the impossible. It was a day of lists. Christmas lists, now one name shorter. Lists of things to handle for Mom's memorial and winding up her affairs.

But Christmas first. Almost everything else can wait.

An hour and a half and three cups of coffee later, it was a civil enough time to call Ann and Vince, in that order. Mike was on the road. Paige had tried Ann the day and night before, but she wasn't at home or work and leaving a message seemed the wrong thing to do.

I sat in my favorite chair, and reached for the phone.

Ann seemed to be waiting for my call. *She knows.* "Mom died last night."

A heavy sigh from Ann, followed by, "Are you alright?"

"I'm managing, but not having an easy time."

"And Paige?"

"The same. I don't know what I would have done without her."

"I should have come, but I had too much to do," Ann said. "What time and where is the service?"

"Eleven o'clock at Duke Chapel, the day after Christmas."

"Oh," Ann said, surprised. "You're doing it at a chapel?"

"Paige and I talked it over. It's a place where Mom's friends, and some of our friends, will feel comfortable mourning her loss. And that's the place where they baptized Brett. They treated me with respect even though I don't share their faith. That goes a long way with me."

"Wow," was all she could manage as a reply.

I remembered to ask Ann about Mom's favorite flowers.

"How about yellow roses. They were always special to her," she replied. "I think it had something to do with Dad."

"I knew you would remember—thank you. I'll call the florist."

I had run out of words.

Ann rescued us from silence, saying, "I'll call you when I have my flight reservations."

I'd only made a phone call, but my shirt was drenched in sweat. It took a while before I was ready for the next one.

Vince's wife answered after the second ring. I struggled with recalling her name, and finally was able to remember. *Pamela.*

"Good morning, Pamela, this is Jack. May I speak with Vince?"

A muffled, "Vince, it's Jack," sounded in the background.

When Vince picked up, I said, "Mom passed away yesterday. Her memorial service is at Duke Chapel the day after Christmas."

Several seconds elapsed before he said, "I am so sorry for your loss. What time is it? May I invite people she knew from work?"

"Eleven in the morning."

"I'm sorry, so very sorry. Mary was such a wonderful person. I thought of her as a member of the family," Vince said with obvious difficulty. "We'll be sure to be there."

Everything that needed to be said had been, except for Vince's ending the conversation by saying again that he would pray for me.

People need to grieve in their own ways. There are times to make a point—this isn't one of them.

Paige was upstairs, and there didn't seem to be anything I had to do this very moment. Instead of getting up, I sat, looked out through the French doors to the pines beyond, let my heart settle a bit, and thought about making Brett's Christmas a good one.

Hanging stockings—milk and cookies for Santa—extra presents—explaining Grandma not being here in a way he can understand—taking him to buy a present for his Mom—and for a drive to see the lights.

Paige's voice called from upstairs. "I'm calling Natalie—do you want Brett home today, tonight, or tomorrow morning?"

I walked to the stairs so I didn't have to shout. "I think it's important to have him at home from now on," I replied. "Why don't we pick him up after we go Christmas shopping?"

"Great," she called down. "And Jack—there's more. Ann called to let us know she's arriving tomorrow night. She was able to get an earlier flight."

The phone must have rung when I was staring out at the trees. Tomorrow night—Christmas Eve.

"How did Ann sound?"

"Absolutely terrible," Paige said. "I tried—but really wasn't able to comfort her."

"Sometimes all you can do is try."

We made it to the car, Paige thankfully remembering Brett's many lists.

Last-minute Christmas shopping has always been on my list of least favorite things to do. But the way this month played out, it is the only option we had.

Brett's list for Santa was daunting—full of popular toys that would likely be out of stock, so I planned for a lot of running around. A big rideable John Deere tractor that would about fill the backseat, a long list of *Star Wars* toys that was both detailed and confusing, and more. Yes, more.

Paige was half-reading Brett's lists out loud as we drove past streets, houses, trees, and churches. "What is an Arteetootie?"

"R2D2—remember the little robot?"

"Got it. Navigator to pilot—let's head to Ace Hardware first. I think their ad said they have the tractor. Let's start with the biggest first."

"Pilot to navigator—roger that."

Paige said quietly "I can't believe I won't ever see your mom again."

"Me either."

Ace Hardware was the closest store. And Paige was right, they happened to have precisely one John Deere tractor left, complete with trailer—to which we eagerly laid claim. Paige had been right when she said "biggest first."

"Paige—this is *ridiculous*—it's bigger than Brett! With the trailer attached it's almost five feet long! Does it come with its own mechanic?"

She gave me the eye. "Jack, he wants it, we're getting it, and you know it. Save the theatrics."

The tractor turned out to be the extent of our luck at Ace. Getting out of there took forever, starting with a long check-out line that concluded with the cashier running out of change. Then, of course, came lugging the heavy metal tractor out and trying to get it into the trunk of the car.

The damn thing feels like it actually has an engine! It really is nice to have things well made...except when you have to carry them.

Stops at two local family-owned toy stores yielded Lincoln logs, Legos, some art project kits, and books. But not the *Star Wars* stuff we needed. They had a fair amount, just not the ones on his list. We weren't going to substitute; Brett had enough disappointments this month.

"Oh no," Paige said at checkout. "This means the mall. It's the 23rd."

I felt like the man in Munch's *The Scream*. I held my hands up next to my face and gave an exaggerated, "Nooooooooo! Not the mall!"

It was a favorite painting of mine, and she spotted the reference. The smack she gave me was only a small one.

Northgate Mall two days before Christmas was pretty much everything one would expect. Traffic was a nightmare, you had to wait to get a parking space, and we encountered a succession of stores in which no special provisions had been made to accommodate the heavy volume of last-minute holiday shoppers.

Jostling, frantic crowds, exhausted clerks, throngs of children running and screaming, and a long line to see Santa that evoked the hopelessness of a Depression-era breadline.

We were far too fatigued to deal with this, but we weren't going to give up. We kept running into people we knew. Not wanting to spoil anyone's mood, we were forced to reciprocate smiles and seasonal greetings.

Having stood in every line, and been hit with every elbow, we finally had every impossible *Star Wars* item on Brett's list, plus a bunch of impulse buys and enough wrapping paper and bows to decorate the Washington Memorial.

We didn't exchange a single word until we reached home, where the packages and tractor were transferred from the trunk of the car and hidden until the time for them to be retrieved on Christmas Eve and placed under the tree.

We went to pick up a sleepy Brett. He didn't ask about his grandma, and we didn't tell him.

After we put Brett to bed, Paige and I stayed up wrapping presents. I had a hefty scotch, and she worked her way through half a bottle of Grgich Hills chardonnay.

We were trying to get back to some sort of grounding, some kind of center in our lives. Simple tasks seemed the way to get there. We didn't talk much, and that was fitting as words had been losing meaning in our lives. What we needed right then was to do, not talk.

Sometimes in the face of large tragedies, simple affirmative acts are the only answer.

Colored paper, ribbon bows, and scotch tape may not seem to amount to much. But sometimes, like that night, they have magical healing powers.

CHAPTER 24

December 24

I woke up in darkness, without even the faintest hint of first light tickling the skies. Paige had shifted against me in the night; I could feel the soft warmth of her leg. Fighting off the urge to get moving—I needed to sort through the first couple of days of this insane week, to discuss with Paige how to handle the day—before getting up.

I have to work through some of my thoughts and feelings, or I'm not going to be in any kind of shape to tell Brett about his grandma. You don't get a second chance on stuff like this with little kids—you have now or never. You get it right or wrong. I need to get this right or Christmas Eve and Christmas are going to be an awful experience and memory for my son. It's not about me, or Mom, it's about Brett.

What a week. His grandma died two days ago—and we haven't managed to tell him. We have to today—not only will he be wondering, but there's always the risk he could hear it from someone else.

I needed to talk to Paige about this before Brett woke up and asked us. She'd spent years teaching kids not much older than Brett and had a better idea of how to handle this situation.

Paige's breathing change and she shifted against me. I rolled over to hold her. "Good morning, sweetheart."

"Mmmm," was her reply. "Is it morning?"

"Yes. Christmas Eve. Brett's not awake yet. But the first thing he'll ask when he gets up is about Mom. We *have* to tell him. He hasn't seen her in two weeks, and he's starting to doubt every-thing we say. And he might hear it from someone else."

"And that's not the only question he's going to ask," she replied thoughtfully. "He'll want to know where Grandma is. That's go-ing to be a tough question for you, Jack. Are you ready for it? What are you going to tell him—heaven or nowhere?"

Why did the theme song from Dragnet come to mind?

"Is he old enough for the truth? How would he react to us tell-ing him she's dead and is nowhere? On Christmas Eve! You know more about kids than I do. What do you suggest?"

"Jack, you may not like hearing this, but Brett isn't ready to hear that, Christmas Eve or not. The best thing you can say is that she's in heaven with God. That's worked for thousands of years. But if you can't get there, telling him she's someplace else is a distant second."

"All right, heaven it is. Then Santa. It really is a day for myths, anyway. Should I go wake him up?"

"In a little while—hold me for a few minutes first."

That was an easy request to satisfy. I cuddled close, trying to draw strength from her warmth for what would come next.

The first rays of dawn told me I couldn't wait any longer. I got out of bed and walked down the hallway to Brett's room, peeking in. He slept in his usual sprawl, secure, safe, and loved.

How am I going to get through this?

"Hey slugger, come on—wake up, let's go snuggle with Mom."

His voice was scratchy, as he half-yawned out, "Daaad…"

I wanted to get into the bedroom with Paige before he asked. "Grab on, sport," I said as I picked him up.

I carried him into our bedroom, laid him down next to Paige, who said, "How's my favorite boy?"

I climbed in after him.

Sure enough, the first words out of Brett's mouth were, "When do I get to see Grandma?" He looked from me to Paige, and back, looking for who would give him the answer.

"Not for some time," I said. "There's something we have to tell you."

Trying to take some of the heat off me, Paige said, "Grandma is no longer with us."

Brett looked at her for a moment, but then immediately back at me.

A second question followed. "Where is she, Dad?" It was clear he wanted a direct answer. From me. Right now.

"She's in heaven with god." There was—nothing else I could say.

Looking past Brett, I could see Paige give a sigh of relief. I knew there had been many times over the years, particularly since we'd moved to the South, when my answers to the contrary had caused some very awkward times for her. I knew she had been worried this would be another of them, and could see her body relax when it was clear that it wasn't.

"How can we get her the present I made for her?" Brett asked.

"First things first, young man. We have to go shopping for a present for your mom."

"Whoa, boys," Paige interjected. "Breakfast first. Then you can go. I'll make pancakes."

"Pancakes!" Brett shouted, vaulting over me, out of bed.

Fortified by pancakes, Brett and I managed to get an early enough start to get to Lakewood Shopping Center as it opened. This is where Brett had spotted the present he wanted to give his mom, at a store called The Four Winds. Apparently he'd been there with his grandma. I tensed for a question—which didn't come.

Brett practically ran through the door—he knew exactly what he wanted and where it was, and he grabbed it, heading for the register.

"Whoa, sport! Let's look at that."

It turned out to be an apron inscribed with "Love and Quiches" and a picture of a quiche cut into quarters. I couldn't remember Paige ever cooking a quiche, but Brett was pretty excited, and that's what mattered. We got it gift-wrapped in the paper Brett picked out—featuring a very red-nosed Rudolph.

It all made sense to him, and he was in a good mood. Mission accomplished.

On the ride home, I asked, "Do you think Santa is packed yet, or are the elves still working?"

"I hope he's not packed yet, I thought of more stuff last night," he said. I gripped the steering wheel in horror. I couldn't go back to the mall, although Paige had said something about a trip back out to Northgate.

I had the realization that all over America, millions of parents were having similar experiences.

When we pulled up at the house, Brett managed to get out of his car seat, out of the car, and to run toward the house—present in hand—before I had my door open.

I caught up with him to unlock the door. The second it was open, he tore into the house, shouting, "Mom, Mom. We got your present." He ran to put it under the tree in a place of honor.

She came down the stairs. "How exciting! Can I open it now?"

"Mom, Christmas isn't until tomorrow!"

"Darn," she said, winking at me. "And Brett."

"What, Mom?"

"Your room is a mess, and Santa is watching. Do you really want him to see it like that on Christmas Eve?"

Brett zipped up the stairs like greased lightning, trying to make sure he stayed off the "naughty" list. We both laughed as we heard drawers being slammed.

"Are you still up to taking him with you to the mall? I need to go to Mom's to clean out the fridge and make sure things are okay until we get a chance to really deal with the place after Christmas."

"That's fine," she said. "There'll be lots of kids, so he'll have fun running around. I'm leaving in a few minutes. How long do you need?"

"A couple of hours, at most. I'm ready to go, so I'll head out now, and see you when you get back."

I parked in front of Mom's apartment and sat for a bit. Opening the door, I encountered a gust of wind. A swirl of leaves engulfed me. Everything felt different since I had been here last.

Inside, in the Saharan heat, I hoped to not encounter anyone, but was quickly disappointed. Mrs. Weston came out to see me, crying. Somehow, she already knew mother was dead. She was clearly upset, and she was also, "So very very very sorry."

She told me she hoped Mom's neighbor Kathleen wouldn't bother me when I went upstairs. Mrs. Weston was like a phantom in a nightmare. I wished she would vanish, but instead she stammered something about hoping Mom had enjoyed living here.

"Yes, of course she did," I replied, and walked upstairs.

At the top of the landing I came face-to-face with Kathleen, or as Mom called her, "nutty Kathleen," an overweight and perpetually overwrought spinster in her early fifties. From her agitated stance, I understood I was expected to engage in some sort of conversation. If I didn't want to risk a scene, that is.

I couldn't remember the number of times and in what context Mom had mentioned this unpleasant woman. Her unkempt hair took up my entire field of vision, and she had a slightly pop-eyed stare. Faced with her, I couldn't remember anything. Nutty Kathleen was just more clutter on top of all the other clutter getting in the way of a clear thought.

She stood too close to me, and talked about Mom as if they were best friends. *I'll bet all your friends are dead.* She needed our conversation to be meaningful, to validate her important role in Mom's life. *Mom just wanted to run away from you.*

I had no idea what she was saying; I kept nodding until she was satisfied and let me alone. I don't think I actually had to say a word—just give her a thousand nods. Eventually, she ran out of words. Her mouth opened and closed several times like a fish. Then she turned a half-revolution around, and waddled to her own room without looking back.

After she left, I found myself in my mother's apartment. The air was stale and close, my breathing was difficult. No one had been in the apartment since my last visit. It was with great difficulty I recalled the reason I had come—I had to clean up.

I opened the door to the fridge, and closed it right away. A stomach-turning wave of spoiled milk and moldy food chased me straight across the room to open a window, and stand, breathing fresh air, until the room aired out. *Should have done that first.*

I opened the rest of the windows and got to work. Flushed the milk and juice down the toilet. Ran the spoiled food that would go down the disposal, put the rest in the trash can, made sure the bag wouldn't leak. Fill it up, quick trip out to the dumpster, repeat. Scour the sink, spray the counters down. Water the plants that seemed salvageable.

Time to go. Just had to close the windows.

I'll sit down for a moment. Maybe with a scotch. There's some under the counter that Mom bought on our trip to the beach in October. Cutty Sark—not the best, but Mom liked it. Two fingers should do it.

Even if it wasn't very good, scotch can still keep you company. It's a good listener, and I had a lot to say that day.

I was in the middle of that conversation, and still on my first glass, when the phone rang. A call was the last thing I expected, and it took me till the third ring to get to the phone.

"You've got to get to the hospital now," a man's voice said.

It can't be Duke calling me again—my mother is already dead.

"Dr. Lewis—Dr. Lewis—are you there? This is Brett's pediatrician, Dr. Summers. You've got to get to the hospital now!"

This isn't adding up—why is he calling me here and how did he get this number—Paige had to have given it to him.

"I'm here."

Dr. Summer's voice was tense. "I'm sorry to bother you at a time like this," he said, "but Brett has been hurt."

Brett has been hurt—my son. Is he dead? How? Where?

It isn't always what things are that cut you—it's what they might be—in that first moment of hearing or seeing. This was a bad first moment, with a deep cut.

It's life—deal with it.

"What happened? Is he okay?"

Several anxious seconds passed before Dr. Summers said, "He'll be all right, but we're afraid that his collarbone is broken."

"Collarbone? How?"

Broken collarbone—not life threatening—but—but—the flu isn't either—look what happened to Mom.

Dr. Summers continued, "I had your wife take Brett to Durham County for x-rays."

That's the hospital where Paige took Mom.

I was dazed, but somehow managed to respond. "I'll leave immediately."

Thirty minutes later, I walked into the hospital, this time through the emergency entrance.

Directly in front of me was the reception desk, with a waiting area off to the left, deserted except for Paige, Brett, and—my eyes were playing tricks on me. Or maybe my conversation with the scotch had been more involved than I realized.

Mother was with them. Couldn't be—but was. She was sitting directly behind Paige and Brett. Paige was doing her best to attend to Brett, who was trying not to cry and leaning awkwardly to his right. Both were unaware they had company until I walked up.

Paige and Brett seemed glad to see me, but the apparition behind them looked concerned.

"What happened to you, slugger?" I asked Brett. He tried to smile in return, but moved ever so slightly and grimaced in pain. Paige was barely holding on.

"We were at the mall, and Brett wanted to ride the train—a few times, as it turned out…"

"I got to ride up front again, Dad!"

"What happened?"

"He was pretty excited and fell, at the end of his third ride."

"Were you having fun?"

"Lots! Until I tripped."

Looking over his shoulder at Mom, I said, "Everything will be just fine."

Brett was being brave, but he was really hurting. For the fifteen minutes it took to see the doctor, Brett squirmed and cried a bit—there was no posture that didn't hurt. Paige tried to comfort him. I tried. Nothing we did worked. All the while, my mother's ghost was mute and motionless, watching us.

"We're going to be fine," I said.

After our name was called, it followed us to the examination room. Brett clasped my arm with his uninjured left hand. Finally, we found ourselves in the examination room.

Minutes dragged. Brett was moaning. "It hurts. It hurts. When is the doctor coming?"

Paige and I were powerless to do anything except alternate in replying. "The doctor will be here soon and you'll be better." Mother's ghost said nothing.

A young male doctor entered the room at last. "Hello, young man. Christmas Eve isn't the time for a little boy to be hurt," he said. "How did this happen?"

Brett briefly explained about the train.

The doctor already knew what the problem was—Brett's pediatrician must have called ahead. "We should take an x-ray to check that collar bone," he said. All our attention shifted to positioning Brett, trying to hurt him as little as possible. Nothing we did seemed to work. Mom looked on.

The doctor warned Brett the screen would be cold against his chest, and they would have to take the x-ray from two separate angles. Brett winced in pain, but he didn't cry, even after the procedure was over and the resident left to develop the x-rays. When the doctor returned, he showed us the x-ray, pointing out to Brett the line that meant he had a fractured collarbone.

"You're going to be just fine, young man. You'll grow up to be an engineer someday, with a locomotive of your own. The same thing happened to me when I was about your age. Mine happened on a swing set. We just need to get a brace on you, and you'll heal up just fine."

Brett nodded his head as if he understood, but he screamed and cried as the brace was applied. Brett glared at me as if something should be done to make things better. Something, anything, should be done by me. I looked around, and Mom was gone. *What did that mean?*

After it was done, I thanked the doctor. He nodded his head and scribbled a prescription for codeine. "Happy holidays," he said.

Brett looked up at him and said, "It's going to be sad because Grandma died and is in heaven."

No one spoke until the resident mumbled, "I'm sorry," and fled from the room.

Paige took Brett home, and I swung by Eckerd's to pick up Brett's prescription. I didn't want to try facing without codeine.

When I made it home, Brett was sitting on the couch in the family room, looking glum despite the mound of presents beneath the tree. I went into the kitchen, filled a glass with water, and gave him the first pill.

"Slugger—this will help you with the pain. Time to get you up to bed."

"But Dad!"

"No arguments, you'll need lots of rest to heal fast."

"Dad!"

"What?"

"You can't forget—milk and cookies for Santa!"

"Right. We'll do that right now. How many cookies, two or three?" I asked as I walked to the kitchen.

"Four!" he shouted.

Four it was, on the floor in front of the fireplace. With a glass of milk. Santa's payoff. Brett wasn't even four, and he had the concept of quid pro quo all figured out. But if that was all it took to get Brett up to bed in a good mood after a day like this, it was a small price to pay.

I just had time to pick up Ann at the airport. On the ride home, I told her of the day's misadventures and Brett's trip to the hospital.

Ann could only shake her head in disbelief.

When we got to the house, she helped Paige and I pull out all the hidden presents and get them under the tree.

She teased me about the John Deere tractor. "Does it mow the lawn?"

After we had finished, and remembered to eat Santa's cookies, the three of us ended the evening with my best single-malt scotch and a toast to Mom.

CHAPTER 25

December 25

I awoke to a silent house. It took a moment, then I remembered—it was Christmas Day, 1980.

It shouldn't be quiet. Where's the 5 a.m. wake-up from my screaming son juiced up on Santa overload. The codeine must have taken care of that.

Brett's collarbone is the last straw—I don't even want to get out bed.

I pulled the blankets up for warmth and protection, and scooted over a bit toward Paige. Ann was either still asleep in the study or had gone downstairs on cats' feet to make coffee.

Ann was probably still asleep. And Brett was still zonked out, or I would hear him.

That's all of us. Paige's family isn't coming—we canceled that when Mom got sick. Mom. Mom's presence will be felt through her shocking absence. I'm not even going to let myself think about seeing her—or thinking I saw her—at the hospital yesterday. That won't happen again.

I have to get through this day—I can't let myself fall apart. Mother's dead. But I have to focus on what I can do, and what I have to do. Leave the rest. Mom's gone.

I can't do this. I can't do presents. I can't do anything.

But I have to. I have to get through today, and the memorial tomorrow. I have to pick up Mom's ashes before the service. Hopefully I can find that place she loved in Duke Forest. That's the place to scatter them. I'm lucky I have Paige to handle things—things that are beyond me right now.

Paige stirred beside me, and moved over alongside me. "Are you alright?" she asked.

"Yes," I lied, knowing she knew I was lying. "And you?" Already knowing the answer.

"Fine," she replied, returning the favor.

I put my arms around Paige and held her in a bear hug. I didn't want to let her go for fear if I did, something would happen to her as well. I hugged her so tightly that—

"Jack—I can't breathe."

"Sorry."

So very sorry for—everything.

Brett's sudden shout from the next room, got us into instant motion.

Paige scrambled out of bed first and switched on the light, replying with a loud, "We're coming, honey!"

My eyes were not ready and took offense at the brightness. I still didn't want to get up.

Overcoming my inner Scrooge, I managed to catch Paige on her dash to Brett's room. There she flipped on the light and cried, "Merry Christmas, honey!"right before my "Merry Christmas, slugger!"

Brett was sitting up in his bed with eyes like saucers. "Did Santa come? Did Santa come?" he asked.

Brett was sitting awkwardly. Because of his injury, his right arm was tucked in close to his body, held there by the brace. There was no way he could have been comfortable. Christmas adrenaline and maybe a residue of the codeine must be masking the pain.

"Yes, didn't you hear him?" Paige said.

Brett's mouth hung open.

"We heard him downstairs last night," I said.

"I heard his sleigh land on the roof," Paige added, not to be outdone.

"Can we go down and see? Can we!" Brett started squirming to get out of bed. Excitement made him forget about his broken collarbone and the brace. When he turned sharply to jump out of bed and lead a charge downstairs to see what Santa had brought—it didn't go well.

His face contorted in pain, and he began to cry. Frozen in place, he was clearly afraid the slightest movement would hurt him again.

There was little Paige or I could do to console him until the crying gradually subsided.

Paige was at his side as Brett slowly rose and took small, tentative steps out the bedroom and down the stairs.

I trailed behind.

"It's time for another pain pill," Paige said over her shoulder, midway down the stairs.

Despite some resistance from Brett, we detoured to the kitchen where the codeine was sitting. Brett stood, pouting as Paige poured him a glass of water. He glared at the the pill Paige put in his hand before washing it down.

"Blech," was his only verbal comment—the rest of his thoughts were obvious. "Now can we go see the presents?" he asked.

As the three of us walked into the family room, I was thinking this wasn't the Christmas morning I'd wanted.

But Brett's loud indrawn breath made clear that our efforts were worthwhile. "A tractor—just what I wanted!"

I watched him stand frozen, not sure of whether to go to the mound of packages under the tree, or to the huge green John

Deere tractor, with its trailer also holding packages. This was closer to what I'd envisioned, the three of us in our pajamas, just like all those years ago Kokomo. I couldn't help but think of Boots the cat.

Ann joined us in her robe as Paige was plugging in the lights for the Christmas tree. Even in the strange light, her face had an unnatural pallor. It was also puffy. She must have been crying. "Merry Christmas," Ann said. Her voice was flat, and anything but merry, but she was trying.

"Merry Christmas, Auntie Ann," Brett said.

"Merry Christmas!" Paige and I said.

Brett's gaze shifted from the tractor, to the fireplace, to the mound of packages under the tree. "How did Santa get all that stuff down the chimney?"

Overlooked for the moment were the four full Christmas stockings hanging beneath the mantle, including one added at the last minute for Ann's benefit.

No sooner had Brett spoken than he began rubbing his eyes with his left hand. He was already acting drowsy from the codeine. The medicine had begun to work its magic. Hopefully, the effect would last.

"I wondered the same thing when I was a little girl," Paige said in mock bewilderment.

"Me too!" Ann seconded.

"Brett, do you want to talk about presents, or open presents?" I asked.

That set him into motion. The battle in his mind between going first to the presents under the tree, or to the tractor, was won by the tractor. He jumped for it, too excited to remember his brace. He stopped after a step—clearly his broken collarbone was hurting.

"Be careful, honey," Ann said, as Paige rushed over to him. But it was too late—Brett was frozen in place like a statue, with a puzzled expression on his face. He was on the verge of crying.

"You sit on the couch and we'll bring presents to you," Paige said. Surprising us all, Brett did so.

I distributed the gifts—starting off by wheeling Brett's tractor over to him.

"You'll be riding around on that in no time," Ann said in her most encouraging voice as I steered it across the room.

I handed him the first package out of the trailer, holding it so he could tear into it with his left—good—hand. "Cool," he said, seeing a pair of UNC pajamas. Both Paige and I had been clear that gifts of clothing were completely unacceptable unless they carried the logos of either the Tar Heels or *Star Wars*.

I alternated the gifts between Brett and the rest of us. This was about the right ratio as Brett got the most presents by far, including a seemingly endless number of *Star Wars* toys and figures.

The floor was acquiring a festive layer of torn paper and ribbon. Boots would have had a field day. I looked over at Ann, caught her eye, and smiled. "I'm so glad you're here."

She nodded back.

Things were winding down, and Brett had unwrapped his last present—*Christmas in the Stars: The Star Wars Christmas Album.* "Thanks, Auntie Ann," Brett shouted.

I looked at Ann and said, "At least I *was* glad you're here." I grit my teeth, imagining the thousand times I was going to hear it.

Ann knew exactly what I was referring to, and laughed.

Brett looked first at the Christmas tree, then to last year's Christmas photo on the mantle. It showed him laughing—with Paige, his grandma, and me. From the look on his face, it was obvious he wished his grandma was here with us now.

Addressing no one in particular, he asked, "Can we go to the restaurant at the Hilton later today to see Grandma in heaven?"

Where did that come from?

I'd been asked some strange questions in my life, by kids, for-
eigners, and drunk people. This one left both Ann and I with our
mouths open. But Paige had been a teacher and was used to odd
questions from kids.

While treating his question very seriously, she used a light
touch to tease out of him the story behind the question, which
showed her how to handle a reply.

The restaurant was at the top of the Hilton, and it was the
tallest building Brett have even been in. He knew heaven was up
above, and on top of the Hilton was the one place he could think
of that would be closest to her. Brett fully expected to go there,
look at the window, and see his grandmother in heaven. It made
perfect sense to him.

I wasn't saying much. And neither was Ann. We'd lost our
Mom. And every reminder of that wasn't just a cut, it was salt in
a wound that would never heal.

"Can we? Can we? Can we?" Brett asked, quickly picking up
steam.

Paige put the brakes on quickly but gently. "That's a wonderful idea sweetheart, but it's Christmas, and everyone at the Hilton is home with their families. We can go there for breakfast this
weekend, when you're feeling better."

Ann and I nodded our heads in agreement. Not Brett. He wasn't
satisfied and opened his mouth to say something in response.

Then it happened—

"Aa-oooooooooow!" he suddenly yelled as his left arm shot over
across his body, so his hand could grip his shoulder. "It hurts!"
followed with equal or greater volume. "It hurts bad!" came next
and was louder yet.

Paige was the first to reach him, followed by Ann and I. It was
considerably more difficult to calm him down than it had been
in his room. And took much longer. But finally we did, and Paige
looked at me and asked, "Is it time for another pill?"

"Close enough," I replied. The post-present Christmas crash, pain of his injury, and codeine sent Brett back upstairs to bed in short order, and with few complaints.

Moreover, his surprising interest in going back to bed seemed to be infectious—Ann and Paige quickly went to the study and bedroom, respectively, to follow his example.

I was left alone for the first time in my life on Christmas day—which was the oddest feeling. Perhaps that was the reason I starting roaming aimlessly around the the first floor of the house. I couldn't figure out what to do with myself. I would have gone out for a wandering drive, but in case Brett got up I didn't want to leave the house.

So much nervous energy—I need to do something. I can't let myself think—the thoughts coming in from the edges are too dark—I can't give in to them.

The family room was a mess. Brett's unusual one-handed present-opening technique had resulted in a confetti-like pattern of wrapping paper, ribbons, tags and packaging debris on, around, and under everything—from floor to furniture.

Throw it away—or burn it?

Mom loved fires during the holiday. I'd stocked the fireplace with a couple of large, well-seasoned oak logs and kindling a while back. With her being sick, this Christmas hadn't turned out to be the kind where we sat down in front of a fire. It had sat there, screen set off to the side, waiting for that special moment that never came.

I really would like to burn this Christmas. It's too bad that Lewis family fires don't come with phoenixes.

Sometimes cleaning is an affirmation—healing or cathartic. Not today, not this Christmas. I didn't clean up the mess—I beat it up. I took as much of my anger as I could get to and put it into my hands, crumpling up every piece of paper, then throwing each as hard as I could into the fireplace—like I was throwing rocks.

Not long after starting, I broke into a sweat. Plastic packaging in the midst of the paper reminded me how much I hated it. Getting into some of Brett's presents to get the actual gift out—had been like breaking into Fort Knox a few times. I started kicking every piece of it toward the kitchen, where the trash can was. It formed into a rough mound.

It would be easier to bring the trash can out here—but it feels so good to kick this stuff. Besides, it gives me a chance to take a breather now and then from all the stooping and throwing.

I was breathing hard and in a full sweat. There was something so satisfying about bending over, grabbing a piece of paper, wadding it up, using both hands to shape it into a fastball, and throwing it into the fireplace. Or mostly into the fireplace. I had my share of misses, which formed an arc out in front of the grate, growing in corresponding proportion as the floor was gradually cleared of paper.

I started in on the pieces of cardboard, and small boxes we didn't need to keep. Tearing up cardboard, using both hands to wring it like a chicken neck, and jamming it in a crumpled ball—this was where things got really satisfying.

Eventually, after getting all the paper and cardboard off the floor and from on and under the furniture, I was down to the ribbon, string, tags, and bows. I gathered those into four awkwardly knotted-up armloads and shoved them in, on top of the logs.

That left the arc of misses. The room wasn't that big, and there were more than I really wanted to count. I could have just kicked them in. But at this point it was down to two choices—throw something, or scream.

Kicking my misses back across the room, into a clump facing the fireplace, I decided to get serious. No more casual throws. The way I was feeling called for Nolan Ryan fastballs.

Picking a spot on the carpet as my imaginary rubber on my make-believe mound, I stood upright, crumpled paper in invisible glove, and looked at the logs on the grate for a sign—as if I had a catcher.

I went into a full-windup, and threw, threw as hard as I ever had in my life. It hit the knot of ribbon on top of the logs dead center. *Dead—don't think that word.* Taking that as an omen, I kept throwing, putting everything—every shred of loss, hurt, anger—into each throw.

I hadn't been much of a pitcher when I played baseball—had no control—but now I was throwing nothing but strikes. Anger gave me focus.

By the time I got down to the last three wadded-up balls, I was getting tired—huffing and puffing, and my arm was feeling the strain.

All strikes. With the last, I stood there panting.

Burn it now? Turn this awful Christmas to ashes? It didn't have to be this way—it could have been special. If Mom was here, it would have been. Our Christmas—Brett's Christmas would have been a good one. And Mom deserved one herself.

I stood there, looking at the fireplace.

Burn it now?

It's not just Mom—or Brett—this year. Or anniversaries of what happened to Dad—or Norman—in the past. It's this year—it's Christ-

mas. It's December. It's everything. There are no words in the language for this. No words in any language. No profanity—no curse. My heart is an abyss. No, it isn't an abyss—it's filled with ashes.

Burn it. Now.

I walked forward and went to one knee, reaching up and in, to open the chimney flue part way—I wanted the fire to last. The box of wooden matches was in reach, on top of the mantle. Reaching down, I opened it, took one out, slid the box closed, and held the match next to the strike pad, hands shaking a bit.

I lit the fire, put the box back on the mantle, tossed the match in, walked across the room, and sat down in my favorite chair.

I thought of my mom as I watched that fire burn. Watched it every moment as it grew, from paper, to kindling, to logs. Watched it burn and felt the heat for hours. Watched as the large logs burned and split, popping and sparking. Watched as the wood turned to charcoal. Watched as the charcoal turned to embers. Watched as the embers lost their last glow and the heat faded. Watched as it all turned to ash, and the room became cold.

That was my Christmas with my Mother. The last one I would ever have.

EPILOGUE

December 26th

I woke up cold. I was under the blankets, and the heat was on, so the chill wasn't coming from outside me—it was coming from my heart.

I have to get away from it—you can't get away from yourself.

I can't talk to anyone—I've got to get out of here before someone gets up.

Sliding out of bed, I found my clothes from last night and carried them with me as I went—as softly as I could out of the bedroom, along the hall, and slowly down the stairs. Dressing in the guest bathroom, I found my car keys and got out of the house.

It was still dark as I drove away from our silent house.

It will be hours before the crematorium opens, hours before I can pick up Mother's ashes. I can go for a drive—go anywhere.

I wound up in the empty parking lot of the crematorium. Just sitting. Looking at the car radio. Not caring enough to turn it on.

Waiting as darkness gave way to dawn. Waiting as dawn turned to day. Waiting. Waiting until the first car pulled into the parking lot, and a man got out, walking to the front door with keys in his hand.

Waiting a few minutes to give him time to get things open before I followed him in.

I'd never picked up ashes before, so I didn't know what to expect. There wasn't much ceremony involved. We hadn't chosen an urn, so Mom's ashes were handed to me in a simple cardboard box in a plain paper bag.

When I got to the car, I set the bag on the hood, and opened the box. It was half full of gray, coarse ash. What was left of Mom.

The box sat on the seat beside me on the drive home.

When I walked in the door carrying the box, I could hear signs of life upstairs—movement, an occasional voice, and what had to be the *Star Wars* Christmas album coming from Brett's room.

I wasn't ready to be a part of that, but downstairs was still quiet. I walked into the family room and turned on the light, looking for a place to put my mother's ashes. The mantle seemed appropriate. Walking over to it, I looked down at the grate, cold and full of ash. The ashes of Christmas.

I looked down at the box. "You deserved to be here with us," I said.

I don't believe in anything beyond death. Mom is gone. And I don't believe in the value of empty gestures or symbolic actions. But I didn't put the box on the mantle.

I knelt down, opened the box, reached for the brass shovel in the rack next to the fireplace, and shifted the screen out of the way.

I reached out with the shovel, dug it deep into the ashes of our Christmas, and carefully tipped them into the box. I couldn't get Mom to Christmas, but I could get Christmas to Mom. It didn't have to make sense to be the right thing to do.

Standing up, I put the shovel and screen back, and took the box out to the car to put it in the trunk.

When I walked back into the house, Ann was coming downstairs.

A bit before it was time to leave for the memorial, I found Paige in the kitchen. "Why don't you and Ann drop Brett off at the babysitter's, and I'll head to the chapel now in case anyone gets there early," I said.

"Sounds good," she said, walking over to give me a hug. "We'll see you there."

When I got to the chapel, the lot was empty aside from a couple of cars. I went in, found the minister and the chapel director. I wasn't myself at all, but I made a point to remember to thank them, not just for this but for everything. Of course, there were flowers, but I willed myself not to notice.

Paige and Ann arrived with the first guests, people from Mom's work and some coworkers from Cornwallis Pharmaceuticals. That's when faces started to blur, although I was still hearing what they said. Until the second time someone said, "She's in a better place." At that point, I shut it all out.

I kept saying, "Thank you for coming. Thank you so much for coming," shaking the hands that stretched out to me from the blurry faces. Paige stood by my side until the last people had arrived. She guided me to our pew, otherwise I don't think I would have made it.

There was some music, and a service—happening around me. A pause, and Paige leaned close, whispering, "Jack, would you like to say something?"

I nodded, and she walked with me, her hand on my arm. The chapel was silent. I stood there, seeing only fog. I had no words for these people. I had a hole in my heart, and could only talk to the woman whose absence had made it.

"Mom—I will always love you with a special love reserved for you and you alone. I'll carry it with me every moment, for as long as I live, never forgetting for a second what you mean to me."

Paige and Ann sat on either side of me until the service was over. They guided me to the door, and people filed out, some shaking my hand, touching my shoulder. They were mist. There was no substance.

Eventually they were gone, leaving only Ann, Paige, and me out in front of the chapel.

"Why don't you two go pick Brett up. I've got an errand to run, and I'll see you back at the house," I said.

After watching them drive off, I went to my car, opened the trunk, and pulled the box out.

Getting in, I set it beside me and drove to Duke Forest.

There was a spot Mom had pointed out once, down a gravel road, followed by a short walk on easy trails. After a couple of wrong turns, I found the place I was looking for, box in hand.

The forest was quiet, the day cloudy with a bit of sun, and bitterly cold. It was the coldest day of the year. The glade Mom had told me about looked over a stream. It was surrounded by poplar, pine, a couple hickory trees, and an oak.

I walked in front of the oak, opened the box and put it on the ground. Holding my hands together, cupping them, fingers curled, my thumbs held in, I scooped them into the box and filled my palms with ashes.

When I looked down into my hands, the ashes formed the shape of a heart. A gray heart, but a heart nonetheless. I cast the ashes of my mom—and our Christmas—onto the roots of the oak.

Walking around the glade, I did the same with each of the trees, scattering a bit of the ashes on each.

When I got to the last tree, there was a little left in the box. I scattered this in the center. Looking around, I willed myself to remember every detail of this moment.

This was Mom's memorial.

dispersed on the soil
of a wooded landscape
lie my mother's ashes

she rests with the
spring, moon, winds,
and falling leaves

she so dearly loved

[Excerpt from the long poem "My Mother's Ashes" by the author.]

www.ingramcontent.com/pod-product-compliance
Lightning Source LLC
Chambersburg PA
CBHW020006140726
47904CB00018B/1975